Stinger in a Sugar Jar

Cynthia Rowe

Stinger in a Sugar Jar

First published by Zeus Publications 2007
http://www.zeus-publications.com

P.O. Box 2554
Burleigh M.D.C.
QLD. 4220
Australia.

ISBN: 9780987455444

ISBN 10: 0987455443

The National Library of Australia Cataloguing-in-Publication

Rowe, Cynthia
Stinger in a Sugar Jar.

1. Mothers and daughters - Queensland - Cairns Region - Fiction.
1. Title

A823.4

This book is a work of fiction and any resemblance to any persons living or dead is purely coincidental.

The author asserts her moral rights.

By the same author:

Our Hollow Sofa

Ants in My Dreadlocks

My French Barrette

Bad Grass

Couscous Threads

Driftwood – poetry collection

Author Biography

Cynthia Rowe has a degree from the University of Melbourne and has taught French and English for most of her working life. She has also spent time in France and the French Territories and was awarded a *Diplôme Approfondi de Langue Française* by the French Ministry of Education. She is a Writing Fellow of the Fellowship of Australian Writers NSW.

Cynthia's short stories have appeared in magazines and been broadcast on National Community Radio. Her poetry has won many awards and can be read in numerous literary journals internationally. She is Editor: Haiku Xpressions; President: Australian Haiku Society; Past President: Eastern Suburbs Branch (Bondi Writers) Fellowship of Australian Writers NSW.

STINGER IN A SUGAR JAR is the third in a series of her books.

For Bruce

Acknowledgments

My thanks to Belinda and her Publicis team, Simon for his interest and input, and Scott Cuthbert for his knowledge of vehicles from boats, to motorcycles and every imaginable car. I am enormously grateful to Amanda of Deli Ink, who instructed me in the fine art of making coffee.

I would also like to thank Ann Haraldson, Peter Wilson, Bruce and Susan Bennetts, Catherine Hammond for her wise editorial comments, and the staff at Waverley Library for its ongoing support. Chris Headford is to be congratulated for his wonderful cover design.

I was privileged to receive advice from the operators of A J Hackett bungy jumping in Cairns, who showed me an impressive cross-section of a bungy rope to assure me how safe the sport really is! And, lastly, I am indebted to Bruce for his willingness to traipse through the rainforest areas of Far North Queensland with me.

Chapter 1

My best friend stole my boyfriend. Which left me hanging out with studyheads and brainiacs—one of the reasons my eighteenth birthday verged on the pits. You see, the studyheads were doing what they liked to do best. And university mid-terms were just around the corner.

Namilly, my mum, was in bed with the flu. So I rocked on down to Acropolis on the Highway with my second-best friend, Hetty Geiger (brainiac, but also wicked), for a celebratory bite to eat.

"Don't forget I'm a raw vegan!" I hitched up my new mature-age calf-length skirt—a gift from Namilly, together with the usual bottle of Miss Dior.

"S'okay," said Hetty, "you can eat moussaka."

"He-llooo? Moussaka is cooked!" A wave of angry French perfume wafted about my head. "You simply don't get it, Hetty. Like, I said—*raw* vegan!"

"There're dips." She flicked her Indian plaits back over her shoulders. "You can fill up on dips, while I pig out on the lamb." Then, "You are *so* difficult, Genna Perrier. Why don't you lighten up like the rest of us, and eat meat?" She glared at me through her black-rimmed, oversized nerd glasses.

"I've tried meat. I ate bougna in Nouméa, but the lot went down the toilet."

"Jeez, Gen, you are so gross!" Hetty was the only decent friend I had, the one person I could joke around with since Win Winstone hooked up with Stefan. "Have dips then, and a Greek salad. *Sans fetta.*" Hetty spoke French much better than I did, despite my origins, and received an excellent ENTER score in her Year 12 final examinations.

We tucked our knees under the waxed, garlic-smelling tablecloth.

After opening Hetty's rite-of-passage gifts—an Australian Electoral Commission enrolment form, a pre-paid driving lesson voucher and two yellow L-plates—I hoed into my Greek salad, picking the cubes of fetta out of the iceberg lettuce and arranging them on the rim of her dish.

Stefan Becker and Win, snogging at a corner table in the rear of the restaurant (café, really), ignored me. They were so hot for each other it was embarrassing. Win—back from tip-rat to being supercool after her mum, Alice's, death—was busy stuffing olives in Stefan's mouth between kisses. His face went as red as his hair as he kissed her back, thereby transferring the pip into her mouth. Win flicked back her ice-blonde locks, spat the pip on his plate, and they both fell about laughing. And began to kiss all over again.

Hetty must've seen my hurt. She nodded to Spiro who wobbled out of the kitchen carrying my cake—shaped like a carrot and composed of compacted raisins and coconut, with a fringe of raspberries—on a marble platter.

I was shovelling cake in my mouth, and feeling a thundercloud bear down on me like a vast blanket over my future, when my mobile phone shimmied in my pocket. Wriggling it out, I pressed *Show*. One text message sat there:

bon anniversaire, tu arrives quand? r

My heart did a little jig. This was my coolest present so far, an SMS from Roch Colline—the guy I called Rocky—wishing me a happy birthday and wanting to know when I planned to visit him.

I considered my response.

Hetty leaned across the table. "Who's the text from?"

I decided not to confide that Rocky was the groovy Kanak kava farmer and freedom fighter I'd met during my stay in New Caledonia. And I wasn't about to tell her he had the most amazing sculpted lips.

"No one you'd know, just a guy who was forced to move from New Cal to the village of Kooracoondoo in Far North Queensland, um, a few months ago." I also decided not to say his Peugeot had been destroyed in a car bombing.

"You've got ver-y secretive since you went on *that* work experience trip to *that* Pacific island," she said, chewing on one of my fetta cubes. "Sometimes I feel you've become different. And, well, *that* hairstyle also doesn't help." She pointed to my dreadlocks, tied back with a fresh ribbon for the occasion. "Where's Kooracoondoo, anyway?"

"Close to Cairns."

"Doesn't your birth mother live near Cairns?"

"Sort of. Sandrine's on the Northern Beaches section of the Marlin Coast."

"Sounds to me as though the two places are not very far apart." Hetty pushed back her chair. "Well, I'm off outside to roll myself a chop-chop cig, while you compose your reply to your new friend." She pulled out her pouch and Tally Ho papers.

I frowned.

"It's only chop-chop," she said. "Mrs B's el cheapo illegal loose stuff from the Zabaglione Woollen Shop, and I did *not* spike the contents of the cliplock bag you took on your trip, *despite* what you may or may not think."

I started to tap out my reply to Rocky's SMS:

thx

As I pondered on how to say the plane ticket was too dear—without sounding like a loser—my mobile phone began to ring.

Sandrine's partner, Claude, whom I'd met once, was on the line. "*Bonjour*. I ring for Sandrine." Had he rung to wish me a happy birthday? "She needs very much to see you."

"Is she sick?"

"*Non*. She is not well."

"Is the illness serious?" There'd been no communication with Sandrine Bas Salaire de Lyon since she briefly spoke to me in New Caledonia, and I wasn't in the mood for guilt trips that evening.

A pause.

I could hear the two of them arguing.

Sandrine came on the line. "Claude is fussing. It's nothing, only problems with my eyes."

"What sort of problems?"

"They're dry." She took a breath. "By the way, the one-bedroom apartment is still vacant if you wish to use it. Situated between Coral Cove and Urupu Point, Glisten Beach is very pleasant."

"Look, I'm busy with my French classes at South Central Community College, like assignments and stuff. I'll think about it. But I don't really have enough money to buy a ticket, and it's kinda expensive."

"I will pay for your ticket." Still not having mentioned my birthday, it was clear she had forgotten.

"I'll see." I gouged a raspberry pip from my front teeth.

I was about to press the Off button when Sandrine said: "*Bon anniversaire!*"

"So, you *did* remember!" I felt myself tear up. Was it the pungent odour of Hetty's rollie seeping beneath the Acropolis' front door? Whatever … no way was that sweet smell just chop-chop.

"Of *course* I remember the day you came into the world! How could I forget crying my eyes out because your father wasn't with me?"

"Us," I murmured. "Don't you mean 'with *us*'?"

She did not reply. The word 'eyes' bothered me. Was this some kind of weird, not so subtle, hint? I recalled Namilly telling me Sandrine's mother—my biological grandmother—went blind not long before she died.

"I might come. I'll let you know."

"*Au revoir*," she said.

My fingers were sweaty as I pressed the Off button. Was Sandrine about to die? My stomach knotted. And then the signing of the Procuration document flashed into my mind, when Sandrine gave up her maternal rights and handed me over to Namilly Perrier all those years ago.

On the other hand, perhaps I should fly up to see her?

Hetty tapped me on my shoulder. "What's wrong, Gen?"

"I'm off, leaving Ravella, going north to see Sandrine."

Her face fell. "Oh no, that's not fair! You *promised* to join me on Catch a Carp Day, at the stream running to the foreshore. The growling grass frog so needs your help from the predatory carp!"

"There's another sort of frog needing my help, and not from the carp, but some mysterious hereditary eye disease."

Chapter 2

Claude was too busy to pick me up, so I took the shuttle bus from Cairns airport to the Amédée Apartments at Glisten Beach.

The complex was massive. The Coral Sea churned before the Beachfront Apartments, while mountains loomed to the rear of the Garden Apartments—shadowy and eerie in the distance. Coconut trees and ferns fringed the boundaries of the entertainment area between the two buildings: a cabana with barbecue and outdoor raffia umbrellas, two pools—one lap, one kids'—and a Jungle Walk through waving palms and melaleucas. All surrounded by a safety fence.

The first thing I did after arriving was ring my mum.

"Hi, Ma!" I said. "It's Genna, touching base."

Grumble, grumble, *grumble* from the other end. (Namilly felt only scorn for Sandrine, and was unhappy I'd gone north to be with my birth mother.)

She began to wheeze—residue of the flu and her bad heart and plain old age—so I decided to change the subject. "I hope you told Win she so ruined my birthday by snogging with my ex-boyfriend *right in my face*! I don't know how you continue to work with her in your recycle shop." I twisted a dreadlock. "She stole him, y'know."

"Stole who? Stefan?"

A sigh burst out of me. "Who else, Ma?"

"I don't like to be called Ma!" A pause. "And you don't *own* Stefan, so I wouldn't say stole. Win needs to relax after a hard day pricing clothes, and Stefan's Nature Shop is very demanding." A longer pause. "After all, you have been away a lot lately."

"It's *gross*," I said, "having your best friend hit on your boyfriend. She is such a hypocrite! She used to say she didn't know how I could stand to touch him!"

"Win needs a steady and caring friend after the trauma of her mother passing on in such a shocking fashion."

"Shocking fashion? If her mum jumped off a cliff, or was shot by a bank robber, *that* would be shocking. Peeing on a hair dryer is just, like, weird. Anyway, Stefan was *my* steady and caring friend. We used to catch blue-ringed octopuses, risk death together. Or don't you remember?"

Hoarse breathing. "You always did tend to have a selfish streak, Genna. You have no empathy."

"*Empathy*? I have buckets and buckets of empathy, when it's appropriate!" I added, "You are *so* wrong!"

"Lack of empathy is a trait, I imagine, inherited from …"

The heat was making me sweat. "You mean my birth mother?" I shouted, scratching my dreadlocks. "Well, she's right here."

Namilly slammed the phone down in my ear.

"She hung up!" I ran a finger over my mobile, still damaged from the night of the car bombing. The cracks and scorch marks on the cover made me think of Rocky's SMS. My response was still unfinished.

Beside me, Sandrine murmured that she wasn't surprised Namilly had hung up. "*Ça ne m'étonne pas,*" she said.

Sandrine's French was as perfect as her English. Her lipstick was almost worn away. She was pale, her eyes bloodshot. From the expression on her face, I knew she hadn't expected me to turn up at the Amédée Apartments so soon. Although red-eyed, she wasn't about to die.

She handed me the key to Apartment No.2—alongside the Management Apartment she shared with Claude. I saw fear take over, a sort of apprehension. Was it regret? Did Sandrine really want me around? Or had the invitation been one of those spur of the moment things? She'd told me, in Jacques Forestier's library, that I reminded her too much of my dad, a soldier who'd died during the bloody Events (the independence uprising in New Caledonia) right after my birth.

"You will find fresh towels in the apartment." She ran her fingers through her bleached-blonde hair; her gaze swept the ground. "You might like to take a shower, after such a long trip. If you need anything, Claude will help you." Turning on her heel, she disappeared into the Management Apartment, beside a door marked Storage.

The sun was low in the sky. Sandrine hadn't asked me to join her and Claude for dinner. *Odd*, I thought. But I was used to looking after myself. At home, Namilly and I had separate kitchens.

The cool from the overhead ceiling fan took over from the heat as I stepped inside my apartment. Placing my suitcase and carry bag containing my laptop on the floor, I looked up and my mouth dropped open. Even from the entrance, the view was awesome.

Directly ahead, the wall was entirely of glass with central sliding doors leading to a terrace. Beyond the terrace was an immaculate fern garden. And, on the other side of the narrow road called Arlington Esplanade, the beach was so close I could almost touch the coconut palms on the foreshore, so close I had no need to climb down a cliff to reach water, as I was forced to do in Ravella.

Bird noise filtered into the apartment. Parrots squawked and squabbled. The palm tree leaves thrashed in the wind, making a pitter-patter sound like falling rain, even though the sun shone. A churned-up Coral Sea turned the waves orange-grey.

Without warning, the sky darkened. The sun whooshed away like a burnt-out light globe. I flicked a switch. Wall lights in the shape of shells surged on, throwing a warm glow across a fish-filled room. Fish frolicked across the floor-length curtains, across the fabric of the two-seat sofa, across matching armchairs, and even atop a tiny television.

A fish-formed vase sat between a pair of palm-leaf candlesticks on a dining table in the far corner beside the window. On a glass coffee table, a pottery starfish held down a letter.

I settled myself on the sofa, pushed aside the starfish and perused the sheet of A4. My eyes scanned the welcome words. Basic beverages were provided, together with soap, toilet tissue, dishwashing liquid and washing machine powder. I read: 'Further supplies can be purchased from the local supermarket.'

Skimming through the hours of the shuttle bus service, courtesy transfers to various bistros and taverns for lunch at 10% discount for

Amédée guests, plus checkout times and luggage storage, I thought: *how kinky is this; how lucky am I to be living in a holiday apartment all my own.*

A warning shiver ran through me. But would Sandrine be welcoming? The letter was standard, no different from the one all the guests received.

Gazing at the sign-off words—'Have a wonderful stay, Sandrine and Claude'—I wondered if I'd done the right thing. She looked fine to me. Her eyes were red, but she was a long way from needing a white cane.

Chapter 3

I decided to turn my trip to Glisten Beach into a positive experience. Pushing thoughts of scheming love rats and cold birth mothers to the back of my mind, I peeled my body off the sofa, keen to inspect my very own fern garden.

Releasing the catch, I slid back the external glass door and went outside to investigate. On the compact terrace sat a table and two plastic chairs, with seats upholstered in faded hessian. The garden reached almost to the edge of Arlington Esplanade, the road along which the Amédée Apartments stretched. Timber edging hemmed the plants in. Did Claude Ponsinet design this yummy display? I hadn't seen Claude yet.

Two chubby women marched along the road, striding with determination.

A hum, crackle and spit. Glancing up, my eyes latched onto the ginormous sign glowing in the air above: ***Amédée Holiday Apartments***

A throbbing bus, with Waveripper painted on the side, pulled up outside Reception. Doors hissed open. Sunburnt tourists with seasick faces tumbled down the steps clutching beach bags. Their towels dribbled sand as they swayed along the path, heading for their units. A lift whined as someone hit the button. Footsteps clanged as others staggered up the staircase.

"Geez, I'm knackered!" said a man in a striped shirt. "And they call this place paradise!"

"'Ave a barbie first up, eh?" suggested a guy with an overweight lady clinging to his arm.

"Nah, I need a swim in the pool. I couldn't eat nuthin'," said striped-shirt man. "Wave piercers? Wave chunderers more like! I feel like hell!"

A massive Indian, barefoot and with his hair oiled, clad in loose linen trousers, slapped the side of the bus with his open hand. "See you lat-*errrr*," he said.

The Waveripper reef bus shook off down the road, brakes gasping and flashing as it turned the corner of the street before disappearing.

Leaving the sliding doors ajar, I went back into the apartment to inspect the kitchen situated in one corner of the living room. Next to the sink was a narrow fridge. Cupboards beneath a return bench housed plates, mugs, cups and saucers, glasses and lots of eggcups. (As a raw vegan, I wouldn't be using those.)

Placing my laptop on the dining room table, I hoisted my suitcase off the living room floor and into the bedroom where fish darted across a lairy spread. I dropped the luggage onto the king-size bed, beside a papaya-shaped lamp on a white bedside table.

After snapping open the locks, I inspected my closet—mirrored on the outside—and found stacks of hanging space, with a bank of drawers at one end.

I'd left the mature-age calf-length skirt Namilly had given me in Ravella, but brought the more appropriate dusky-pink beaded pareo—purchased in Anse Vata, and making Stefan blush on the one time I'd worn it. Folding the pareo carefully over its special hanger, I placed the funky matching kitten-heel sandals on the cupboard floor and slung hipster jeans, cut-offs and minis on the hangers provided.

Having tucked Hetty's L-plates gift in the side pocket of my luggage (just in case), I dumped the rattling plates on the living room coffee table.

I extracted a toothbrush for scrubbing my dreadlocks and made for the bathroom, where feature fish flitted across the shower screen, to wash away the grime from the voyage. Removing the ribbon from my dreads, I threw back my head, let the water run down my face and began to soap myself with the shell-shaped starter bar. Two minutes later, my happy grin turned to a not-so-happy scowl as the hot water turned cold, and I found myself trembling in the muggy heat. I scrambled the soap suds off my body with the aid of icy water.

Refreshed, with a towel wrapped around me, I ambled from the bathroom.

My eyes popped. The Indian I'd seen slapping the Waveripper reef bus was in my apartment. Examining my L-plates. Sitting on my sofa.

"Get out, *get out*, GET OUT!" I jabbed my finger at the doors leading to the terrace, now open.

The large Indian made no attempt to leave.

"I'll call the police!" I cried. "The owners of this apartment are friends of mine!"

The chicory man continued to sit there. He picked up the welcome letter from the coffee table, and hit it. Tap, tap, tap. "You merst *rrr*ead Sandrine's instructions!"

"What instructions?"

"PS. When retiring at night, please ensure that your balc*ooo*-ny door is locked," he read aloud. He glared at me. "You might be *rrrr*aped!"

I gasped. "You're Claude! Sandrine's, um, boyfr … er"—I was in a tizzy, and unable to think of the right word—"like, partner."

"Co*rrrr*ect!" He pushed himself off the sofa and gave me a *bise* (French air kiss) on each cheek.

"It's the hair!" I gazed up at him. "I mean, what happened to the incredible 'fro you wore when I came here with Marcel Manet, and Sandrine didn't want to see me." I could hear myself babble. "It, it was, well, the biggest 'fro I'd ever laid eyes on!"

"I oil my hairs for her." Claude turned his head side on. "You like? Sandrine tells me I resemble an Indian prrrrince." He looked back at me, and said, "Do you 'ave any food?"

Did he want something to eat? "Well, there are biscuits provided." Or was this the dinner invitation I'd been expecting? I stuttered, "I d-don't even have an apple, and I don't, like, eat biscuits anyway, as I'm a raw vegan."

I waited for the invitation to eat at the Management Apartment. Imagining a nice green salad and a platter of tropical fruit, my mouth began to water.

"I will drive you to Fraiche Mini-mart," said Claude. "You can buy your food there, please."

Hauling on shorts and a T-shirt, I slid my feet into an old pair of thongs, locked the apartment and scurried after him.

"I must warn Sandrine to mind Reception while I am gone," he said.

"What time does Reception close?" I panted, struggling to keep up with him.

"Nine o'clock. And we commence at six in ze morning."

"Phew, that's a long day!"

Reception was open to the sea and the esplanade on one side, the walls on the other three sides lined with pamphlet-stuffed shelves. Inner and outer reef cruises tempted tourists, together with scuba diving, boom netting, guided snorkelling and ocean walking. Four-wheel-drive safaris, white water rafting and rainforest adventures beckoned. Opal mining. Rodeos. Wildlife by night. Feeding a crocodile called Fergus.

Claude went behind the counter. He disappeared into the living quarters.

I could hear weeping sounds.

As I pretended to trawl through Skyrail and Scenic Rail timetables, car rentals, bistros and bars, bottle shops and T.A.B. leaflets, I heard Sandrine say, "I am *not* crying."

The noise of the television took over. Burying my nose in hot air ballooning and all-you-can-eat buffets in local taverns, I stood there wondering what to do. I felt like running off to the wetlands, immersing myself in aboriginal culture—anything but stand there like a derrbrain.

Shuffling my feet, I gulped at the price of a dinner cruise.

Claude reappeared. He swiped car keys from a row of hooks beside a freezer filled with cold drinks.

"Sandrine is much fatigued." He made clicking noises with his tongue. "See you lat-*errrr*, darling!" he called out.

He led me from Reception to a salt-stained Commodore station wagon with mag wheels and a pink flamingo dangling from the rear-vision mirror.

"Good evening, Claude." A woman with a frizzy coiffure and wearing polyester shorts walked past.

"*Bonsoir*, Madame 'Ays-Bert!" Claude gave a beaming smile.

Giggling, Mrs Hays-Bert veered left to the area behind the stairs where the lift was situated. She turned, smirked and said, "Oh, Claude dear, the bar on my squeeze mop has snapped. Could the apartment owner see his way clear to replacing it?"

"See me in Reception, Madame, in, ah …" He checked his watch. "Twenty minutes."

"I can walk." I touched Claude on the arm. "You direct me to the Mini-mart."

He shook his head.

I climbed in.

We passed tennis courts where the overhead lights steamed in the humidity. People whacked a ball across a net. And, up close, Claude's hair smelled of ti-tree oil, making me homesick for Ravella already.

The flamingo swayed. We drove in silence.

And then, "You are back 'ere again."

"Yes, I decided to come 'cos I was worried about Sandrine's health. But I can tell she didn't *really* expect me to turn up, at least, not so soon. I wouldn't be here at all if it wasn't for Pascal Manet."

"Brother of Marcel?"

I nodded. "Yeah, Pascal's the guy who runs Jacques Forestier's work experience programme in New Caledonia. But he's not always cool." I recalled Pascal's accusations. "Y'know, I never smoke dope, only chop-chop."

Claude shrugged.

"Have you ever smoked, um, chop-chop?"

He indicated he hadn't.

"Well, chop-chop is tobacco, sold on the sly by Mrs B, a friend of my mum, so it can't be *too* illegal. Hetty Geiger, brainiac buddy, gave me some as a farewell gift when I went to New Cal." Claude's eyes began to glaze over. "So, to cut a long story short, the gendarmes made me leave the territory even though I'd done nothing wrong!"

Claude seemed unimpressed.

I continued on, "In fact, Jacques Forestier …"

At the mention of Jacques' name Claude tightened his fingers, his hands clamped, and his knuckles turned into huge brown lumps.

"Jacques Forestier … argghh!" He squeezed the steering wheel so hard I thought it would break. He ground his teeth. His eyes bulged. He looked enormous.

Chapter 4

"We have a lot in common then." I grinned. "We both hate Jacques Forestier."

"You is rrright!" Claude flashed me a smile as even as sugar cubes.

He must've seen me stare.

"Vinyl coated!" Ungluing a finger from the wheel, he touched his pearly whites.

"Amazing!" I said. "Where did you have those teeth done? They must've cost you a fortune."

"Surfers Paradise, when Sandrine and I own a bathing costume shop." He eased the station wagon into a parking spot outside Fraiche Mini-mart. "You may buy your food here."

"Does Fraiche mean the food is fresh, you know, like the French word?"

"*Non*," he said. "Shop is owned my Mister Fraiche. No circumflex in 'is name."

"What do you mean?"

"Do not ask me to explain such things," he sighed. "Sandrine say so." He looked at me. "She is educated at a fine school in Sydney." His eyes softened at the mention of her name.

"Her English is very good, like her father's," I said, and then, "Oops, sorry!" hoping he wouldn't fly into a rage again at the mention of Jacques Forestier.

"I am not lucky like Sandrine. I learn to speak English in Australian pubs," he said. "I leave school when I am only twelve years in age. I work in Koné in Northern Province of *Le Caillou* ... as we call our homeland. Zen I come down to Southern Province, and work in nickel mine." He dragged on the handbrake.

"That's how you came to know my grandfather, and met Sandrine?"

Nodding, he climbed from the car.

Eddie Fraiche had a beer gut and a face like an overfed phantom. In the harsh fluorescent lighting, he stood behind the counter, pasty and curious.

Skirting the freezer in the centre of the shop, I passed fishing tackle, bait and beachwear as I headed for the cereal section.

"G'day, Claude," said Eddie. "You've got a new guest, I see. Stocking up for the duration, eh?" He suppressed a burp. "The wet 'as been pretty mild this year, so I guess them tourists are startin' to come up north."

Claude smiled as Mr Fraiche fluffed on about the weather and tourism.

Lifting a packet of natural muesli off the shelf, I began to read the contents.

"Lucky the blurry cyclone that went and hit New Caledonia didn't move on to us, eh," said Mr Fraiche.

I put the muesli back.

Claude approached.

"Food is not good?" He pointed to the cereal.

"It's got honey, and I don't like exploiting bees." Pulling another brand from the shelf, I scanned the ingredients.

And then I realised that, having been forced to take the shuttle bus, I was almost skint. I would have to be careful. Placing the packet on the shelf, I circled the open freezer, went back past the fishing tackle and grabbed an apple from the vegie section.

I held up my fruit. "This'll do for dinner. Let's go!"

Claude stopped talking to Eddie Fraiche. "You will need more to eat than zat."

"I'm a bit short at the moment. I lashed out on a flash dress in New Cal." I felt myself go beetroot.

Delving in his pocket, Claude produced two fifties. "You can recompense me lat-*errr*, when you 'ave found job.

Did he say job? I wondered, in alarm. I had planned to stretch out on the beach and sunbake.

Pulling the muesli off the shelf again, I added soy milk, sun-dried sultanas, vine-ripened tomatoes, organic walnuts, bananas, a mango and an interesting star-shaped carambola to my goodies.

The lights of the cars raked Claude's strong profile as we headed back to the Amédée Apartments. Silent at first, his words then came out in a rush. "Sandrine say she not trust ADN test. She wishes you will have another."

My jaw went slack. "Is *that* the reason you persuaded me to come all the way up here? For a DNA test? That is so off!" I hugged my groceries angrily.

"So you will not do zis?"

"Marcel pinched a piece of my hair, so I never even *knew* about the first DNA test! No, I *won't* have another!" I felt like catching the next plane right out of there, and then I remembered Roch Colline. And Kooracoondoo. And Rocky's sister, Douce—who I hoped to meet.

Still fuming, but determined to stay cool, I noticed we'd turned into the drive. We cruised past the Garden Apartments and into the car space reserved for management.

Hoisting my purchases, I was about to climb out when I heard Claude murmur, "Sandrine is very sick, sick in her heart."

"I can't help that," I said. "Sandrine gave me up when I was a baby. She has to live with the consequences!"

A strumming banjo sound filtered from the fourth floor as I scrambled from the car.

"Evening, Claude!" A guy carrying a plate of sausages reached to open the latch of the safety gate, leading to the cabana and barbecue alongside the kids' pool.

"*Bonjour, Monsieur Ponsinet!*" cried the dumpy lady with the frizzed hair. Now wearing a boomerang-print dress (two more boomerangs across her behind than the average person), she waited on the path leading to Reception. Her perfume was as bad as her French accent.

Her leer told me Mrs Hays-Bert was flirting with my birth mum's boyfriend. And she was welcome to him. I couldn't have cared less if I never saw Claude Ponsinet again.

Chapter 5

A rap on my apartment door woke me the following morning. I yanked on cut-offs and an Indigo singlet, and hoicked back the safety latch. Claude stood there in white trousers and a floral shirt so bright it made my eyes twitch.

His own were clear as he said, "You are ready for a lesson in 'ow to drive?" Keys swung from his long dark fingers.

"Driving lesson? I'm not even up yet!" I rubbed sleep from my lids. "What time is it?"

"Eight am. Our rrreef bus did not wake you?" He gave me the same smile I used whenever I wanted something: a narrowing of the eyes, head placed beguilingly to one side. "I see your L-plates when I am 'ere and I speak to Mercurio. And *voilà*!"

"Hang on a tick, Claude. I'll grab some breakfast!"

Fabbo, I said to myself. A driving licence meant wheels, and wheels meant freedom. I slipped into a pair of thongs, ran to the kitchen and plucked an apple from the wooden bowl.

"Coming," I called, "and do you want the L-plates?"

"*Oui*, your little plates are essential."

Digging my teeth in the fruit, I followed Claude to a ratty old Ford Falcon sedan with pink bingle patches along the side, and buffalo horns painted on the bonnet.

“Why this heap? What’s wrong with your car?”

“Mercurio’s car ’as gears,” he said.

“Who’s Mercurio?”

“Our excellent cleaning man.” He extended his arms wide, as if to emphasise the task of caring for forty-five flats, and then pointed to a guy scrubbing guano off walls on the top floor of the Garden Apartments.

Munching on my apple, I hopped behind the wheel. After jamming my L-plates in the front and back bumper bars, Claude heaved himself into the passenger seat beside me. The car leaned left as he pulled both feet in—still unshod—and slammed the door to.

“First we do gears.” He indicated the worn knob. “Take hold of your handle.”

Giving him my half-eaten apple to look after, I grasped the gearstick.

Thumb and index finger around the fruit, he said, “Now put your foot on clutch, rrright down, and draw little handle towards you. You will be in Number One.”

Having put the car in first, I said, “Shouldn’t I turn the ignition on?”

Claude shook his head. “You are permitted to do zat when you understand importance of gears.” Waving my apple, he said, “Up, up and left, and up, up again. And now you find yourself in Number Two.”

Thinking this was a cinch, I did what he told me.

“Now straight back and, *voilà*, you are in Number Three!” His breath smelled of toothpaste.

“Can I turn the ignition on yet?” I was hanging out to start the motor, hanging out to go all the way to Cairns—and my licence.

“Back into Number One,” said Claude. “Up, up, ac-rrrossss, down, down, down and towards your body.”

“The stick is stuck.”

“And where is your foot?”

“Oops!” I thrust my left foot down on the clutch.

“Now you may use key.” He leaned across until his oiled hair was in my face, a cloud of ti-tree essence overriding the mouldy smell of the vehicle.

At the twist of the key, the car gurgled and chugged. I pressed my right foot down hard. Bellowing out black smoke, we jounced forward.

The engine shuddered, and stopped.

We sat there in silence.

"You must start again!" Claude suppressed a sigh. "Think of big aarsh!"

"Aarsh?"

"Aitch," he said.

"Oh, I get it. The gear stick's in the form of the letter H."

We went through the process for what seemed like three years, and yet we were still sitting in the driveway of the Amédée Apartments. In the rear-vision mirror I saw Sandrine emerge from Reception with a hibiscus in her hair. After a brief look, she went inside.

"I was wrong. This is *not* so easy."

Soon I began to get the hang of it.

"Now we will go to Arlington Esplanade," he said.

We kangaroo hopped our way around the block. "Listen to your car!" The Falcon's engine screamed. "She *cries out* to be in Number Two!" The Ford jerked up and down the road, until—"*Arrête!*" said Claude.

"What's wrong?" I planted my foot on the brake.

"I see rubbish!"

He pulled a plastic supermarket bag from his pocket, threw open the door, pounced on an ice-cream wrapper and stuffed it in the bag. Back and forth we went, until I found myself doing snappy double declutches every time Claude sighted anything, from torn Frisbees, to yellowed newspaper pages and perished beach balls. Even a discarded disposable nappy.

"That is so yucky! Shouldn't *they* clean it up?" I said as he jumped back into the car, bag bulging, outside the All Day Breakfast Café.

"Now we go on Cook."

"Cook?"

"We will venture to our highway."

Driving along the highway was easy—apart from the road trains, which passed me at a thousand Ks per hour. I was packing, but relieved not to have to wrestle with the gears, relieved not to have to deal with Number One and Number Two. Barrelling along in top gear, sugarcane whipping past on either side of the road, I was super confident of my driving abilities. Even Claude began to look relaxed.

"Where's Kooracoondoo?" I asked.

He flapped his hand at the distant mountains. "A town famous for 'is bungy jump."

"Bungy jump? Wow, how do I get there?"

"You may take a bus, or borrow a train."

As I concentrated on Claude's explanations, everything came undone. A guy with beige hair and beige skin, clad in beige shorts and a beige T-shirt, pressed the button on a pedestrian crossing just before the town of Jamesville. I'd never thought about traffic lights. I'd never practised at traffic lights, never *seen* any traffic lights.

I panicked. I planted my foot on the accelerator.

"*Putain!*" Claude shouted. "*Les freins!* The brakes! Hit ze bloody *freins*!"

He dragged on the handbrake, and we came to a juddering halt on the crossing. Mr Beige walked on, heading for the shopping centre, oblivious.

My armpits were clammy.

Claude yelled, "*Descends de la voiture!* Out of my car!"

"You mean Mercurio's car?"

"Out! Out! Out!" His face went purple.

My right thong stuck between the brake and the accelerator as I pushed open the car door.

"I change my mind," he said. "Get back in! I will take you 'ome."

"No way! If you're going to yell at me I'll definitely get out!"

Scrambling from the vehicle, I hopped onto the median strip thinking I'd be forced to hitchhike back home with only one thong. I had no money, no mobile phone, not even the key to my apartment.

Burning rubber, Claude did a U-turn and headed back to Glisten Beach leaving a trail of stinking smoke.

Sticking my thumb in the air I set off, trudging beside the sugarcane. The sun beat down as the cars flashed past, slipstreams flipping my dreadlocks. My body was melting. But no one pulled up. Nobody offered me a lift. The road trains and B-doubles heading north with supplies for the glitzy tourist resorts weren't interested in stopping—until a shiny prime mover, fresh out of its wrapping, trembled to a standstill.

The driver, good looking, with straw hair and hip wraparounds, threw open the door. I was about to climb in when I spied the gun rack welded to the dashboard.

"You wanna ride, or dontcha?" His onion breath blasted from the cabin.

"It's okay." The roadside was searing into my right foot. "I'm waiting for a friend."

The vehicle surged off into the distance. I shoved up my thumb again.

Before long, I heard the splutter and cough of a bucket of bolts moving slowly behind me. Some creep was gutter crawling, and even worse, in the daytime. I did a surreptitious glance. A rusting ute with bullbar and spotties, and a brown dog in the back wagging its tail and sniffing the breeze, was tracking me.

I seemed to be attracting weirdos and losers. Was I giving out unwanted signals: SKANKY AND AVAILABLE? I pulled in my thumb, kept my head down, and limped along as if I was taking a stroll along the highway wearing one thong and minding my own business.

The passenger door squeaked open.

My heart started to thud.

"*Mademoiselle*," the driver called out. "*Putééé. T'es jôôôliiieee!* You come wis me. I will show you good time."

Oh heck. Now the creepy gutter crawler was telling me I was pretty—in French. But hadn't I heard those words before—*somewhere else?*

Chapter 6

Turning, I saw the sun-kissed face, the red-gold curls of Roch Colline—this time, free of the beanie he used to wear. He wore a hoodie, with the hood thrown back.

"Rocky!" I screamed.

My grin was so wide I felt as if my cheeks would split in two. I pulled off my remaining thong, and waving it in the air, hurled myself into the cabin of the ute. The dog whimpered, and wagged its tail.

"My Kanak accent gets you in every time, Genna!" Rocky laughed out loud as I threw my arms around his neck. "And why do I always find you wandering along the side of the road?"

I shook my head dumbly. "Claude kicked me out of his car, for almost killing a pedestrian." I gazed at Rocky's incredible sculpted lips. "I thought you were dead," I whispered, clinging to him, burying my nose in his curls, and inhaling his earthy smell, "for such a long, long while, and it so scared me, until I read in the paper … no I didn't, Pascal said Marcel rang to say you were safe. And, I dunno, everything was okay then."

"You look fantastic!"

I wasn't wearing lipstick, I hadn't taken a shower and I was sweaty from the heat. Big time. I pulled back, twisting a dreadlock. "Like, I'm kinda grungy."

"*Au contraire.* When did you do your dreads?"

"It's a long story. Pascal Manet, you know, French examiner, teacher …"

"… and brother of my close friend, Marcel."

"Well, outside the nakamal … the kava bar … as I stood there waiting after you left, he jumped me right as your car exploded!"

"I'm sorry I caused you grief." His grey eyes locked with my dark gaze.

"I passed out, and when I came to I was at Pascal's place." My breath caught. "And I thought you were killed, stuck to the road in melted cinders and I sort of did my dreads as a statement, you know, solidarity." My body shook, as though I had a fever.

"Let's drive to Pandanus Beach. We can sit and talk there."

I clung to Rocky's arm, afraid to let go in case he vaporised. "What's the dog called?" I murmured, "He's very brown."

"His name is Chocolat."

We did a jerky right at the next roundabout, chugged past private gardens filled with palm trees, and turned right into a pot-holed road beside sand dunes. Rocky eased the ute into a parking space, nudging a bollard, and pulled on the handbrake.

"How come you nearly killed a pedestrian?" His slow smile relaxed me.

"Sandrine's partner was giving me a driving lesson, and this guy dressed in beige appeared from nowhere. He pressed the pedestrian lights and dummy yours truly hit the accelerator instead of the brake!"

Rocky gave a soft chuckle. "I almost killed many people when I first learned to drive, and there weren't a lot *to* kill in the Brousse where we lived."

Chocolat sprang from the back of the ute as we climbed from the vehicle. His tail was like a scruffy duster as he scampered onto the sand, bounded to the water's edge and began to chase waves.

"Let's sit here, in the shade." Rocky indicated a spiky pandanus, and kicked off his T-Boots.

"Wow! This feels, like, so good!" I collapsed into a sitting position beside him. "It's not easy walking in one thong, and the pavement is hot."

"I keep asking you to come and visit, and you never reply." He shrugged off his hoodie to reveal a black sleeveless muscle tee with

ASSASSIN on the front in green. There were scratches on his left arm. "So when were you planning to tell me you were here?" His eyes were accusatory. "Or were you going to stay a few days, and then get on the next plane without contacting me?"

"Hey, I only arrived in Glisten Beach last night!"

"Well, I've desperately needed someone to talk to since arriving in Australia. I am suffering very bad homesickness, and you are my sole connection with *Nouvelle-Calédonie*." He lifted a bandaged hand.

"What about your mum, your sister?"

"Douce doesn't know she's from *Le Caillou*, and doesn't speak French."

"But she must've been rapt to see her brother after all this time."

He slowly shook his head. "It's complicated."

"Complicated? You said that in the letter you sent, but I don't get it."

His mouth was a thin line. "Douce can't read or write." He leaned back on his elbows, letting the sand trickle through his toes. "And sometimes she gets lost, *and* she's older than you might think!"

"Her name means sweet and gentle in French, appropriate by the sound of it."

"Mm, she is interesting."

The hair beneath Rocky's armpits matched the hair on his head. In the bright light, his body resembled a bronze you might see on a hall table, or on a mantelpiece beside a gilded mirror.

"Want to tell me about it?"

"Not yet."

"Your hands, what happened?"

"They're nearly better, although the burns were so bad at first the fat under the skin was exposed." He shrugged. "I was fortunate not to need a skin graft. Lifting boxes and cartons for my mother, I need to protect them." He pushed aside a piece of driftwood. "Douce also has a stall at the Kooracoondoo Markets. She sells *trucs*, little knick-knacks, and threads beads for my mother's clothing stall." He showed the bracelet around his wrist.

"That's fab. She can't be *too* confused then?"

"She's fine as long as Jeanne keeps an eye on her."

"Your mum must've been over the moon when you turned up?"

He said nothing, chewed his lip.

I was bothered by the odd bits of information Rocky was feeding me. I told myself he'd fill me in when he was ready. I rolled onto my stomach. The sun was almost directly overhead, and the shade from the pandanus was narrow, a squiggly line.

"I'm getting marks from my singlet. I can feel it." Wriggling my arms through so that Rocky couldn't see my boobs, I eased the straps over my shoulders.

"Take your top off."

"Oh no, um, noooo, nup, no way, I couldn't."

"There's no one around except me, and that couple way down the beach." He gave me another slow smile. "After all, I am used to seeing girls sunbake topless. At Anse Vata everyone does it." His eyes crinkled at the corners. "I was a wild kid after my mother left." Then: "Go *on*, take it off!"

"I'm like, well, you know." I squirmed with embarrassment at my miniscule mountain ranges. "I'm not … I don't have …"

"I won't look!" He turned away as I removed my top, whipped his head back before I had a chance to hide. "They're perfect!" he said.

"You cheated!" I rolled onto my stomach again. "You said you wouldn't perv!"

"I lied. And I *am* French. It's our culture." He grinned. "I don't mean the lying, only the perving. Appreciating pretty girls is our national sport. No, it's our national *duty*."

"Yeah, right." The sun beat on my back as I sank into the sand. "This is soooo good."

Tail thrashing, Chocolat bounded up with a sausage, dropped it and played with it. He buried the food, dug it up again and, saliva swinging, wolfed the lot down.

"Imagine what the dog's insides are like with all that sand! He must have a whole beach in there!" I glanced at Rocky. "Did you know your other dog died?"

His face fell. "*Non*. No one told me."

"I went to your farm." I felt a moment of panic, but ploughed on. "Did they tell you your house was burnt down too?"

"Pascal rang."

Lying on the sand, my own life seemed unexpectedly safe and comfortable. "And did he say all, well most of, the kava plants were stolen?"

He nodded. "One of the reasons I cannot go back."

"But your cat is still alive!" I sat up, forgetting about my naked chest, but he seemed not to notice. "And the cagou bird and its chick are okay too!"

He said nothing. The breeze ruffled his curls.

"Your dad was holed up in the Manet house." I gave a fake laugh. "And I found him a pair of Capri pants, Madame Manet's, to wear." I was unable to stop burbling.

Rocky looked away.

Holding my singlet against myself, I clambered up. "I'm off for a swim!"

"Will you drop that bloody top!"

I fled, thinking: *me and my big mouth.*

Rocky stayed behind, pensive.

Shucking my cut-offs, I dived in. Warm brine flooded my yellow-spotted knickers as I headed for the bottom, hoping to see a wonderland of coral and brightly-coloured fish. But churned-up sand swirled about me, and my toes were invisible. Thoughts of stonefish and cone fish, and creatures with spikes, invaded my brain until I could only make out lethal shapes.

Paddling around in the murk, I remembered the stripy poisonous sea snakes in New Caledonia. Did *tricots rayés* exist in Australian waters? Mostly I remembered box jellyfish. One sting from those suckers and no one would ever find me in this muck.

A sea creature latched onto my leg. I struggled to resurface. Had a shark or moray eel chomped a piece of me? Kicking out as hard as I could, my foot collided with a solid mass. A Great White?

In my haste to get away, I gulped in water.

Chapter 7

Coughing and spitting, I shot to the surface. Nearby, Rocky was also spitting water. His hair was plastered to his cheeks; his undies were designed like the Kanaky flag—blue, red, green and gold.

"You kicked me!" He indicated his fully sick sixpack.

"I thought you were a shark!" I gasped in a lungful of air. "You could've *drowned* me!"

"I'm sorry. Those things you said, well … stuck in this place, I feel helpless." Now bandage-free, his left hand was lumpy from the car bombing burns.

"Sorry, I should've kept my big mouth shut." The word mouth reminded me I'd only had an apple for breakfast. "I'm hungry. Is there somewhere we can get a bite to eat?"

"Didn't you tell me you follow a raw vegan diet? I have a bag of oranges in the tray of the utility."

The oranges were fat and juicy. We sat by the water eating, and chatting, and slurping. I said to myself, *Here I am, with Rocky, and the rain's not bucketing down and there's no cyclone and I'm having a great old time and I'm sitting here* TOPLESS. In that moment, I understood Sandrine's love of the monokini. I had never felt so at ease with my body.

"You're lucky you don't have to worry about becoming sunburnt," I said.

"*Si*, I do." Leaning across, he wiped a dribble off my chin with his forefinger.

"Then how do you know when you're sunburnt?"

"Simple. My skin becomes hot and painful and, after a few days, itchy. I peel, like everybody else." He touched his arm and I noticed one of the wounds, so long after the accident, still suppurating.

"Your left hand looks bad. Tell me what really happened that night at the nakamal."

"The Nouméa Accords were only a partial victory," he began. "Soon only the sovereign powers of justice, public order, currency, defence and foreign affairs will be left with France. But there's no pride in partially controlling a country which rightfully belongs to the Kanak people. We need to keep chipping away at the edges." He absentmindedly tossed Chocolat an orange. The dog picked it up, bounded back and dropped it at his feet. "I better not eat this one by mistake," he murmured, chucking it away again.

"No, I mean the explosion, after we left. What did you do? Where did you go?"

"I remember being thrown by the blast, hard into a doorway, my legs jammed against the wall, splayed apart. The detonation blasted off one of my shoes. I could feel my toes." His voice was low. "They hurt so much I knew I still had them. My body screamed with pain and I had trouble opening my eyes, swollen, lashes gone from the flames."

"Did the beanie you wore, which I saw you turn into a balaclava as you ran off, save your face?"

He gave a brief nod. "I knew something was afoot, so I pulled the brim down. But I never imagined they would wire my car. I remember coughing up sputum, the spit curling into a crack in the bitumen. I drew my legs into the doorway and lay there, watching an airline sign flicker down the street. I knew K-Mel, my papa, would be waiting for me, and I had to alert him."

"When Pascal and I saw your dad, he whinged about you never being home."

"Y'know, my father is not as vague as he seems. That night, I was warned. They told me they would seize my kava crops if I didn't watch out, saying the last delivery was a bad batch. The ground kava had been cut with grain, the whole roots supplied of poor quality." Sand trickled through his fingers. "They told me the piper methysticum had no feeling of numbness when mixed with water and sipped. They threatened to take even the old kava plants, the valuable pepper trees with the most potent roots."

"And they did. They slashed and burnt the lot!"

Rocky ran his tongue around his lower lip.

"What happened next?"

"My eyes streamed, and I could hear gendarmes shouting. A *flic* ran past, flashing his torch, but I must have resembled a heap of old rags." Chocolat ran up with a sandy orange; Rocky shoved him away. "I must've passed out, because I woke to find myself shivering and drenched. They had taped off the area, removed the body of the guy who wired my car. The wind was howling, and I knew I must hurry before the cyclone arrived."

"The French examiner, um, Pascal, shoved me in his Merc, and took me to his house."

"You were lucky. He probably saved you." Rocky gave me a brief look. "Fortunately, I was able to walk. I pushed myself up, still planning to return to the Brousse … a long way when you no longer have a car." A pause, as if he was trying to recall. "It occurred to me that Noah's hoons might be waiting, that K-Mel would stand a better chance by himself, and maybe they wouldn't harm an old man."

"They sliced off his fingernail."

"*Ouais*, but they didn't kill him." Rocky hugged his knees to his body. "I knew I would have to quit my homeland, and I remembered the postcard I received from my *maman* many years before." He took a heavy breath. "I managed to find my way to the domestic airport where a Cessna was preparing to leave. The rain was pounding down, the dogs know when a cyclone is due and they were barking. The pilot, an Aussie, agreed to take me. *Voilà*. That's how I got here, ahead of the cyclone until we reached Far North Queensland."

"And your mum was rapt to see you?"

"The sun is burning you," he said, ignoring my question. "I will get my jacket."

He loped to the pandanus, retrieved our threads, and placed his hoodie over my shoulders. We sat at the water's edge, playing with his dog.

Rocky began to sing: "*She wore an itsy, bitsy, teenie, weenie, yellow, polka-dot bikini …*"

"I'm wearing my knickers, not a bikini."

"Douce wore a pair like yours when she was about eighteen months old. *Maman* used to sing the song to her before they left for Australia."

"You must've missed your sister and your mum."

"Yes, as did Pascal Manet. Sometimes Marcel and I would turn up after hunting *roussette*, the giant bat, and we would see him run off, face red, as if he'd been crying. I guess he had problems, and came to confide in Jeanne."

"Where was your dad?"

"Oh, planting kava in the gully, or down at the market selling his bananas."

"Pascal's hands were damaged in the car bombing." I inched the hoodie up against my neck. "He applied kava leaves to make them better."

Rocky blew out a sigh. "If only I could find kava in Far North Queensland my life would be easier."

He grinned. I saw his gums were pink and healthy as they'd never been before. Despite his wounds, his nails had lost their yellow tinge. We sat there chucking oranges for Chocolat and chatting, until the sun went behind the palm trees and the parrots began to squawk. The wind picked up along the foreshore.

"It's getting late. I must get back with the supplies. *Maman* needs them for tomorrow. She'll think I've had a crash. I'm still not proficient on the left side of the road."

We rinsed our hands in the sea.

"Your mum must be happy you're with her again and, um, able to do things."

Again, at the mention of his mother, Rocky said nothing.

Chapter 8

Chocolat leapt into the tray. Rocky re-bandaged his hands, and turned the key in the ignition. A phone rang. Reaching beneath the seat, he pulled out a mobile held together with rubber bands and pressed the button.

"*Oui, Maman.*" He clamped his teeth together. "*D'accord*, Jeanne!" He spat her name out. "I'll be home soon, *Jeanne*!" he said, pronouncing her name in the French way.

Tension crackled across the airwaves. The engine stalled, and we sat there in silence. My singlet was chaffing my back, and I ponged of sand and sweat and orange juice.

"You need Number One," I said.

He stared. "I do not! I did *pipi* in the sea!"

"Number One is Claude-speak for first gear."

Rocky laughed. His shoulders relaxed. He backed the ute away from the bollard, made a U-turn, and we headed for the highway where the streetlights were starting to glow. I had been with him for most of the day, which was fine. I was a free agent. I was a long way from home, with no one to answer to.

"Do you still have the same boyfriend, the guy to whom you sent all those text messages?" he said out of the blue.

"Nope, Stefan ditched me. The rat called it off by SMS. Now he's on with my best friend, Win."

"*Je suis content*," he murmured in French.

Rocky was glad? A smile snuck over my face. Did that mean he was interested? I didn't dare hope. The groovy kava farmer was way older than me, a freedom fighter, and a twenty-something guy.

We did a right off the highway, and wound through streets towards Glisten Beach.

"You know the way to the holiday apartments?"

"I do." His lips tightened.

We turned left into Arlington Esplanade. A cop car was parked outside Reception. A policeman in shorts and a wide-brimmed hat climbed in and drove off.

"Trouble in paradise?" Rocky steered the utility into the kerb a block from the Amédée Apartments.

"You're not dropping me at the door?"

He shook his head.

"Thanks for the great day." And then: "Why'd you park so far away?"

"I do not want your mother to see me."

"Whoa, Sandrine's not my mother!"

"She is your mother!"

"No way." I twisted a dreadlock. "Namilly's my mum."

Rocky became stroppy. "The Caldoche, white people born in my country, don't change, even when they emigrate. *She* thinks she is better than the rest with her aristocratic name, Bas Salaire de Lyon!"

"My biological mother was Forestier before she married *into* that name! And she's not rich. She has mortgages!"

"Sandrine would not like her daughter … or should I say 'genetic offspring'? … spending time with me." He stuttered the words: "I h-have *peau mate*. She would be bothered by the colour of my skin."

"You're not making sense. Claude is a Kanak!"

"But I am a mongrel, with unusual hair colour, and she does not like me." Rocky sounded petulant. "I asked her to let you know I survived the car bombing. My phone was broken, and the monsoon rains were pelting down along the Marlin Coast, and I needed a place to stay before I went on to Kooracoondoo."

"Whoa, back up. I've got no idea what you're talking about."

"The Aussie pilot landed his plane in Townsville." He spoke slowly. "I hitchhiked up the highway to Cairns, and then headed towards Glisten Beach and the Amédée Apartments. Marcel had told me Sandrine owned the big place on the foreshore."

"Sandrine doesn't *own* the flats, only the apartment I'm using. She bought the management rights with Claude, and oversees the units for people who live in Sydney or Melbourne …"

"She looked at me like I was worthless." Rocky's expression was stubborn. "And I had plenty of money."

I remembered the rolls of cash the nakamal proprietors gave him for his kava. "I'm sure you did, but what were you wearing? The beanie you wore when I last saw you in the Latin Quarter?"

"Pffttt." His French accent was coming through. "So, she is only at the *plage*. She is not in a big city."

"And your clothes? Your hands were covered in bandages, I imagine? Did they stink of burnt flesh and dirt?"

"Pffft. I speak to her in French, and she looks in computer and says she 'as a room on the fourth floor beneath roof. And then a *boudin* comes in."

"*Boudin*?"

"A fat lady enters Reception saying, 'Bon-*jewer*, Madame'. She has just flown in from Melbourne."

"Did she have scrunchy hair?"

"I only know she was very ugly. And she asks if the other bridge ladies have arrived. Claude Ponsinet appears and gives her a big white smile and, *bang*, Sandrine says she has made a mistake. The room is taken!"

Rocky continued to complain.

The Waveripper reef bus surged past, hissing to a halt outside Reception. Claude, barefoot and in the same shirt he'd worn that morning, climbed aboard. He moved down the aisle of the bus, waving his hands and looking concerned. Had there been an accident, someone left in the Coral Sea, snorkelling near the diving platform, and forgotten when the tourist boat turned back from the day's outing?

"Hey, I'm no fan of Sandrine but I'm sure it was a misunderstanding." I opened the door to climb out. "Look, something's wrong. I'd better see if I can help."

"You will come to our Kooracoondoo Markets? Maybe have a bungy jump?"

I recalled the final communication from Rocky's mother in the side pocket of his Peugeot door, the postcard with the bungy jumper on the front, her face frozen in terror. I struggled to hang loose, to appear cool and unimpressed at the thought of plummeting earthward attached only to a piece of three inch elastic.

"Sure I'll have a bungy jump! I'm big on danger!"

Rocky touched the beads on his wrist. "Take these, so you don't forget."

"That's sweet of you, but they'd be too big." Plunging my hands into the pockets of the cut-offs, my fingers touched something rough.

Rocky snapped off the bangle. "Memory wire!" His eyes caressed my face as he gave me the jewellery. "Douce uses memory wire to thread her creations."

"It's beautiful. And I have something for you." I handed him the heart-shaped kava leaf.

"Where did you find this?"

"Oh, it was on the ground." I remembered sleeping with the leaf under my pillow. "I found it at your farm. You might like it as a sort of keepsake?"

As I spoke, I noticed the worried looks on the tourists' faces. People talked in groups on the footpath beneath the Amédée Apartments sign. A man paced along the gloomy sand. Was he searching for a body?

Claude slapped the side of the Waveripper reef bus. "See you lat-*errr*!" His voice was subdued; he turned and went into the building.

"Sorry. Gotta go!" Distracted, I pushed the beads onto my wrist where they clung.

Rocky clutched his treasured kava leaf. "*À bientôt!*"

He waved a bandaged hand. The ute shuddered off.

Chapter 9

A cry went up: "Isn't that her?"

Someone said, "*Geneviève*."

"The girl's got dreadlocks!" another shouted.

People pointed, and made comments: "Doesn't look as young as 'e described!"; "Smaller"; Fairer"; "Darker"; "Skinnier"; "Seems Aussie to me"; "Nah, somethin' foreign, Caldoche!"

A backpacker chewed gum.

A guy with sun-streaked hair said: "Are you Genna?"

I reeled back. "Yes, I'm Genna. What's wrong?"

"It's her! She's safe!" he announced to the crowd beneath the neon sign.

"You weren't kidnapped at all, dear?" A woman reached to touch me.

I dodged her fingers. "Kidnap? I don't think so."

A hush as I passed. Guests hung from balconies. Clapping erupted. Mrs Hays-Bert wore a broad smile.

Sandrine clicked around in killer heels outside Reception. Her eyes, no longer bloodshot, glittered as she said: "*Where were you?*"

"Nowhere."

"Claude!" she screamed. "She's turned up!"

Claude came running. He threw his arms around me.

"Ouch, I'm sunburnt!"

"I am ve-*rrry* sorry I get angry. Do you forgive me?"

"We reported you missing to the police!" Sandrine adjusted her hibiscus. "*Where have you been, Geneviève*?"

"My name is Genna."

"Very well. Where have you been, *Genna*?"

"I met someone, and it's none of your business what I do."

"Who did you meet? And it *is* my business." Her finger stabbed the air. "Where are your shoes?"

"One thong's in Mercurio's car, the other is in, um, a ute somewhere." As I said 'in a ute somewhere' I realised the words sounded slaggy. As if I'd been up to no good, while they were contacting Missing Persons.

Sandrine's ears pricked up. "In who's ute?"

"You are not my mother!"

"I *am* your mother!"

"Well, you've got a pretty funny way of showing it, signing that Procuration document. You've got no right to interrogate me!"

Beside me, Claude nodded. "Genna is correct. You 'ave no right."

"How dare you, Claude! It's *your* fault she ran away!" They began to argue in French, so fast I hardly understood a word.

The crowd dispersed. Guests scuttled inside. Apartment doors closed. Mrs Hays-Bert left. You could've heard a pin drop throughout the complex, apart from Sandrine and Claude getting stuck into one another. I could just make out, "What would the *nounou* think?" from Sandrine. And I found it weird that, after all this time, she was concerned about Namilly Perrier's opinion.

Claude switched to English. "I will nev-errr understand you, a Caldoche, handing over your precious *petite* baby as you did."

"You were happy not to have a child around your neck at the time, if I remember rightly!"

He ignored her comment. "And you take photos of someone else's infant to send to your papa. It make me *sick*."

"You didn't *stop* me taking the snaps of the next door neighbour's child!"

"*Non*. But I am ashamed of myself, of your be'aviour. And because of this I throw up in *toilette*!"

They say it takes seventeen muscles to smile and forty-three muscles to frown. I used up at least forty-two of those frown muscles. The frown melted away and I got that stick-in-your-throat feeling. My mouth went squashy as I listened to the hurtful words. And I understood, in a small way, what my friends went through when their olds ripped into one another. I scratched my dreadlocks, fiddled with the beads on my wrist. Should I leave, I asked myself, or stay and watch? What was the protocol in this type of situation?

Knowing I'd start blubbing, I turned to go.

Claude ran after me. He lifted the catch of the safety gate leading to the lap pool. "Come wis me!" He put his arm round me again—gently, this time. The smell of his ti-tree oil made me relax.

Although hanging out for a shower and the cool of my overhead ceiling fan, I went with him. We sat by the edge of the pool, dangling our feet in the water.

"I will call a cat a cat," he said.

"It's okay. I know about the photos. Marcel filled me in." I nibbled on a nail. "But, y'know, after having gone to Jacques Forestier's deer farm I can *understand* why she did it." I remembered my grandfather making me watch his vicious dogs rip a stag apart. "He is ruthless."

"An evil father is no excuse for daughter to be ze same." Claude gave a heavy sigh. "I also am apologising for my own be'aviour. I have a very naughty temper sometimes."

"It's all right. We ventured onto the highway too soon, that's all."

"I am not 'appy killing people on pedestrian crossing."

"Guess not." Reaching down, I cupped my hands and sprinkled water on my arms.

"This is lovely jewellery you were not wearing this morning, brown garnet, horn from Africa. I have cousin who sells *bijoux* at Thursday evening markets in Anse Vata." He eyed the softly glowing beads. "Did you go to shops today?"

"Um, nup."

Claude knew I was skint. How to explain away the bracelet? I decided to change the subject.

"What's wrong with Sandrine's eyes?"

He screwed up his lips. "Very dry."

Carrying a plate of bloody meat, a guy in gladiator sandals came through the gate. "Okay if I use the barbie, eh?"

Claude gave a nod.

"You forgive me?" He wrapped me in a bear hug.

"Ouch," I said.

"I am very surprised you 'ave sunburn." He pushed himself up.

"You're right. I don't usually burn. But I overdid it this time, coming up from Victoria where the weather's turned cold and then taking off my … oops!" I covered my mouth with my hand.

"I mean you are too dainty for sun to ever find you!"

"Well, um …" I was speechless.

"I will get you cold tea," he said.

"I don't, like, drink tea."

"For applying to your back so you may sleep, as my *maman* used to do to me when I 'ave pain from lying too long on a beach."

People opened their apartment doors. Cooking smells filtered through the night air.

Claude cleared his throat, and I wondered if he planned to ask me once more to have a DNA test in exchange for iced tea. Instead, he walked me to a shed on the fence line of the car park, close to the path leading to Reception. "This is workplace where I make repairs." Tools were arrayed on a bench.

He opened the door of a narrow cupboard attached to the outside wall, revealing a row of books—dog-eared paperbacks with damaged spines, and dripping sand—donated by people heading home at the end of their holidays.

"I will pay you one hundred dollar for each month if you care for our tiny library. And I will forget about money you owe me, zis time."

Thinking one hundred bucks a month still wouldn't be enough to cover the cost of my food, I was relieved to start with a fresh financial slate.

"You're right. I need a job. Do you know of anything?"

"Can you work coffee machine?"

"Sure!" I lied. "I can brew the most amazing coffee!"

As a fib, this was a whopper. I had only ever earned money stacking shelves at The Store back home. I didn't drink coffee, let alone make it, but I was familiar with the retro and unused espresso machine in Mrs B's haberdashery shop in Ravella. I'd pulled levers in there, and pretended to serve cappuccinos to my friends. However, I had never juggled a real-life steam dooverlackey, or whipped up frothy milk.

Claude's smile glowed in the gloom. "Dominick Nicks will 'elp you!"

Chapter 10

Night-time, my skin was like crispy toast.

After tipping Claude's metal jug of iced tea over my back, I tried to get some shut-eye. I needed to be calm and collected for my job interview. My back was burnt. My front was burnt. My mountain ranges were killing me.

I tossed and twisted, listening to the tropical chatter in the palm trees. I could hear Claude fuss around in his shed, and I wondered if he and Sandrine were speaking again.

Use of the pool was banned after ten pm. I heard the final splash of a swimmer. The front and back buildings of the Amédée Apartments became silent. Was everyone in bed, exhausted from reef snorkelling, white water rafting, boom netting or exploring wet tropic rainforests? Was gawping at crocodiles really so enervating? I wondered.

Midnight. I continued to wriggle on my king-size bed. Clambering out, I turned the ceiling fan to high, removed my T-shirt and lay there topless and briefly cooler.

My dreadlocks flipped beneath the swirl of the blades, and I thought of Rocky. I fiddled with the beads he'd given me, admired their glow and wondered if they were a form of friendship ring—a fidelity bracelet of some sort. Or had the gift been a spur-of-the-moment thing? I knew he was homesick for his country. Did he regard me as a link to his homeland?

My mind moved to wondering why Rocky refused to talk about his mum, Jeanne Colline. I'd overheard his telephone conversation. Why hadn't she let him call her '*Maman*'?

My eyes went round and round, watching the blades of the ceiling fan. My brain whizzed at a zillion miles a second, and I wasn't even close to dropping off. Bones aching, I staggered out of bed and hobbled into the sitting room. Printed fish flashed past as I swished the curtains back to peer through the palm trees at the ocean.

The neon apartment sign crackled and spat overhead. And I noticed the Vacancy word highlighted. Which made me think of Rocky again. Had he really been turned away by Sandrine? Perhaps she'd simply reacted in the same way I had when I first saw him? Until I saw those awesome lips, his eyes you could plunge into and never want to emerge from ever.

I pushed the beads he'd given me up and down, and back. I had heard Rocky's mates talk about taking over the cigar-shaped island of New Caledonia, of cutting the fibre-optic cable running up the coast. A thought skidded into my noggin: if a coup occurred, who would be president? The separatist leader I'd met—Yannick Boudaou? Or Rocky Colline? Was Rocky planning to make his move from Australia?

"Nup, the sunburn must be doing my head in." I rejected the idea.

Outside, the waves seethed onto the shore.

I blinked. The Amédée Apartment sign flickered and flashed and went dark for a moment, before surging back on. And then I saw a shape—a man with dreads tucked into a Rastafarian bonnet—standing between the palm trees.

I blinked again. The man was gone.

Had I imagined it?

A sweet odour, like the rollies Hetty sometimes smoked, filtered beneath my sliding doors. Was the dreadlocked man sucking on swamp? I gave a hearty sniff. Or was the smell coming from Storage? I sniffed again.

Or was my birth mother a pothead, and the aroma flowing from the Management Apartment?

Chapter 11

The Waveripper reef bus didn't wake me. Squabbling rainbow lorikeets in the mango tree at the northern end of the lap pool catapulted me out of a nightmare. I was simmering in a pot surrounded by salivating cannibals.

Creaking out of bed and into the bathroom, I ran myself a tepid shower and stood there until the water went cold, and the heat from my sunburn calmed. Wrapping a towel around me, I hurried to the bedroom, wondering what I should wear for my job interview.

Selecting a modest mauve mini and a putty-coloured Indigo singlet, I eased into the duds. I tied my dreads back with a ribbon, then gulped down some soy milk for breakfast. Grabbing my wallet and mobile, I slipped into flatties.

Passing Storage on my way to Reception, I turned the knob. The door opened with a rush, revealing a row of padlocked cages. Laundry bags in the first cage were stamped with AA. To indicate Amédée Apartments? Oiled sacks leaned against the wall of the farthest cage, beside wooden crates with rope handles. A length of metal, like the barrel of a slug gun, gleamed. Was the weapon Claude's, a gun he'd used on hunting trips in New Caledonia?

I pulled the Storage door to.

A guy in a green linen suit with a briefcase waited near the lift. He was way too overdressed for a tourist. His clothing resembled the Kenzo outfit I'd seen the French examiner wear, and from behind, his hair was also similar. I decided I was imagining things. Last heard, Pascal Manet had taken up the post of director at the Alliance Française in Melbourne.

Sandrine wasn't overjoyed to see me. Nor was she fizzed off. Her hair was tied at the nape of her neck, and her expression was cool and business-like.

"Claude said Dominick Nicks might have a job for me." I locked eyeballs with her. "I'll be brewing coffee, or waiting tables, or whatever. Where does Dominick hang out?"

Sandrine, in hot-pink shorts and a matching blouse tied at the front to reveal a neat midriff, scribbled an address and telephone number on paper with an Amédée letterhead. Her arms were tanned, but I noticed a bruise. Had Claude hit her? He had admitted having a 'naughty temper'. Then again, he seemed crazy in love with her.

She saw me eyeing the bruise, twisted her arm, and handed me the piece of paper.

"How do I get there?"

"Our complimentary shuttle bus is just leaving."

"Complimentary?" I scowled. "Wow, I paid forty dollars to get from Cairns to Glisten Beach when I arrived."

Sandrine gave me a sharp glance. "Was Wesley the driver?"

"He didn't give his name."

"Probably a fill-in being opportunistic." Sandrine sounded resigned, as though dealing with scams was part of her daily routine. "I'll look into it."

She opened a cash box. I tucked the fifty she gave me into my wallet, together with Dominick Nicks's address.

"The shuttle drops you off at Jamesville Mall." She added—as if worried I might be tempted to flag down a passing ute: "At four pm the last bus of the day returns."

Guests in straw hats clambered aboard as I ran to the humming vehicle.

"I'm Wesley," said the unfamiliar driver. "Any queries, eh?"

We wound our way through the side streets, and onto the highway. Beyond walls of sugarcane, smoke cast a pall in the sky.

"They're burning the sugarcane," said Wesley, sucking in his cheeks, "to destroy them taipans that kill the cane cutters in two shakes. These days mostly they use machines, cut the cane with big mothers."

"Are there *really* taipans in the sugarcane?" I asked.

"Blood oath!"

"And are these poisonous creatures only in sugarcane? Or do I have to be careful *everywhere*?"

"Yeah, or is only the beach safe?" A guy scratched his belly.

Wesley snorted. "Taipan was seen on the foreshore of Glisten Beach the other day."

My stomach dropped.

"And them things are deadly, worse than a cane toad in the bowl of your loo. And that happens more than you'd expect. Worse than crocs, and there's been the odd one of *them* seen in the bushes on Glisten Beach. Crocs come outta the creeks."

We turned into the Jamesville Mall car park.

"This shuttle bus is continuing to Cairns." He yanked on the handbrake. "Next bus back to Glisten Beach in an hour, otherwise you gotta wait 'til this arvo."

"When this arvo, mate?" someone yelled.

"Four … or thereabouts. And if youse wanna stay on lingering longer, imbibing in the Jamesville Tavern, another shuttle bus connecting tavern to resorts departs every hour to bring you back to Amédée Apartments."

"We're off to Lavender Bale's T-shirts, have our names hand-painted on a croc, or a green tree frog!" The wife of the gladiator-sandals man turned to me. "Are you going there too, dear?"

"I'm off to a boring interview."

"Well, luck was on your side yesterday. The kidnapper let you go. So I'm sure you'll be as fortunate with your job application."

"But I wasn't kidnapped!"

Not interested, she hurried off with her husband.

Flopping down the stairs of the bus, I wondered: *How to persuade Dominick Nicks I'd spent years making coffee?*

Behind me, I heard Wesley say: "Watch out for them taipans!"

I plunged into the cool of the mall, scanning the retail outlets for Dominick Nicks's coffee shop. I scooted along the concourse, sweaty and edgy. At the far end, I spied a sign: NICK INTO DOMINICK'S. Beneath, was a smaller sign: *For your Fix!*

Heart clattering around in my ribcage, I touched the beads Rocky had given me three times for luck.

Chapter 12

Only one customer sat drinking coffee in the sea of bentwood chairs and tables. Posters on the walls advertised foreign films and community events.

Wearing a T-shirt printed in large green letters with NICK INTO DOMINICK'S, Dominick Nicks peered at me through horn-rimmed specs. His cheeks puffed in and out as I approached.

"I'm Genna Perrier," I said. "I've come about the job."

He led me straight to the Expobar espresso machine with cups and tumblers heaped in wonky piles on top.

"Claude tells me you're almost a barista, eh, Genna!" Dominick twisted a peace ring on his pinkie. "Even if true, I can only afford to pay you the base food and beverage rate. Bit over thirteen bucks an hour."

"That's fine!" My heart was still pattering with nervousness. "But I'm not *that* good. In fact, it's a while since I, like, *used* a coffee machine, so I've probably forgotten everything I ever knew."

"It's like riding a bike." He indicated the grinder at the side of the Expobar. "Two shots for your normal cup of coffee, bucket for excess and empty it at the end of the day." Pause. "I'd be relying on you to keep the end of the steamer clean to avoid getting a build-up of milk on the wand, very unhygienic, eh."

"Tell me about it!" I said, doing my best to sound hip about steam wands.

"Oh, and the bubbles." He fixed me with his gaze. "Always bang the milk jug down to get rid of the bubbles, don't want big bubbles. If you haven't done this for a while I should emphasise fine foam's the go these days. Far trendier to have a low froth in your cappuccino, smooth is what they like, even this far north. And remember we also get our fair share of tourist drop-ins!"

I nodded.

"I don't have to stress, if you don't have a crema on the coffee, throw it out, don't muck around. I've had that many smart arses trying to fix a bad coffee. Don't fiddle with it, start again. But you already know that, eh?" Removing his specs, he rubbed the bridge of his nose with thumb and forefinger.

"Absolutely!"

"A 'why bother' is more popular with the locals than the tourists. Soy, half-skinny, half-decaf. I don't s'pose you have many of those fairy-tale coffee types in Sydney?"

"I'm from Melbourne," I said, not daring to tell Dominick I came from a hick seaside town on the Mornington Peninsula.

"Well, well, you come from a *real* coffee city … big Italian community down there!" A thoughtful pause. "I run H2O through the machine to clean it every day … oh, and water's connected directly to the plumbing … or the coffee tastes burnt and disgusting. Girl before you used to let the coffee build up so you couldn't even get the filter on. By the way, never touch the steam pressure."

A chick carrying a clipboard marched to the counter. "Latte please, Dominick!"

I prayed he wouldn't ask me to serve her. He hit the grinder like a pro—two shots—and packed, slammed the lever in place, whipped a glass beneath the spout. The slogan—*For your Fix!*—rippled across his back as the coffee dribbled into the glass. He filled a stainless steel pitcher with skim milk from the fridge, plunged in the steam wand and moved the pitcher as the froth rose up. He poured in the frothed-up milk.

After handing over the latte, he took the cash. "Of course, I'd expect you to clean the machine before you leave at night."

Alarm bells rang. "Night?"

“Didn’t Claude say?” Dominick rubbed his forehead hard. “Start at four, finish at ten, or later. We get students from Reef University up the road, marine biologists and such, come in for a coffee after the last lecture of an evening.”

I’d been hanging out to visit Kooracoondoo, see Roch Colline, meet Rocky’s family and go to the markets. Maybe even have a bungy jump. My social life was about to enter the zilch zone.

“Fine by me, I like working at night.” My stomach sank. “When do I begin?”

“Tomorrow.” His eyes flicked over my dreads; he ran his hand over his own hair, slicking it forward from the crown to the top of his forehead.

“What’s wrong?”

“You’re bright and attractive, but I’ve got another possible for the job. I should speak to her first.”

“I’m very reliable. I’ll turn up no matter what, cyclone, tidal surge … tsunami.”

“Nope, changed my mind, can’t hire you.”

“Why not?” My voice became high-pitched.

“It’s the dreadlocks. They’re unhygienic, all that peanut butter and muck you put on ’em. Customers don’t like it.”

“Oooh, nooo! I never used peanut butter!” I explained about the toothpaste, honey, eggs and Stately Homes of England beeswax.

“That so?” His eyes began to glaze over.

“What if I had ’em cut off?” My scalp itched; I resisted the urge to scratch. “Would you employ me then?”

“Mmn.” Dominick eyed my ‘do. “I s’pose, if you do it straightaway. See Seranella, a friend with a salon in Jamesville Mall. She does an okay job, and she’s not expensive.”

“Citronella?”

Dominick grinned. “It’s an Italian name. You must’ve passed Seranella’s Locks on your way here!”

Chapter 13

Midway down Jamesville Mall, I discovered the salon.

"Hi, I'm Genna," I said to the girl behind the desk. "I'm here"—and I peered at her name tag—"um, Sofia, to see Seranella about my dreads."

The receptionist scanned my hair. "Need our special wash, do you? Sometimes you find bits and pieces of nasties in dreadlocks caused by the peanut butter. Even insects."

"Ooh, nooo. I never used peanut butter. But I did have ants at one stage. I used honey, and it fermented." I gave a little groan as I remembered Pascal Manet falling about laughing when he spotted the ants on my scalp. "It was so embarrassing!"

"Yeah. It's worse if someone else notices 'em, a bit like nits." She rolled her liquid eyes in a clockwise motion. "So what do you want done then?"

"Dominick Nicks said …"

"Dominick, eh? Old friend of ours!" Sofia sounded excited.

"Well, he'll employ me if I cut off my dreads. He says they're too unhygienic for, y'know, handling food."

"Sure, we can do that. It'll be short, though, a bit butch. She won't be able to remove *all* those tangles. And I imagine the rubber bands you used will have fused with your hair by now. She'll do the best she can, but."

"That's fine." I gave a resigned shrug. "I need work. I'm skint."

"I'll gown you up then. Seranella prefers to snip off the dreads first, wash the hair and then sterilise the scissors."

Sterilise the scissors? I felt germ-infested.

Sofia installed me before a mirror.

A leggy dudette, also with liquid eyes, loomed up behind me. "Hi!" She addressed my reflection. "I love doing this!"

"Love what?"

"Cutting off dreads. They are *so* unhygienic!"

By now, I was getting the picture. The shopkeepers of Jamesville Mall believed I was a walking bag of germs. I was surprised Dominick had allowed me to enter his coffee shop. I was amazed he hadn't suggested sheep dip.

Seranella snapped the blades of her scissors. "Ready for the big cut, eh?"

"Right on." Shivers of apprehension ran along my arms.

"Excellent!"

"But what if I hate my hair? I've never worn it short."

"It'll grow back. In this climate, whoosh, it'll be shoulder length, but!"

Pulling off my ribbon, she inspected a dreadlock and wrinkled her nose. Sawing at my hair, she said, "Sheesh, it's like rope. You've sure got some muck in here. Whatever did you use?"

Again, I listed the ingredients, and confessed about the ants.

"Stuff happens," she murmured. And then: "With all this shit, Dominick can pay to have these sharpened!" She continued to saw and snip, pant and complain, changed scissors and kept going. "Keep your head down, Genna, so I can do the bits underneath."

After what seemed like ten years, she announced, "All off! Don't look yet, but. You'll freak if you look before it's washed!"

She went to put her hand over my eyes. Too late. I clamped my lips together to stop the scream. I resembled a feral kid, with a dunny brush on top.

"What've I done?" I groaned. "I am so gross! I look like a jailbird, a loser, worse than any bogan!"

I ran my fingers over the beads around my wrist, lifted the memory wire and let it snap back. "I've just lost a potential boyfriend. He's older than me, and he'll flip when he sees how scungy I look! It's like I'm wearing a fright wig!"

Seranella placed another towel around my shoulders and led me to the basin. The warmth of the water helped me relax. I lay back and let her scrub. She dragged a comb through my remaining thatch, clucked and muttered and used lots of products.

Finished, she walked me over to the mirror.

I stared. "I'm like a bloke!" My voice was hoarse with horror.

Seranella sounded shocked. "Noooh, you are bellissimo. You're kinda European, eh. Where are you from originally?"

"I'm Aussie, but I was born a Caldoche in New Caledonia."

"That so? Well, now everyone can see your pixie Caldoche face, and those awesome eyes of yours. Wait 'til I've finished blowing. You'll be rapt!"

My hair was darker than I remembered, and glossier. But that short-back-and-sides cut sure was severe. She must've seen the doubt on my face.

"We could do some highlights next time, eh? Even put in extensions?"

"Extensions?"

She held up a long, skinny straw-coloured piece. "Like this!"

"How do you attach it?"

"Dab of glue near the top of your head."

"More glue?" I said, doubtfully. "Dominick wouldn't like it if I had more glue. It's what he complained about in the first place."

"A proper hair product would be totally acceptable with Dom!" She removed my gown. "Like some hairspray?"

"Sure."

She squirted. A blob of lacquer landed on my skirt, leaving a mark the size of a ten cent piece.

"It'll dry out in two jiffs!" She dabbed at the stain with a towel.

My head felt strangely light as I went to the desk.

"Seranella, what's the damage?" shouted Sofia.

Busy sweeping up bits of hair from the floor, the hairdresser stopped what she was doing and shook her head.

"My sister used to date Dom," Sofia said in a hushed voice. "She'll get the money out of him. In my opinion, he had a terrible cheek telling you to cut off those dreads. So forget about paying, eh! We'll watch the moths fly out when we gouge out the moolah!"

"Thanks." I glanced at my still-stained skirt.

"BTW, I love your neat bracelet!" Sofia's glance zeroed in on the beads around my wrist. "How's it done?"

"Memory wire." I headed for the door of the salon, anxious not to miss the shuttle bus. "A girl called Douce makes 'em and sells 'em at the Kooracoondoo Markets. Go check it out!"

Dudes in fish-print shirts flogging reef tours shoved flyers in my face as I sped along the lengthy shopping centre. Pushing past pale southerners in hats, and locals with beer guts looming above crocodile belts, I burst into the sun.

The car park was filled with tourist buses, flat-bed trucks, sedans and utilities. I could see no sign of the shuttle bus. And Wesley wouldn't be back until four pm.

Chapter 14

At a stall overflowing with tropical fruit, I bought a banana. Trawling along Jamesville Mall, window shopping and munching and filling in time until the next shuttle bus, I halted outside Lavender Bale's T-shirt shop. Tourists looked on as a woman hand-painted their names atop laughing crocodiles and green tree frogs.

The shop was packed. I reminded myself to come back later.

Alongside Lavender Bale's, was an army disposal store. Sale signs were plastered across the Drop Zone Army-Navy window. Camo clothing was trendy, and I still had the money Sandrine had given me. With the bucks left over from the hundred Claude had paid me for looking after the Amédée Apartments library, I had enough for new duds. I spied a fab pair of paratrooper fatigues—reduced to $14.99—and decided to investigate.

Inside the shop, I found an impressive range of soldier apparel: BDUs, military warm-up suits, sweatshirts and anoraks. As I paused to admire some nifty boots—paratrooper, combat and jungle—the sales guy with a to-die-for tan approached.

"Hi, we've got a great range of headwear too. Patrol caps, poly-cotton boonie hats, berets and head-wraps. Like to try 'em, eh?" His gym junkie muscles bulged as he talked.

"Headwear?" I suppressed a glare. "Are you bagging my new short-back-and-sides?"

"Whoa!" He lifted his palms in a defensive gesture. "Who said anything about your hair? It's hot outside. You might like something to keep the sun off, but."

I relaxed a little. "I'm feeling a bit fragile. I had my dreads cut off and it's like I'm, well, sort of …" I raised an eyebrow.

"Name's Anton."

"Yeah, well, Anton, I feel like a bloke right now."

"A bloke, eh?" He gave a brief laugh. "I don't think so."

Hoping he hadn't noticed the flush creep up my neck, I said, "The paratrooper fatigues in the window? Do you have a pair in my size?"

"Dunno. You're quite small, but. I'll go have a look." Anton disappeared. He re-emerged, holding up a pair of camo army pants. "These orright, eh?"

"If you get me a matching tank, I'll try them together."

"Solid colours go best with camo." He handed me a khaki tank top from the pile. "The tank's a good buy for eight bucks."

"Where do I try these on?"

He indicated a curtained space.

"Oh wow, *those* are great!" I said, passing a bunch of bags on my way to the change room.

"Mechanics' tool bag is twenty bucks, duffle for twenty-five … nah, I can give you the duffle bag for twenty as well, if you like."

Closing the hessian, I whipped off my Indigo singlet and undid the zipper of my mini. As I wriggled out of the soiled, maybe ruined, skirt, I decided I could hardly rock on back and complain after receiving a freebie haircut.

Piling my things on a table in the corner, I hauled on the camo fatigues, pulled the tank over my head and admired my reflection. Running my fingers through my new cropped hair, I tightened the ankle drawstring and did a twirl in front of the mirror. If I bought the duffle bag, too, I'd still have change from Sandrine's fifty, I told myself.

"Whaddya think?" I pushed aside the hessian.

"Sex-eee!" said Anton. "Some chicks look butch in camo. You look great, but." He touched me on the arm. "Stay in the sun too long, eh?"

"Yeah, I arrived from down south, and spent yesterday on the beach."

"Ouch!" He grinned. "But with skin like yours, you'll be a native in no time." Pause. "Like a patrol cap, or a head-wrap, to go with it?"

"Nup, I'd look as though I've joined up. I'll just take the fatigues and the tank, and one of those duffle bags."

"Wanna wear the threads now?"

Nodding, I gave him my fifty and accepted the change.

Anton removed the price tags. "What about a camo canteen, only six bucks? Or a military marching compass?"

I giggled. "No, really."

"Ever go camping? Need an anglehead flashlight? A tri-fold shovel?"

Was Anton trying to come on to me? I looked at my Swatch. Darting back behind the hessian, I stuffed my skirt, singlet and mobile into my new duffle bag.

"Gotta go! Thanks. I'll see you around."

"Wait a sec!" Grabbing an army beret, Anton jammed it on my head. "Finishes the outfit off, eh!" He handed me a pair of dog tags.

"I don't need those, can't afford 'em!"

"Beret and tags are on me, but."

"That's grouse of you!" I gave him a glowing smile. "I'll give *you* a coffee in return, gratis."

Swinging the tags over my head, I adjusted the beret and hurried down the mall to the car park. Still no shuttle bus. I began to wonder when Rocky expected me in Kooracoondoo. It would be dark in a couple of hours and, with my new job starting tomorrow, I'd be forced to go up the mountain early in the morning if I wished to see him. Pulling my mobile from the duffle, I dumped the bag back on the ground and searched for Rocky's phone number in my Contacts list. Pressed the digits.

My tank top was sticking to my back. Gathering my things, I retreated into the cool of Jamesville Mall and called him.

"*Laissez votre message*," said the voicemail.

My signal was weak. Only one bar left. I composed an SMS, punching out the message with my thumb:

cd u text me yr address as I plan 2 c u

Keeping one eye on the car park, I saw the shuttle bus arrive and hefted my duffle bag. Wesley didn't recognise me when I climbed aboard.

"You just arrived in our Deep North, eh?" he said, as I installed myself in the front seat close to the air-conditioning. "Backpacker?"

"No, not backpacking. Don't you remember me? I'm Genna, Sandrine's"—the 'daughter' word stuck in my throat—"um, friend."

The driver seemed doubtful. "You look different, but."

"I cut my dreadlocks off."

"Sort of like a soldier or somethin'." Wesley continued to appear puzzled. "So, if yer not backpackin', did ya join up?"

"Nup, I shopped in a disposal store." Pressing OK, I sent my SMS to Rocky and waited for his reply.

Shaking his head, Wesley plucked his iPod from the dash. Plugged in, he tapped his feet to one of the ten thousand songs stored in his device. We waited. No one else arrived.

"Others must be imbibing in the Jamesville Tavern, doncha think?" he muttered.

"It's hot enough." I adjusted my beret.

"They'll 'ave to get the hourly shuttle back to Coral Cove if they don't get a move on." Sighing, Wesley turned the key in the ignition.

I checked my mobile. Rocky hadn't responded to my text.

Speeding along the highway to Glisten Beach, I watched the sugarcane stalks waving, fluffy and pale. "What are those feathery things on the cane?" I leaned forward.

"Them sugar flowers?" Wesley said over his shoulder. "They don't grow the cane from that, but. They strike the cane from pieces about twelve inches long."

"Like kava?" I recalled Rocky telling me they grew kava the same way.

"What's kava?"

"Oh, it's a plant whose ground roots make a muddy tasting drink. You go to a special place, a nakamal. And you feel a most amazing calm sweep over you, and your muscles relax and everything becomes crystal clear."

"That so? Reckon I'd prefer a XXXX."

Again, I checked my mobile screen. Rocky still hadn't answered my SMS.

"Mind if I drop you at the back?" Wesley's voice took over from the aircon whoosh. The shuttle bus slowed and pulled up at the rear entrance of the Amédée Apartments.

“That’s fine!” I fiddled with the wisps of hair poking from my beret.

“Watch out for them stingers, eh!”

I clambered off the bus. Swinging my duffle bag over my shoulder, I sauntered past real estate signs tacked to the fence advertising Garden Apartments for sale. The place seemed deserted. Fewer cars were in the parking spaces. Was everyone snorkelling on the reef, tramping through rainforests, or maybe feeding Fergus the crocodile? Through the safety fence, I saw Mercurio cleaning the pool, his tatts inky in the sunshine.

The whip of a sulphur-crested cockatoo stripping branches off a gum tree competed with the hush of a carpentry plane. Recalling my promise to help Claude with the Amédée Library, I headed for his shed.

Chapter 15

I remained at the doorway. "Dominick Nicks hired me!"

Claude continued to work on the wood with his plane, and I wondered if he'd heard.

"I thought I'd put an exercise book in the library," I shouted above the noise, "with the titles borrowed listed. And a pencil tied to a piece of string."

Giving out a waft of ti-tree oil, he put down his plane and picked up a ruler.

"Did you hear me? It's Genna!"

"I 'ave heard you." He concentrated on measuring. "Go see Sandrine. She 'as paper and pencils and fings like zat."

"Cool, I'll ask her." I turned to go. "Oh, there's a bird making a mess of your drive, stripping off branches."

"It 'appens often." He kept his back to me.

As I left, the sulphur-crested cockatoo balanced on the tip of a branch, gnawing. The branch broke off. The bird nosedived, and then swept back up into the gum tree. *He's playing games*, I said to myself.

Taking the path beside the Beachfront Apartments, I adjusted my beret again and strolled into Reception. In the same outfit she'd worn that morning, Sandrine worked at her computer. A warm breeze blew off the sea. She seemed at peace.

She glanced up. Her eyes were dreamy, until she saw me. Her pupils dilated. Her mouth dropped open, and a scream exploded from her lips. Goose bumps danced along her arms. Was someone behind me with a gun? I spun around. There was no one else in Reception. My hands were sweaty and trembling as I swung my duffle bag down, and hauled up my camo fatigues—now slipping to my hips.

Sandrine screamed again. Clapping her hand over her face, she reeled away from the desk. Colliding with the door leading to the Management Apartment, she bounced off the architrave and disappeared.

Claude pounded up from his workshop. Thrashing past ferns in planter boxes, he burst in. He took in my appearance and his face became thunderous. "*How could you do zis?*" His lips went purple.

"Do what? *What have I done?*" Beneath my feet, the ground felt spongy.

He grabbed me by the shoulder, shoved my face before a shell-enhanced mirror. "Look! Look! Look!" he bellowed.

I gazed at my short hair, at my newly-acquired beret set on a jaunty angle. "What?"

"You *de-liber-ately* upset *mon amour*! 'Ow could you do zis to Sandrine?"

"I'm sort of butch, a bit blokey. But that's not enough reason for her to break out screaming and run away as if she'd seen a ghost. I don't get it."

"You dress up as soldier, and you still don't GET IT?" Claude's face was so close I almost passed out from the ti-tree oil. "Who do you very much resemble?" Again, he pushed my face against the glass.

"I du-n-no. I really, I mean, I only came in to ask for a pencil and string and something to write on." My bottom lip went rubbery. I clamped my teeth to stop from snivelling.

"You are *nasty* girl!" With that, Claude went behind the counter. He disappeared into the Management Apartment.

I could hear Sandrine sobbing, a terrible, bereft sort of weeping. Finally, the sound became muffled. In the dimness of the apartment, I saw Claude take her in his arms and clasp her tightly. And I recalled the photograph I'd seen: Sandrine with my father, her in a bikini, him with his hair in a military style. I had brought back memories of my dad, quite innocently, by wearing camo gear.

Hefting my duffle bag, I trudged off.

Near the entrance to the Jungle Walk, Mercurio peered over the safety fence. "What's goin' on, eh?" He flicked his ponytail, fiddled with his skimmer.

"Nothing." I inserted the key in the lock of my door. "Just family business."

"Aw, right. Thought someone 'ad their throat cut, but!"

He went back to scooping the leaves off the lap pool.

Letting myself into my apartment, I collapsed on the sofa and gulped back tears. I desperately needed someone to talk to. Scrabbling for Hetty's number on my mobile, I pressed the button. Her phone rang and rang. Eventually, she picked up.

"Hi, um, hello, Hetty, I was like …" Struggling for words, I almost chickened out of the call.

"What's up, Gen? You sound kinda stressed."

"Um, well, I cut off my dreads, and it's, like, kind of had repercussions."

Hetty heaved a sigh. "Look, mate …"

"Only Stefan calls me mate!"

"Okay, Genna! In case you forgot, I've got exams, French 101." She heaved a second gust of air down the phone. "I'm up to my ears in Imperial France. People are having their heads hacked off, and you're freaked about losing your *shitty dreadlocks*! That is *so* pathetic!"

"No, it's more than losing my dreads. I bought these camo pants on sale, with a tank to match, and the guy gave me dog tags and a beret"—I heard her sigh once more—"and when Sandrine saw me she screamed and collided with the door leading to the Management Apartment."

Silence the other end.

"Um, she ran into the door, desperate to get away from me. I reminded her of my birth father, and I don't know what to do." My body went slack. I played with my dog tags.

Hetty's voice battered my eardrum. "Come back home then!"

"But I just got here, and I found a job working in a coffee shop."

"Look, Gen, this chick's got issues. Anyway she's not really your mum. Namilly Perrier brought you up. Sandrine let you go when you were a little tacker, in fact didn't even know you were gone for about five years." She reefed in a breath. "Frankly, I don't know why you're roaming around the country serving coffee, dropping out of your French course at South Central Community College. Your mum's not well, either." She sniffed. "Plus Win's not pulling her weight in the recycle shop. What's it called? Re-sale Rose?" Hetty was in lecturing mode.

I knew one response that would shut her up. "I will."

"You will what?"

"Come home!"

"Good! Now I can return to Imperial France!"

She hung up.

Chapter 16

I was determined to forget about Sandrine. I made up my mind to leave Glisten Beach and return to Ravella. This trip had turned into a ginormous disaster. Rocky hadn't responded to my SMS, I knew zilch about making coffee, and I'd chopped off my dreads for no good reason.

Changing out of my fatigues into comfy drawstring pants and a shapeless Mambo T-shirt, I pulled my mini from the duffle bag. I tipped soap powder into the bathroom basin, and scrubbed until the hairspray stain came out. Giving the skirt a final dunk, I rinsed and hung the gear over the towel rail. I dragged my suitcase from the cupboard.

First, I decided to make myself a plate of salad. Chomping moodily on a vine-ripened tomato, I heard my mobile rap dance on the coffee table. Was Rocky, responding to my text at last?

I rushed to the phone. *1 message received.* Heart paddling, I pressed *Show*.

address is 8 sugarcane lane, plse come have gr8 news

Gazing at Rocky's SMS, I wondered: *What great news did he have?* I changed my mind about leaving, but I needed to fix my hair. *How could I look less butch?* Tips, as the hairdresser had mentioned, or should I have extensions?

Grabbing my wallet, I pulled out Dominick Nicks's card and dialled.

The proprietor picked up. He sounded breathless.

"Dominick? Genna, here. I desperately need to ring Seranella's Locks." A buzz of talk in the background; coffee cups clinked.

"Speak up. I can't hear you!"

"The hairdressing salon? Do you have the phone number?"

"Not off the top of my head, and the girls lock up at five."

"What hour do they open?"

"Hang on a moment." I heard him take an order for a macchiato; he picked up again. "What do you wanna know?"

"What-time-does-Seranella's-Locks-open-in-the-morning?"

"Ooh, about eight. Who am I speaking to, eh?"

"Genna."

"Who?"

"Genna Perrier!"

"Boy, Genna Perrier, do I have a bone to pick with you! Are you and Seranella involved in some sort of shakedown regarding yours truly? That bitch has cost me a fortune!"

"Whaddya mean 'shakedown'?"

"I'll see you tomorrow arvo. We'll discuss it then."

"I'm not sure if I'll be coming."

But he'd hung up. I pressed the Off button on my mobile.

A rap sounded on my door. Sandrine stood there.

"I wish to apologise." The whites of her eyes were like road maps.

"What, for scaring the tripe out of me?" My lips tightened. "For making me feel like, um, a piece of *merde*?" I glared. "I had my dreads cut off only so I could be employed. Do you think I enjoy going around like some sort of lezzo?" I wagged a finger at her. "The job was all part of Claude's grand plan, and I don't even know how to make coffee." I inhaled. "I don't think *you* should be making my life worse than it already is."

"Would you like me to show you how to make coffee?" Dimples showed at the corner of her mouth as she smiled.

"Wow, you have your own machine?"

"We have a small one, for our use. Would you like to try it?"

"Um, like, um, I dunno."

She glanced at the dining room table. "Finish your meal, and when you come, don't go through Reception. Knock at the side entrance to the Management Apartment." She added in French, "*À tout à l'heure!*"

Having said she'd see me shortly, she clicked off down the path, beaded sandals twinkling.

Disinterested in finishing my salad, I wrestled cling wrap over the plate and shoved it in the fridge. Not wishing to upset Sandrine further, I wondered how I could make myself appear less like my father. Had his eyes been as dark as mine? In the full-length bedroom mirror, I was unable to see where my pupil ended and the iris began. And then I knew the answer. If I plastered on mascara and eye shadow, it'd take away any blokey, unwanted, soldiery butchness.

In my makeup purse, I found lilac shadow and matching mascara. I caked the gunk on in layers until I was almost skanky, and smeared on a purple lippy. Hair ribbons? A satin ribbon lay among my knickers. I tied a squirt of hair into a bow upon my head.

Inspecting my reflection, I wondered if I should change into something more feminine to go with the makeup. I held up a day-glo skirt. Was a skirt too formal? Flicking hangers along the rack, I fingered my lemon butter shorts. Would a boob tube go with shorts? Or was the look too beachy?

I was still agonising over what to wear when the wall phone connected to Reception rang. Knocking over a palm-leaf candlestick, I snatched it from its cradle.

"Have you decided not to come?" Sandrine sounded concerned.

"Sure, I'll be there. I'm, um, like, doing the dishes." I righted the candlestick.

"There's no need to wash up in the sink! You have a dishwasher. Surely I left powder in your flat?"

"Mmmn," I murmured. "You did leave some powder. But I don't know how the machine works and I sorta like doing dishes by hand. It's the sudsy feeling." I was squirming in a tangle of porkies. "I'll be there soon, in a sec, in a mo … whatever..."

"Good! We'll have fun making coffee! Claude is minding Reception this evening, so there'll be the two of us!" She sounded almost joyful. Was the feeling genuine? I wondered. Or had Claude persuaded her to invite me?

Berating myself for caring about what Sandrine thought, of tarting up my appearance to please her, I scuttled back to the bathroom and yanked the ribbon from my hair. I frantically rubbed the goo off my face with a tissue.

With raisin-coloured marsupial eyes, and still in my T-shirt and comfy pants, I grabbed my keys and let myself out.

Chapter 17

I was surprised to find the Management Apartment not much different from mine. Apart from framed parrot pictures and a print of a cagou bird, little in the way of personal items such as books and knick-knacks were on show.

The soccer table in the corner, beneath a criss-cross timber-work wall mirror, bore the *Baby-foot* logo. It was as though my birth mother and her partner were ready to pack and leave at any moment. A record player belted out *Non, je ne regrette rien*, and I detected a pungent smell, suspiciously like dope. Or was the aroma caused by French cigarettes?

Sandrine had changed into a strapless dress, with a floaty over-shirt. She switched off the CD and flicked on a pineapple-based lamp. Pulling back the curtains, she slid open the patio doors. Waves dumped in the moonlight. Palms and eucalypts swayed in the tropical breeze. The Amédée Apartments sign cast a rectangle of light across the soccer table.

The breeze cleared the room of the dodgy odour.

Sandrine led me straight to the kitchen, saying, "Did you have a nice day?" as if I'd just come home from school and she was the mum who'd always been there, as if she'd never screamed at the sight of me in my camo duds. *Was she about to offer me milk and cookies?* I wondered.

"I, um, had my dreads cut off."

"I liked your dreadlocks!"

"Dominick Nicks said they were a health hazard."

She eyed my wrist. "I also like your bracelet. Did you buy that at the Kooracoondoo Markets?"

"Um, yeah," I lied, rather than mention Rocky.

"Now *this* is where you will practise for your new job."

Her coffee maker was miniscule in comparison to Dominick's. A packet of Gitanes Blondes cigarettes, blue with a gypsy dancer holding a tambourine, lay on the bench beside a chunk of white coral. I recalled the odour of the Gauloises Blondes, smoked by both Pascal and Marcel Manet. Did Gitanes smell different?

I forced myself to concentrate. "You sure this'll help me work Dominick's machine?"

"It's the identical principle. Hot water through the coffee, steam wand through the milk. And *voilà*!" Her hand wafted a scent of Miss Dior—the perfume Namilly gave me each birthday and Christmas—in my direction. "Unless he has an illy."

"An illy?"

"A hundred thousand dollars for one of *those* machines, the Rolls Royce of coffee makers!"

"He has an Expobar."

"Well, here is the filter holder, and this your filter." She opened a gold foil bag containing the freshly-ground beans. "You pack the coffee in the filter, although, of course, you'll have a grinder. One shot if it's …"

"… weak, two shots if it's strong, which will mostly be the case."

"You're catching on already!" Lipstick showed on her front teeth when she talked. "Now, you make the coffee while I tell you how." She cleared her throat. "Lift the lid, unscrew the cap and fill the machine with water, and don't overfill! Now plug in." She looked at me. "I suppose Dominick's machine is directly connected to the plumbing?"

"I think, ah, he said … it … was." Doing my best not to spill water on her bench, I pushed in the plug. "Now what?"

"Place the filter in the filter holder … have you tamped the coffee? … and connect the holder to the unit." She gave me a cup. "Put this underneath, turn the lever and wait. Easy, *n'est-ce pas*?"

"Except Dominick's espresso machine is computerised, with symbols." I watched the coffee spit and dribble from the outlet.

"So press the appropriate symbol!" Her laugh was tinkly. "Now the milk." She handed me the stainless steel frothing jug. "Fill with milk, preferably skim, and place the steam wand inside."

I moved the steam nozzle around in circles as I'd seen Dominick do, thinking this was simple.

Until she cried, "*Attention!*"

Too late.

As I lifted the nozzle above the level of the milk, my T-shirt became covered in hot spots.

"Are you burnt?"

"I'm okay, I think."

The liquid pricked against my skin and, with a shaky hand, I tipped the foam in the cup and handed her the coffee.

"*You* have it!"

"I'm raw vegan. I don't, like, drink coffee. Milk is in there, and the coffee's roasted."

"Oh no, roasting means they send hot *air* over the green beans. So the beans are not really cooked. And the water *runs* through the coffee, so you couldn't say it's cooked, either." She dipped a finger in the drink. "Now that is the correct temperature for a good coffee. You should be able to touch it without burning your skin. Logically, you could say coffee is an uncooked drink!" She smiled. The lipstick was gone from her front teeth.

"But there's milk in there."

"Well, I'll drink this one and *you* drink the next, without milk! As I understand it, dairy food is forbidden." She cocked her head to one side. "Why did you decide to become a raw vegan?"

I refused to admit Namilly's greasy cooking had pushed me in a vegan direction. I didn't plan to provide Sandrine with ammunition to use against my mum.

In Reception, Claude was persuading a Sydneysider to buy a three-day yacht cruise.

"When do you have dinner?" I asked. "I mean, it can't be easy as you've got tourists rocking up all the time."

"Dinner? We don't have dinner!" Leaning against the bench sipping, Sandrine stared at me in a strange way. "We have a snack, after we close at night." She paused. "Clarissa Hays-Bert occasionally holds the fort so Claude and I can have a long lunch together."

"It's like that seven days a week?"

She pushed herself away from the bench, and I saw a fresh bruise on her arm. "Now a coffee for *you*, Genna!"

I found myself exchanging hits of coffee with Sandrine while she grilled me about the proportion of milk in macchiato and latte and cappuccino. She instructed me on the difference between an espresso, a long black and a ristretto, plus the art of making mocha with an added dash of chocolate. I made cups of coffee, over and over, until I got the correct amount of crema on top.

"The Colombians put water in the cup first and top up with coffee," she informed me.

The room spun from the caffeine. "Am I meant to know that?"

"Only if a Colombian walks in." She burst out laughing.

Lighting a Gitane, she led me to a fish-print sofa, blew a smooth stream of smoke in the air, and installed herself with a half-finished short black.

I sat down beside her.

"So have you been happy living with *her*?" Picking up a Paris Match magazine, she idly turned the pages.

"Her?"

"The *nounou* who ran off with you."

"Her name is Namilly, and she didn't 'run off' with me. In Nouméa car bombs were exploding, people were dying and she rescued me!" I pushed myself off the sofa. "I'm sorry I upset you earlier."

Impassive, she took a puff of her cigarette.

I went to leave, and then blurted: "Okay, I'll have the DNA test. You organise it with the doctor."

"We'll do it now!" The magazine hit the coffee table with a splat as she stubbed her cigarette out in a nautilus shell.

"Do it *now*?" My knees went wobbly.

"I have the test kit ready. We take mouth swabs, and I mail them off with a cheque."

My head reeled. "To France?"

"No, Italy!"

"I don't un-understand," I stuttered. "Marcel Manet had DNA tests done, confirming I was your natural daughter." The indignation rose up. "He pinched bits of my hair!"

"Oh, Marcel did a similar thing with me, on my father's perverted orders."

"Why do we need to do it again?"

"Papa told me Marcel sent the tests to France. At the time, such things were banned. I trust Pascal, a teacher and a loyalist, but I do not trust his younger brother." She took a breath. "You were born with blue eyes, I distinctly remember."

"Aren't all babies born with blue eyes?" Curious, I asked, "Why don't you trust Marcel?"

"Marcel is a playboy, attractive, but sometimes I wonder if he is using my father for his own ends. One moment he is a separatist, a committed insurgent, the next attending loyalist meetings. Poof!" She threw her hands upwards.

Claude locked the external doors to Reception. Yawning, he entered the Management Apartment. "I will wash my teeth and go to my bed, *ma chérie.*"

Sandrine made negative signs with her fingers. "*Mon amour*, I need cotton tips from the bathroom first!"

"She 'as agreed then?" He spoke as if I was not there.

Sandrine nodded.

He strode to the other side of the room and jiggled the *Baby-foot* levers. He rammed red plastic men at the ball, rattled a goal through the net, before retrieving the ball from the goal box with his left index finger and playing again.

"Come, we will leave Claude to his games." Sandrine led the way to the bathroom.

Under the glare of a fluorescent tube, we took our cotton buds and, as though performing some bizarre ritual, ran them inside our mouths.

"Here!" I gave her my bud, shiny with saliva.

She placed the soggy samples in a cliplock bag, murmuring, "Now *that's* done, I need to join Claude. It's been a long day, and the reef bus will be here at six. We must be up bright and early, looking our best for our tourists!"

"Bye, then."

As I passed Storage on the way to my unit, I heard Sandrine clatter behind me in her glittery slides, and turned.

"Claude said to give you these." She thrust an exercise book and pencil at me, a length of brown string and a packet of thumb tacks. "Before I forget, I should warn you if someone hands you a copy of Maigret, *Maigret et la Grande Perche*, for example, a paperback in the original French, pass the book on to Claude immediately. *Do not* place it in the library! Claude will know what to do with it."

She hurried off.

Chapter 18

Night-time, I was as frisky as a freshly-opened packet of bran. Unable to sleep from the unaccustomed caffeine and Sandrine's warning about the Maigret book, I lay gazing at the whirring ceiling blades.

The clock radio burped numbers. At precisely 2:05 am, needing someone to talk to, I clambered out of bed. Knowing Hetty'd still be awake and book bashing, I also knew she'd be fizzed off if I bothered her again before she had finished her exams.

I unzipped my Cartoon Network carry bag, pulled out my laptop and, connecting the computer to the phone on the wall, went online.

The *birthmother.com* chat room was in full swing. Did these people never sleep? I asked myself. To fend off any potential stalkers, I called myself Garnet. It was cool to be a net chick once more. I chatted for twenty minutes, bragging, saying I'd found my birth mum, that she'd welcomed me by showering me with (ahem!) gifts. I even said she'd made me feel as if I'd never been away.

My cyberspace chums repaid my porkies by telling me that chat rooms were for those searching for their origins, not those who'd *discovered* their origins. And didn't I know how *bad I was making them feel*?

I logged off. Prowling around the apartment, I drew back the curtains to admire the reflection of the moon shafting across the Coral Sea. I could hear the putter of a boat. Was someone out there, fishing in the middle of the night?

As I peered, the glow of the Amédée Apartments sign began to fade. After a final spit and crack, the entire display turned black, just after I'd spied the person in the Rastafarian bonnet again. The dreadlocks were long and thick and, from the back, the man resembled the Kanak separatist I'd met in New Caledonia.

The glow of a cigarette penetrated the gloom. Slinking between the palm trees, he headed for the water. The moon edged behind a cloud. Puzzled, I turned away. Who was this person? And what was he doing on Glisten Beach?

I could smell sweet tobacco, like swamp. The aroma snuck beneath the crack of the door. I sniffed, sniffed again. Someone was definitely smoking dope. Was it the man on the beach, a tourist, or was the smell coming from the Management Apartment? Was the odour simply Sandrine's Gitanes cigarettes? Surely she wasn't toking on ganja?

A rustling sound came from the direction of the Jungle Walk, as though someone was in there. The sprinklers started up, clicking as they rotated. I heard "*Merde!*" Had the Jungle Walk intruder become wet? Every cell of my body was alert, every pore at attention.

A sharp rap on a door rang out, coming from the Garden Apartments at the rear of the complex. A voice called, "Pizza!" A door creaked open. There was low talking, the jingle of money. The door closed. Footsteps echoed down the concrete stairs as the delivery guy left. These were normal noises.

In an effort to calm my nerves, I tore paper from Sandrine's exercise book. Cross-legged, I settled myself on the floor and composed some words informing people about the Amédée Library. I wrote:

Amédée Free Self-Service Library

Guests,
Select your books, enjoy, and return prior to departure. Donations of books greatly appreciated.
Thank you.

Unsure whether to call myself Assistant Librarian or Chief Librarian, I opted for the top job. I completed with: *Chief Librarian, Genna Perrier.*

The Amédée Apartments sign surged back on. A golden glow, spattered with shadow dots, spread across my knees. Dot reflections? Was this the onset of rain?

I heard a pounding. Pushing myself up, I saw a waterfall of wet. Ropes of moisture drummed against my patio, cutting off my view of the beach and blotting out the boat sound. A chair clattered across the tiles and into the garden, settling among a clump of tree ferns. The effect of the caffeine was wearing off. My eyelids had that scratchy feel.

In the bedroom, the clock radio blinked 3:20. Did the early bus go to Jamesville Mall, I wondered, as I climbed into bed. In no time, I was dreaming of pirates and smoky dreadlocks, and cane toads in the bowl of my loo.

Chapter 19

The sun was peeping through when the Waveripper reef bus woke me. Hyped at the thought of seeing Rocky, I showered and dragged on shorts and a day-glo boob tube. Changing my mind about the shorts, I eased myself into a day-glo skirt, clingier and sexier. I decided on the shorts again—more practical for a trip to the Kooracoondoo Markets. I slung wallet, mobile and shades into a metallic tote bag and rushed off.

I almost tripped over a parcel lying on my doormat. Ripping the paper off the package, I discovered a copy of Maigret in the original French. Not *Maigret et la Grande Perche*, but a different Maigret: *Le fou de Bergerac*. I'd been awake most of the night; whoever had left it had been stealthy.

Claude was sipping coffee behind the desk when I entered Reception. The coffee smell made me want to puke.

"That's for you!" I handed him the paperback.

"*Merci*." Giving a cautious smile, he placed the book in a drawer beneath the counter.

"Sandrine said anything French should be handed to you. I guess not many tourists would be able to read 'em anyway."

He gave a hint of a nod.

"I composed a few words, like, to stick on the library door. If you give me a bit of wood, I'll paint 'em on."

"I will seek one in my shed."

"Is there a shuttle bus going soon to Jamesville Mall? Or should I go to the highway or Coral Cove for the shuttle there, or … phew, it's humid today after that rain!"

"I am picking up planter baskets for our balc*ooo*-nies, so you may come wis me if you wish." He grabbed his keys.

Sandrine entered Reception. Clad in a hot-pink pareo, she yawned and shot me a wan smile.

Scuttling along beside Claude as he headed for his car, I said, half-joking, "I don't s'pose you want me to drive?"

He shook his head. The springs squeaked from his weight as he installed himself behind the wheel. I clambered in beside him. An awkward silence descended, and I listened to the blast of the air-conditioning, thinking: now I'd given Sandrine the mouth swab, did Claude feel no need to be nice to me anymore? Did he still resent me for upsetting her—twice now? The pink flamingo swayed. We turned onto the highway.

I was curious to discover more about Sandrine. "Did you never want children?"

"*Si*," said Claude. "We try, but no succeed."

"Considering Sandrine doesn't totally *hate* children, why didn't she acknowledge me as her daughter in the first place?"

"She 'as *fausse couche* ... miscarriage … in week before you arrive."

"Oh, I'm sorry." I remembered Sandrine's cigarettes. "However, she does break the law by dragging on those things."

Claude's hands tightened on the wheel. "What are you meaning?"

"She smokes Gitanes cigarettes, bad for babies!"

His shoulders relaxed. "You are right. It is no good for 'aving infants." He added, abruptly, "I 'ave times when I wonder if she wants Kanak baby only to annoy 'er papa."

"What an awful thing to say! She loves you very much!"

"*Oui.*" And he sighed.

We turned into Jamesville Mall car park.

"*Elle m'aime*. And I, also, love 'er and I will go *anywhere* to be wis Sandrine." He looked me in the eye as we pulled up. "Anywhere!"

I arrived at Seranella's Locks as Sofia was opening the salon door.

"I desperately need highlights," I panted, "and a few of those extensions. My birth mum nearly fainted at my hair. Actually she screamed, and I'm going up to Kooracoondoo this morning."

"I've never heard of anyone having their hair done for the Kooracoondoo Markets before!" She switched on the lighting. "Your mum must be easily upset, eh?"

"I bought camo gear as well, a tactical error. My father was a soldier."

"Was? He's dead?"

"He died from dengue."

"Ooooh, there's a lot of dengue in Far North Queensland! Was he in the Cairns' area?"

"Nup, he was bitten by the Aedes mosquito on, um, the island of Ouvéa."

"Where's that, eh?"

"New Caledonia."

"Oh, right, you said you were a Cal-something."

"A Caldoche."

"Seranella's just grabbing a coffee for brekkie. I'll get you a gown."

The hairdresser walked through the door, sipping and groaning. "Oh, my head!" She paused when she saw me. "You back already?"

"Her mum freaked at her new 'do, thought she was a soldier!" Sofia fastened the studs at my neck.

"Bit off the wall, style wasn't *that* bad, but!"

"I'll go mix up the colour." Sofia headed for the screened-off area. "Her hair's dark. Tawdry Tan in the front, and Bashful Blonde extensions at the back?"

Nodding, Seranella crushed her paper cup and tossed it in a wicker bin.

"How long will the extensions last before I have to redo them?" I asked.

Sofia reappeared with the colour.

"Protein bond, or glue, gels with your own hair, and lasts for, oh, about three months. After that the extensions start to look like spaghetti."

I ran my fingers through my thatch.

Seranella picked up a foil. "You won't be able to do *that* anymore, but you can wash as normal, and comb. Not the roots, but."

"How much will this cost?"

"I can't touch Dom for the money this time. He chucked a mental yesterday, asked me once again for his friendship ring back!"

"Y'know, I had trouble getting the hairspray stain out of my skirt."

"Tell you what. I'll do the 'do for sixty … no, fifty … as you're not happy with what I did yesterday."

"Can I pay in instalments?"

"Sheesh! Are you really so hard up, eh?"

"Close." I knew I was now committed to my job serving coffee.

Sitting back, I did my best to relax. After completing the foils, she applied her hot iron. She held up a hand mirror to show the effect from all sides.

"Like your new 'do? Tawdry Tan at the front, your own dark in the middle, and Bashful Blonde long bits at the back. Looks cool!"

"Wow! That's excellent. For the first time, ever, I'm kinda funky. The extensions leave those daggy old dreads for dead! Wicked! Thanks!"

"Not a problem." Her eyes met mine in the glass. "You gonna have a bungy jump today?"

"Dunno, bungy jumping is not my bag. And it could muck up the 'do."

"Go on, have a go, eh! It won't hurt your hair, and it's great! Bungy Malachi makes it *veeery* spooky. He dresses up in brown leather, with a mask over his face, like a hangman. He cackles as he places the straps around your ankles, the harness round your waist."

"Sounds scary," I murmured, admiring my new 'look'.

"Yeah, and he's got this amazing Irish accent that really turns you on, a chick magnet thing. Mind you, he's got a wife, Siobhan, and seven kids."

"Didn't Bungy Malachi kill someone once?" said Sofia. "Or was it an accident?"

In the mirror, I saw Seranella frown at her sister.

Chapter 20

The Cassowary Rise bus sputtered and groaned up the mountain, heading for Kooracoondoo.

Heat rolled over me in waves. I sat there nursing my tote and wondering who the bungy man had killed. The reek of diesel fuel clogged my nostrils as we gasped and shuddered along the winding road. Passing eucalypt forests, bougainvilleas, curtain fig trees and ginger plants, we trailed behind a row of kombi vans spewing smoke from tailpipes. I chewed my nails, musing about Malachi.

Beside me, a woman in a peasant skirt grasped a green recycle bag. Smelling of cheap eau de cologne, she muttered to herself each time a road worker held up a red and white Stop sign. She rubbed her eyes as the traffic wound past us down the mountain.

I turned in my seat. "Excuse me. They say the bungy man, Malachi, killed someone. Is that true?"

She shrugged her shoulders.

"How long before we get to Kooracoondoo?"

"Town's next after Barrabull Falls, dearie, if ever!" She muttered some more, and rearranged the shopping at her feet.

Moments later, the bus heaved to a stop beside a sign saying Barrabull Falls. In the distance, I could see rock canyons, escarpments and a wisp of white water tumbling from a ledge high above a river.

"Falls are almost dry," I said.

"The wet didn't turn up this summer, did it, eh?" She shuffled in her seat.

"Do you know Sugarcane Lane?"

"Only one street in Kooracoondoo, and that's Sugarcane Lane!"

"Can you tell me where I'll find number eight?"

She simply exhaled. Her breath smelled of aniseed.

We continued to jerk our way up the mountainside through lush jungle, with the occasional banana plant waving flag-like leaves from the undergrowth.

"Kooracoondoo Markets!" the driver called out.

We pulled in alongside a hoarding riddled with bullet holes.

Scrambling off the bus, I brushed dust off my clothing and wondered whether to go to 8 Sugarcane Lane first, or look around. Tourists jostled outside the Kooracoondoo Markets. Slinging my tote over my shoulder, I joined the crowd.

A cramped, packed-earth path opened into a vast space filled with stalls, a shadowy maze of shopping lanes beneath a giant canopy of melaleucas. Muddy puddles from last night's rain created a brownish mist of humidity. The traders' faces streamed with sticky sweat as I picked my way past. Twisting mobiles, aboriginal art and wooden dinosaurs tangled with eye diagnosis, colon therapy and mozzie coils.

Beyond emu oil, pot hangers and sun visors, I found birdhouse feeders which looked interesting, in the shape of roosters—and called *Le Coq du Bonheur*. Had they been manufactured by a Frenchman? I pondered, continuing around a bend. As the slope wound downwards, my gaze lit on the words: 'Joanie's Clothing Corner.' Rocky'd said his mum sold clothing. But her name was Jeanne, not Joanie. Then I asked myself: wasn't Jeanne the French equivalent of Joan?

The stallholder had a hard face. She wore no lipstick; her brown hair was cropped and sensible. She was unlike the photo I'd seen of Jeanne Colline. Rocky's mum had been a hippie chick with her hair in skinny beaded Rasta braids, laughing as though she hadn't a care in the world. This woman appeared as tough as the gear she had for sale—hardwearing skirts for outback safaris, khaki cargos and jackets with long pockets. My vision latched onto a string of beads, like the ones I wore on my wrist. A cascade of sparkly garnets, horn and crystals decorated the open neck of a safari shirt.

Standing beside his sign: 'Aussie Cold Comfort Neckties', a vendor called out, "Eh, Jeanne, you look buggered! You could do with one of them icy cold granitas from Curly's!"

The tuft of hair beneath his lower lip quivered as the woman laughed. Her face lit up, and I knew it was Jeanne Colline. She had fled, as had Namilly—and, ultimately, Sandrine—from New Caledonia. Had those terrible Events changed her so much?

Not game to ask Joanie—or Jeanne—about Rocky, I trawled along searching for Douce's stall. Next to 'Iris Veivers: Pearls for Girls', I spied a sign. The 'Douce's Trinkets' stall overflowed with the same glittering necklaces, and bracelets threaded on memory wire.

I approached the apple-cheeked girl manning both stalls. "Excuse me, I'm looking for Douce Colline."

"No one of that name around here." She looked thoughtful. "The Douce I know is Douce Hill."

"Hill? Name is definitely Colline."

"Well, she's the only one in these parts called Douce, and it's not the most common of names. She's wandered off for a sec, should be back soon." A pause. "She does that, a lot."

"Wanders off?"

"Yeah. Douce and I were in the same class at school. That was, when she bothered to turn up instead of roaming along the banks of the Barrabull River, or the railway line." She tucked her hair behind her ears. "If you do happen to bump into Douce, say Iris is sick of flogging her jewellery for her." She sighed. "I've been *that* busy with 'er bangles."

The penny dropped. "Colline means Hill in English!"

"Does it, eh?"

And then I wondered if these name changes were the reason Rocky continually steered the conversation away from his mother and sister.

"What does Douce look like?"

"Oh, Douce is *stunning*!" Iris met my gaze. "I thought you said you knew her, but?"

"Nope. I only, um, know her brother."

"It must be the wrong Douce, then." She indicated 'Joanie's Clothing Corner'. "Douce lives with her mum. And there's definitely only the two of 'em!"

"Does she have golden-red hair, skin like whipped fudge?"

Iris shook her head. “No way! Douce has chestnut-coloured hair and skin like whipped *cream.*”

A wave of disappointment flooded through me. “She’s the wrong person then, must be two girls with the same name.” I flicked an extension back over my shoulder.

Iris stared. “You’re wearing one of Douce’s bracelets!”

I grinned. “Yeah, gift from the guy with the whipped fudge face. And I, um, thought he might’ve been her brother.”

“Uh-uh! No Koori in Douce!” Iris began to serve a customer.

I was about to protest that Rocky’s origins were Kanak, when a scream echoed across the markets.

“What was that?” I gasped.

“Oh, just someone bungy jumping. Well, good luck in your search.” She turned back to the customer. “They’re on memory wire, madam. They bounce back, fit on any sized wrist. And they never forget their shape!”

I threaded my way past hammocks, gourmet soap and Queensland boulder opals until I came to the food section. Yummy macadamias, pecans, German sausages and fresh Turkish bread gave way to a fast food area where people on benches munched hot dogs. Others ate pies and licked ice creams.

Heads turned towards a metal tower.

Seeing a crowd against the railing, I went to look. A girl with flowing hair and pale skin plunged to the ground, arms outstretched, skirt around her waist. She screamed so hard, I thought her lungs would burst.

On the platform above, a man in brown leather pumped his fist.

The jumper rebounded, plummeted again, screamed even louder. *Would I drop myself like a stone on a piece of elastic, just to please Rocky?* I wondered.

A thought ran through my mind. Was the bungy girl Douce, having a break from selling her jewellery?

Chapter 21

A man in a cowboy hat yelled, "Goodonya, Diane!" to the bungy jumper.

I left the Kooracoondoo Markets and headed along the main street. Sugarcane Lane had a hippie feel. The street was lined with shops selling bongs, herbal 'heat' and 'cool' packs, floral skirts and T-shirts painted with parrots for the tourists.

At a place called 'Fresh Juices and Rainforest Yoghurt', I bought myself a crushed mango and pineapple drink. On the other side of the road, outside the fire station, Koori kids were ripping into one another. Hollering and punching, they made off down the road to the Kooracoondoo railway station. They settled themselves on the edge of the platform, skinny legs dangling and swinging, faces wreathed in smiles like sliced watermelons.

The street numbers were becoming smaller. After twenty, they ceased. *Where was No. 8?* I wondered.

Sweat ran down my legs. As I mopped up the perspiration with a 'Fresh Juices and Rainforest Yoghurt' paper napkin, I heard someone singing. Straightening, I turned to see a long-limbed chick with foaming hair. She wore a micro mini, and gorged from a plastic tray of Tim Tams.

"Zits, zits, glorious zits. Nothing quite like 'em for looking the pits. So follow me, swallow." She stopped singing, stuffed a chocolate biscuit in her mouth and chewed furiously. She gulped the biscuit down and greeted a passer-by in a caftan. "G'day, mate!" Her mouth was smeared with chocolate and biscuit crumbs. "Like one? Before I finish the lot, and get fat?"

Shaking his head, he handed her a tissue-wrapped package and murmured, "Can you fix this?"

I heard her mention a 'supplier' and some beads called 'Chicko'.

Continuing on I came to a house of peeled weatherboards, surrounded by palms with lianas crawling up their trunks. A ute like Rocky's, with bullbar and spotties, was parked on the ragged nature strip. A brass sign, '8 Sugarcane Lane', hung beside the flywire door. Was this Rocky's home?

Edging past the dead snake tacked to the gatepost, I picked my way along a broken path lined with wild orchids, and knocked.

No answer.

"*Merde!*" I was annoyed at having come all this way for nothing.

Close by, a steam train shushed and whooshed. I went to leave.

"Can I help you?" The chick with the foaming hair stood before me. Her eyes, like shot taffeta, grey with a trace of blue, were as huge as headlights. A rainbow of crystals descended from her earlobes.

"I'm looking for Rocky Colline." I sidled back past the dead snake and into the street.

"Mama's supplier?"

That word again.

"Supplier?" I said.

Surprised, I heard Rocky's voice at the side of the house. "Douce, get back to your stall! Stop wasting time talking to strangers!"

Her beautiful face went taut. "What right do *you* have to tell me what to do, eh?" She wiped the sticky crumbs from her mouth with the back of her hand. "It's not as if you're part of my *family*, or anything!"

Was I witnessing sibling rivalry?

Rocky appeared. Hair fiery in the rainforest light, wearing a mud-coloured muscle tee with GIGOLO printed on the front, he folded his arms across his chest. Beside him, Chocolat sniffed the breeze. Rocky's face lit up when he saw me.

"Genna, what have you done to your *hair*? You are like a charming bush creature."

Behind me, Douce breathed: "Whatever …"

"Um, I had the dreads cut off for this new, kinda, job I've got serving coffee." My heart jiggled around in my chest; I turned crimson.

Rocky strode across. Gripping me by the shoulders, he gave me a *bise* on each cheek.

Doing my best not to giggle, I said, "So this is Douce, your sister?"

"*Sister?*" Unfolding the tissue from the package Douce pulled out a necklace of rose quartz mixed with jasper, and arranged the beads over her collarbone. "I don't think so! I'm a single sibling. Mama only did it once!"

This was not what I'd expected.

Confused, I said, "I mean, I thought …"

"You are so wrong about us being related." The words poured out. "Mama's just soft-hearted. I was out back one afternoon, doing my threading. I use fishing line for my necklaces, well, it's sort of like fishing line, and I heard the front door slam shut. Then I heard snivelling and sobbing. So I peeped through the crack in our parlour door and I saw Mama hugging him." She jabbed a finger in Rocky's direction. "And she was weeping, 'cos she's got a very tender heart, and he was weeping too. I walked in, thinking this was *sooo* strange, and Mama told me the supplier was broke, and he had nowhere to live, and she'd agreed to take him in. Wasn't that kind of her, eh?"

Rocky's face was like granite.

"Are you his girlfriend?" She indicated Rocky with her chin. "Are you the supplier's squeeze?"

I was gobsmacked.

"Douce, this is Genna," said Rocky.

"Well, Genna, I'll let you into a secret." Douce swung her hips. "The supplier told me he had a girlfriend when I went into his bedroom and tried to hit on him one night. He's got *such* a good body, and you should've seen how scared he was. He was starkers, hugging the sheet around him, and packing."

A snake slithered down the tree behind her as she talked.

"Watch out!" I cried.

"D'oh. It's only a python, and they are so not poisonous!" Grabbing the snake by the tail, she smiled as it writhed around her wrist.

Rocky glanced at the time. "Douce, you have customers to look after!"

She released the python.

Chocolat chased the snake into the undergrowth.

"I had to come back, gotta fix this, and get more Chicko beads." As she fingered the necklace, I noticed a butterfly tattoo on the side of her neck, a Ulysses Mountain Blue.

"The beads are glass! Their correct name is 'Czechoslovakian'!" Rocky's lips became a hyphen. "Can't you even *try* to get the word right?"

"Whatever …"

Douce disappeared inside the house.

"You texted me. What's the great news?" I asked.

"Look!" Rocky held out his hands. Not a mark was to be seen on the back of them, the left one cleared of all suppurations. The welts and scratches on his left arm were gone.

"That's sensational. How did they cure so quickly?"

"The kava leaf you gave me!" A slow smile spread across his face. "I crushed the leaf with a pestle and mortar, and then soaked it for a few hours before applying it to my hands and arm. And *voilà*!"

I ran a finger over his healed skin. "You have excellent hands!"

"The hands of a kava farmer, exiled from his country and going crazy!"

"Well, I'm glad some good came from keeping the leaf."

He didn't ask me why I had kept the heart-shaped memento, simply led me into the house.

"Watch it, you two, eh!" Douce walked back along the dim passage, tossing beads from one hand to the other. "Don't do what Mama did once! You might end up with a brat like me! And that would be a disaster!"

I didn't know where to look. "It's not like that."

"Sure it is." The beads gleamed in the gloom. "Hey, are you goin' for a bungy, Genna?"

"I, I don't know. Do you bungy jump?"

"No way! Malachi offers me jumps in exchange for doing it … boom boom! … with him, and he *really* knows his way around a woman's body. He says I'll be bungy jumping in paradise."

"I heard he had a wife." I was startled by her slaggy talk.

"Siobhan's fault for getting banged up all the time!" She pulled at her knickers. "God, my snatch is raw! Norks, too!"

Flicking back her luxuriant hair, Douce sashayed off, slapping the flywire screen shut behind her.

"OMG, did she say what I thought?" I locked eyeballs with Rocky.

"I'm learning words I will never be able to use!" He sighed.

"Okay, fess up. What's going on? What's this about the two of you not being related, about you being 'the supplier'?"

"You have a nice suntan now." He briefly touched my shoulder.

"Don't change the subject."

"You see, Genna, when you become burnt you always recover if you give it enough time."

"Is that a metaphor for something?"

"Come with me," he said.

Chapter 22

He led me into a formal front room. Photos of Douce were on display: first day at school, on the swings, in a Halloween costume, holding a balloon … I lost count. But I could see no photos of K-Mel, none of Rocky.

I heard the pride in Rocky's voice as he murmured, "Isn't she beautiful?"

"Douce is awesome, but there are no photos of you."

He said nothing.

"I guess your mum didn't expect you to turn up?"

"She did not." He sounded bitter. "She wanted nothing to do with me when I first arrived in Kooracoondoo."

"That's terrible!"

He shrugged. "I discovered Jeanne's whereabouts at the markets when I saw an advertisement for her clothing. I knew Jeanne meant Joan in English. But, when I approached, she told me to leave, even seemed horrified to see me. I came to the house later. Finally she gave in, and let me stay."

"Douce doesn't seem to know you are related. Why?"

"Jeanne is worried that if my sister knows her origins, knows about K-Mel, that I am her brother, she will leave Kooracoondoo, and join us in *Nouvelle-Calédonie*."

"What's wrong with that?"

"My mother is afraid of the independence movement. She believes the Kanaks will rise up again." He turned to look at me. "And they *will*, sooner than anyone realises. She is terrified Douce will be killed … the thought overwhelms her." He inhaled. "All these years she's been hiding, changing names, just a little, but enough … except she made one error."

"Which was?"

"She never left the place from which she sent her final postcard."

"Perhaps she hoped you'd find her?"

His shrug was imperceptible.

I threaded my way past the tapestry-covered chairs until I came to a recent photo of Jeanne, her arm linked with Douce's, on a side table.

"Your mum's changed a lot since you were a kid."

"How do you know?" He tensed up.

"I saw a photo of her in Pascal's house in the Brousse, beside your dad's mattress."

"K-Mel still loves my mother."

"Well, he sure doesn't love Pascal!"

"Oh?"

"Your dad spat at Pascal. I've never seen such hatred between two people!"

"There is bad blood between them." Rocky rubbed his chin with his thumb. "And I have never been able to work out why. Even his brother Marcel is unable to enlighten me, and there are no secrets between *us*. Pascal has been good to me, though, and yet I do not understand him."

"Being stabbed as a teen during the Events must've changed him, don't you think?"

Rocky's forehead creased. "His aloofness predates that."

"He sure is aloof." I laughed. "Did you know Pascal was my examiner in my Year 12 final exams?"

Rocky shook his head.

"He said my French was *affreux*! *Affreux*, I mean how bad is *that*?"

"Let me show you the rest of the house." Rocky's tone was abrupt. "*Maman*'s bedroom." He pointed to a closed door opposite, and then walked me along the passage.

At the entrance to a room adjacent to Jeanne's, he said, "Check this out!"

In the pretty, wallpapered room soft toys were piled upon soft toys, so high you could barely see Douce's bed. Propped on white-painted shelves were teddy bears with missing limbs, koalas with chewed ears, legless Barbie dolls with knotted hair.

A board with a horseshoe-shaped groove for setting out the beads to be threaded lay beside a cane basket overflowing with coils of memory wire and string. Coloured baubles spilled from plastic bags, rolling over the wooden floor as if their owner had tired of playing with them. On the dressing table a box of makeup sat beside a comb, its wonky teeth stuffed with hair—the only evidence the person living here was an adult.

A sheepskin rug lay beside a single bed.

Puzzled, I asked, "I'm eighteen. How old is Douce?"

"About your age."

"Is she, like, retarded?"

"She never learnt to read or write, only her name and a few words. Jeanne does the books for her stall at the Markets. I remember being told Douce was different, and she is light-skinned. But she seems intelligent enough, street-wise at any rate." He stopped before a room. "This is where I sleep."

Cardboard boxes and crates clogged the small space. A narrow bed stretched along one wall under the window.

"I'm sorry. I didn't know you were coming." The sheets were crumpled, the bed unmade; a Scrabble board was set up on a wooden crate. "I've been trying to teach my sister how to create words."

"I love Scrabble!"

"Show me how good you are then!"

Placing my tote on the floor, I settled on a stool by the makeshift table. I removed the tiles from the racks, and scrambled the letters face down in the lid of the box.

"Pick a tile, and see how close it is to A."

After selecting a tile, he laughed, revealing the letter X.

"Okay, my turn." I held the letter B.

"Already you are beating me." His lips twitched. "You will get double points for your first word."

I tried not to look smug.

As we both selected our seven tiles and began to place them on our racks, one of my tiles flew to the floor. We both reached to pick it up. Our hands brushed. The touch of his skin zapped through my body. We froze, as in a game of Statues. Slowly Rocky raised himself off the stool and, leaning forward, kissed me on the corner of the mouth. Gently.

"You smell of sunshine," he whispered, his lips moving across mine, giving me tiny kisses. Nibbling his way along, he eased his tongue inside my mouth. His fingers slid beneath my boob tube. I closed my eyes, head swirling from his earthy smell.

"Don't do it!" said a voice.

I jumped back, and hastily rearranged my top.

"Don't even think about it." Douce's head poked around the door, the beads to be repaired still around her neck. "He doesn't have a franger." She giggled. "I checked."

Rocky came to his senses first. "But you do?"

"Did you check?" she gurgled, going pink.

"No, I didn't." His gaze narrowed. "Why aren't you at your stall serving customers?"

"None o' your business, but!" As she sauntered down the passage, she added, "I've been mucking around with some Koori kids at the railway station."

My heart still lurched around in my chest. "I must leave. I'm due to start work at a coffee shop in Jamesville. I'll need to catch the bus."

"I'll drive you down the mountain, if you promise to have a bungy jump first."

"Now?"

"Douce!" he called, striding down the passage. "I'll give you a lift." Pushing the flywire door ajar, he put his fingers in his mouth and whistled. "Chocolat! *Viens*!"

"I can't bungy jump today," I said, puffing along behind him.

"Why not?" Rocky opened the door of the vehicle.

"My boob tube will fall off!" I clambered into the ute. "And I'm scared."

On the front seat lay Rocky's ASSASSIN muscle tee. "Put this on." He grinned. "It needs washing. You'll be so bothered by the smell you will not have time to be afraid."

We cruised along Sugarcane Lane, searching unsuccessfully for Douce.

"She's an airhead, like a kid, kinda ditsy."

"She is," he agreed, "and that creates a dangerous situation, particularly with regard to her, ah, becoming pregnant. Jeanne and I have discussed it, in French, so she doesn't understand."

Had Douce meant it when she said she'd gone all the way with Malachi? I wondered.

Outside the Kooracoondoo Markets, Rocky said: "Now for your bungy!"

I grasped around for reasons not to jump. "But-but the chick who did my hair said Malachi killed someone!"

"You, *ma puce*, are safe. He will not kill you with hundreds of people watching. All you will have is a wonderful experience."

Chuffed that he'd called me 'sweetie' in French, I joggled Rocky's muscle tee over my head and followed him to the tower entrance.

Chapter 23

Rocky handed ninety dollars to a chick with hennaed hair and a stud in her nose. Packing polenta, scared spitless with terror, I clutched the ticket with sweaty hands. *Was I insane?* I asked myself? I was about to place my body in jeopardy—*just to please Rocky.*

He accompanied me along the boardwalk towards the steps leading up the side of the steel structure.

"What happens when I've d-done my bungy?" I quavered. "Do they winch me back up?"

"See Malachi's son." Rocky pointed to the stretch of muddy water beneath the tower.

"Um, yeah." A raven-haired guy sat in a rubber dinghy, waiting.

"He will remove your harness. You've nothing to be afraid of. Young boys on the Island of Pentecost in Vanuatu drop thirty metres, feet secured only by vines. The sport is very safe in this country."

"But Malachi killed someone!"

"How did he do that?"

"I don't know."

"Well, I am certain it must have been an accident, or he would be in jail."

Another guy dressed in white shorts, T-shirt and sneakers watched as I tried to wriggle out of doing my jump.

"I've done a hundred and I'm still here!" he said, taking my ticket.

Rocky pushed me gently up the first few steps. As if in a dream, I kept going. A scorching wind swirled about me. I told myself I was nuts. Was I a total desperado? *Would I do anything to impress a kava farmer?* Would I leap off any imaginable object for a potential boyfriend? Sweat poured down my face. Inhaling the BO from Rocky's muscle tee, I did my best not to look at the ground. As I climbed my ears buzzed, my chest was constricted and I felt like throwing up. My throat was dry, as rough as sandpaper.

After what seemed like forever, I arrived at the platform.

Rigged out in brown—leather singlet, trousers and lace-up boots—Malachi waited. From behind his mask, black hair hung to his shoulders.

His onyx gaze glittered. "Have you asked forgiveness for your sins, darlin'?"

"Um, like, wow … I dunno."

Tatts ran down his oiled arms: inky blue hearts with daggers jostled beside skulls and crossbones, the word MOTHER, a crucifix and a snake. A wedding ring was tattooed on his finger. My eyes latched onto a Ulysses butterfly on his neck, identical to the one Douce wore. And I briefly wondered about her relationship with Malachi.

His hands were deft. Whipping a harness between my legs and around my waist, he pulled the webbing tight. Cuffing my ankles together, he connected the shackle to my waist with another loose, dark cord. Securing it all with a humungous silver clip, he attached my feet to a fat elastic rope hanging from an overhead beam and covered in woven fabric. Feverishly, I noted the rope seemed sturdy.

"No twistin' and turnin', darlin'. Just a smooth, neat dive, straight down and you'll be havin' the time of your life."

My tongue refused to work.

For the benefit of the people gawping at the railings in the fast food section of the markets, he boomed: "And what will yer final words be, sinner?"

Trapped like a bug in a spider's web, I surprised myself by shouting, "Such is life!"

"Ladies and gentlemen, it is Ned Kelly's granddaughter to be sure!" he intoned, breathing out a whiff of grog. "She's a horse thief, fired five shots into a walloper, and she's about to meet her maker!"

My heart was in free-fall.

Softly, he added, “Move forward, darlin’, right to the edge.”

I peered at the ground. My extensions suddenly felt claustrophobic, as though aliens were running around on my scalp. Tree ferns swam and twittered, tiny fluffy dusters from where I stood. The billabong where the guy in the rubber dinghy sat seemed as puny as a puddle.

The dreaded moment was inevitable. My knees were like overcooked pasta; I was unable to control my legs. I trembled and shivered while people yelled: “C’mon”, “Jump”, “It’s only a bloody bungy”, “Typical girl”, “Yeah, whaddya expect!”

The smell of hotdogs wafted upwards. Way down, Rocky’s hair was on fire in the sunshine as he stood beside a stand of palm trees. He waved, gave a thumbs-up. Everyone was having a bee’s knees time. Except for yours truly. The foliage below was hypnotically green, but still I shivered.

Placing his hand on my shoulder, Malachi turned me to face him. “I suggest ye do our Backward Swan Dive, darlin’,” he whispered. “It’s easy as pie that way. Just put yer arms out as wide as ye can, fingers apart, and smile. Give a *great big* smile, as wide as a map of Ireland. Now lean back.” His voice was like honey. “Drop and ye’ll be bungy jumpin’ in paradise, with Seamus to catch yer.”

A cheer billowed up as I fell back.

I resisted the urge to twist and turn. My noggin filled with blood. The horizon was bathed in an upside-down purple haze. The earth rushed towards me, and I knew I was about to be splattered into a million pieces.

Miraculously, my body was being lugged back into the air, like bouncing on a trampoline. My new hair fanned out, flopped and bounced and wiggled. In a nanosecond, I was a convert.

“Yee-haa!” I screamed. “Woweeee! Yeah yeah yeah! Scoobydoobydoo!”

My boob tube slid under my chin and the green ASSASSIN word flashed before my eyes. Up. Down. Up. Down. I stretched my body upright, let myself drop down again. Upside down. Right way up. I was having a ball.

“Keep going, keep going, keep *going*!” I hollered. The momentum slowed, and a feeling of sadness washed over me as strong hands guided me into the rocking dinghy. Still trussed, I watched Seamus take the cuffs off my ankles so that Malachi could haul his gear back up.

“Have a good time?” He gave a cheeky wink.

"AMAZING," I said. "Far out! The best! Beyond excellent!"

"Dad's got his gear back if you want to go again?"

Rocky strode across, an enormous grin on his face. Pumped from my death-defying 'wonderful experience', I leapt out to greet him.

"Wow! That was unbelievable! It felt so reeee-al!" I screeched.

"I thought you'd enjoy it." His locks danced. "Like another?"

"Thanks! But I need to go to work." I had seen how much he'd forked out.

☆

As we drove down the mountain, I wriggled around inside Rocky's muscle tee pushing my boob tube back into place. I removed the borrowed clothing, and stuffed it in my bag.

"I'll wash your top, and return it to you next time."

"*Merci*." He turned the wheel of the ute.

"Did you know the bungy man has a butterfly on the side of his neck, like Douce's?"

"I didn't know, and I'm not sure what that means." A heavy pause. "Douce did hers with a safety pin and a bottle of ink, not long after I arrived. In the bathroom, blood was spattered all over the place."

"She's creative, talented."

"I would prefer it if she could read and write. I worry about how she will care for herself if something happens to Jeanne."

"She'll be fine. Douce is just scatty."

"I've heard her talking to her toys. I don't think that's normal."

"No, sounds a bit wacky." I patted my extensions. "You *really* like my new 'do?"

"You're growing up!" He gave a half-smile. "When I saw you in the airport at Tontouta, I thought you were a kid with your serious French plait. Now, look at you!"

I decided not to tell him I'd originally thought *he* looked like a creep. The bus in front belched out thick smoke. I covered my nose with my hand.

In the tray of the ute, Chocolat whimpered.

"In France, the buses run on canola oil," said Rocky.

"I wish they did here. That diesel!" I gasped, "Quick! Stop the car!"

"I can't! We are on a bend, hemmed in by traffic!"

My stomach collided with my throat. Panic pulsed through me. Twisting open the passenger doorhandle, I leaned out to throw up on the road.

"*Arrête*, Genna!"

Rocky jammed on the brakes. The tyres screamed. The ute swerved, and I clung to the swaying door. A thud: something hit the bitumen. An ominous feeling ran through me.

Had I just killed Rocky's dog?

Chapter 24

The traffic screeched and slid about. Bumpers collided in the hot mist. Wheels slewed sideways into the edge of the rainforest as the driver of the beaten-up bus floored the brakes. People gripped the backs of seats, and clutched the silver poles. Passengers' possessions flew into the aisle. The vehicle bounced and yanked, belching out even more smoke.

As the vehicle ground to a halt, I saw the Cassowary Rise sign: the same bus I'd taken up the mountain earlier.

The ute shuddered to a standstill, bullbar nudging the number plate in front.

"*Putain!*" Rocky leapt from the cabin. Threading his way through the stationary traffic, he ran to Chocolat. The dog lay there, unmoving.

"Hey, mate. You aimin' to kill someone, ruin their vacation?" A red-faced motorist leaned out his car window.

Rocky's accent surfaced. "Eet ees my dog."

"Bloody Frog! Learn to drive on the left-hand side of the road, will ya?" Red face wound up his window.

I panted up to Rocky. "Is Chocolat dead?"

Not responding, he crouched down and placed two fingers on the furry throat. Concern lines furrowed his forehead.

"He's alive." He ran his hands over the motionless form. "But I think he has a broken leg."

People gathered.

Rocky looked up; his expression was antsy. "Have you vomited, Genna?"

"I beg your pardon?"

"You said you needed to vomit." His lips tightened. "Go on, *vomit*!"

"The feeling's passed. I, um, don't want to throw up anymore." My voice became squeaky. "Sorry, I didn't mean to harm your pet."

Chocolat's tail gave a feeble flick.

"His dog seems to be okay," said a nearby guy to his girlfriend.

"Well, I'm not." The chick clasped her stomach. "I almost lost my Devonshire tea!"

The couple climbed into their dust-covered four-wheel-drive. The vehicle revved as it backed, turned and took off up the road.

"There's a blanket in the tray." Rocky pointed. "Could you get it, Genna? I'll use it as a sling to lift Chocolat. He needs a vet."

I reached into the ute and pushed aside boxes, tools and bits of clothing. No sign of any blanket. But my gaze fixed on a woollen object tucked in the corner. I examined the beanie. This was not the old burnt one. This was a new beanie, but with similar holes in the brim. *Was I holding a balaclava?* The weather was humid, and Rocky had no reason to hide his hair. *So why did he need a balaclava?*

"The blanket's not here," I yelled.

"I need something to wrap around my dog." Pushing himself up, he waded through tooting vehicles, tapping on windows as he went. "You have a blanket, tarpaulin, anything I can use?" He sounded like a beggar.

The driver of the rattly bus engaged the gears. I checked my Swatch. I'd be late for work if I didn't hurry.

I scurried to the bus door. "Can you take me down to Jamesville?"

The driver thought for a bit, ran his tongue over his lips and nodded.

"Hang on a sec. I'll get my things!"

As I grabbed my tote from the ute I saw Rocky having a discussion with a bread van driver, who held out a hessian sack for his approval.

"Rocky, I've gotta run! I'll be late!" I shouted. "Text me! Let me know how Chocolat is! And best of luck at the vet's!"

Scowls and sighs greeted me as I swung aboard the bus.

I held out my hands in a defensive gesture. "Sorry, my, um, boyfriend's dog was thrown from the tray of his ute."

"So why aren't you back there helping?" A guy with a box stamped Roo Shoes glared at me.

"I've gotta work." I placed my bag on the seat between us.

"With that attitude, I'm amazed you've even got a boyfriend."

Sunshine dappled the leaves of vines, palms, flowering coral trees and melaleucas on the side of the road as the bus chugged down the mountain.

"Did you have a bungy jump?" I turned towards misery guts.

"Me? Don't be silly. I've heard things. No way will you catch *me* jumping!"

When we pulled in at Jamesville Mall bus stop, I was still wondering about Malachi. What crime had the bungy man committed?

Inside the mall I caught a ride on the mini tourist train, arriving at Dominick Nicks's coffee shop on time.

"Ready to rock 'n' roll?" The proprietor pointed to my new 'do. "Your hair's better." Pause. "Oh, your dad dropped by to see you."

"Dad? I don't have a dad. He's dead." I placed my things on the floor behind the counter.

"Well, the dude said, 'Tell Genna Dad dropped by to see her', or words to that effect. He wasn't so easy to understand."

"Did he say 'her dad'?"

"Just Dad."

"Don't know who that could be. What'd he look like?"

"Blue eyes, wavy hair, tallish, conservatively dressed."

"Mmmn, could be anyone." I tied an apron with the NICK INTO DOMINICK'S logo on it around my waist. "Must be someone playing a joke. Does the guy live here?"

"He said he was working at Reef University."

"I don't know anyone at Reef University."

"You soon will." He pointed to a student with a ringbinder; her face was festooned with zits.

"Espresso, please," she said.

I attempted to delay my defining moment. "Weak, strong, hot, or not so hot?"

Dominick frowned.

"Dunno, just a short black, oh, and one of those finger buns." She indicated the pastries in the glass case beneath the counter.

Dominick took the money and gave change.

Heading for the grinder, I said over my shoulder. "Have here, or take away?"

But she was already seated at a table, flicking through her notes, scribbling in the margin with a ballpoint pen.

After tamping down the coffee, I locked the filter handle into the brewing head, whipped a cup underneath and pressed the appropriate button. The coffee spluttered into the cup and I had a chance to look around. I saw a second door leading outside to a terrace with five tables, advertising different brands of coffee on the flapping umbrellas: Vittoria, Lavazza, Mocopan, Mokador and Segafredo.

I handed the student her coffee and finger bun.

Dominick had almost finished restocking the sugar sticks on the tables when a crowd in hats and thongs burst in. They chatted and giggled as they discussed their close shave with an estuarine crocodile. "He was lying on the bank right beside the WARNING/ACHTUNG sign," screeched one, "saying a crocodile attack can cause serious injury and death! He would've made some handbag!"

I tensed up. My first cup had been a breeze. But how would I cope with serving so many at the same time?

Behind the counter Dominick took the orders, sticking Post-it notes along the machine while I made the coffee and mentally thanked Sandrine for coaching me. I put lattes in cups, flat whites in glasses and, despite Dominick hissing in my ear, no one complained.

Having scalded my fingers when cleaning the baskets, I ran them under the cold tap and sent a text to Rocky:

thx 4 a gr8 time 2day hope chockie is betta

Twenty minutes later he replied:

still at vet dog unconscious

I SMSed him back:

unconscious?

In less than two minutes I received his response:

operation leg Bing set

As I contemplated whether I should say I was praying for his dog, or if this was an over-the-top response to an injured pet, I felt Dominick's breath on my neck. "You're here to do a job, not chat to your girlfriends by SMS. Get the milk off the steam wand and make sure that jug is cooled down."

"I'm not chatting to my girlfriends. It's my boyfriend, and his dog is really badly injured, in fact almost died, and he's a bit peed off."

"I'm not interested in your boyfriend's dog. I'm paying you to work." Blending with the frame of his specs, his eyebrows became one long eyebrow. "You can wipe down the tables outside."

I scuttled off. Would Dominick sack me when I'd barely started? I still owed money for my hairdo.

The remainder of the evening passed uneventfully. When it came time to leave, I put a last load of coffee cups, rims trimmed with every shade of lipstick, in the dishwasher. Dominick offered me leftovers from the fridge: lettuce, tomatoes, bananas, and a half rockmelon in cling wrap.

I opened my tote.

Pointing to Rocky's muscle tee, he reeled back. "That yours? It's a bit on the nose, eh?" I was about to reply, when he added, "Hope it's your boyfriend's! If not, have a good long shower before tomorrow!"

I giggled.

"What does your boyfriend do?"

"He's a kava farmer."

"I didn't know kava was grown round these parts, although aboriginal communities in the Gulf region promote kava as an alternative to alcohol."

"He's from New Caledonia."

"Like Claude?" Dominick adjusted his glasses. "Claude says he's an Indian. Do many Indians live in New Caledonia?"

Not wishing to expose the fib, I said, "Um, quite a few live in Nouméa." Remembering Claude was from Koné, a predominantly Kanak area, I added, before Dominick could pound me with questions, "Gotta go. Where do I catch the shuttle to Glisten Beach?"

Dimming the lights, he pointed to the outside door. "Jamesville Tavern, south end of the mall, a few hundred metres away. You can't miss it. The sign on the bus says Coral Cove, but it'll drop you off at the Amédée Apartments. Say g'day to Claude for me." He fingered his peace ring. "And tell him, if I can get the time off, I'll catch up at lawn bowls next Saturday."

"I'll do that."

Letting myself out, I headed for the lights and noise of the tavern.

The night was steamy. Under a cone of streetlight I waited for the bus, inhaling the smell of beer and listening to the clink of glasses. Amid a buzz of chatter, backpackers boasted about their adventures.

Behind the lattice screen, a fair-haired student said, "What do you think of our new lecturer?"

"Monsieur's arrogant, but it's to be expected. The French are like that. He sure is sexy, though," her friend replied. "Those lines at the side of his mouth when he smiles, world weariness, as if he's suffered anguish in his life."

"Yeah, his clothes smell sexy, too, must be the Gauloises cigarettes!"

Although I'd never thought of him as sexy—too pompous—their description fitted the French examiner. He had been through suffering in his life. But … Pascal Manet was currently working at the Alliance Française in Melbourne. Or was he?

Chapter 25

One other passenger boarded the shuttle bus home. Ripped and reeking of beer, the sleaze sat down beside me, and began to run his fingers over my knee.

The radio was low. Missy Higgins' groaning made way for the calling of a horse race. I pushed past, moved to another seat further back—on the aisle. The sleaze-bag followed. A string of hair hung from his chin like a stray worm. Was this facial hair a beard? Or was it a dribble of beer foam? Seated on the other side of the aisle, he leaned across and touched my arm.

I moved again.

Sleaze moved, too.

It was pitch black outside, and the air-conditioning was chilly. Goose bumps rippled across my skin. As I sat there shivering, a gust of beery breath blew on my naked shoulder. I saw the reflection of the slime-ball's slobbery face, topped with a greasy crop of mustard hair, loom in the glass.

"Excuse me!" I called to the driver—not Wesley. "A man's harassing me."

No response.

Grabbing my things, I pushed past again and plonked myself in the front seat. Tottering, the pisspot followed. Slumping onto the floor beside me, he put out his tongue and tried to lick my leg.

I screamed, "Go away, you *creep*!" and shoved past, fleeing to the back of the bus.

Sleaze-bucket followed.

Hurtling to the front, I tapped the driver on the shoulder. The driver smiled, nodded and turned up the radio as he listened to a trotting race in Cairns. Barrelling along the highway towards Glisten Beach, tracts of sugarcane flashed past and I had a bad feeling. What if this lowlife was a guest at the Amédée Apartments? Would he follow me to my unit? I knew Reception would be closed.

Snatching the Emergency cord, I yanked as hard as I could. The driver planted his foot on the brake. We screeched to a halt beside the sugarcane.

"What's wrong?" he said.

"I told you, *he's* harassing me."

I pointed to the plonker, who poked his tongue out, and wiggled it. Back and forth went the slimy object.

"Gross! I'm leaving, hitchhiking!"

"Ya can't, it's dangerous out there!" shouted the driver.

"Not as dangerous as your bus!" I scampered down the steps.

The doors hissed shut. The bus took off, and I began to tramp along beside the highway, thumb out, praying the taipan snakes were asleep inside the sugarcane. Cars passed, trucks and road trains, but no one stopped. Thinking I'd be forced to walk home to Glisten Beach, I heard a car slow and turned. A gunmetal Lexus with gleaming hubcaps cruised to a halt.

The driver opened the door. "How much?"

"I beg your pardon?"

"For the night, how much?" His eyes were pale and cold; a vein throbbed at the side of his bald head.

"Whoa, it's not like that. I just wanted a lift!"

"Get in!" He jabbed a nicotine-stained finger.

"I've changed my mind! I don't want to go with you!"

"I told you, get in!"

Wishing I was still on the bus with the slobbering drunk, I backed off. Baldy climbed from the leather-seated vehicle, grabbed me by the shoulders, and dug his nails into my skin.

"Get in!" He hissed hot breath in my face.

Cars passed. Nobody stopped.

Wrenching myself from his grasp, I ran. Baldy followed, chasing me along the side of the road. I tripped, almost fell, and regained my balance. The rockmelon banged in the tote bag, thumping against my side as I stumbled towards the sugarcane and those terrible taipan snakes.

A sudden flood of light, the grumble and putter of an engine, and the sky lit up. Unable to see, I whipped around, heart surging. Was this a chopper? Was I about to be rescued by pigs in space?

My pursuer fled to his vehicle, leapt in, floored the accelerator and fishtailed off up the highway. I stood there, caught in the spotlight. A door squeaked open.

My head clanged with agitated thoughts.

Still unable to see, I heard the weary words, "*Putééé*, Genna. Why do I always find you on the side of the road? One day, you'll get yourself killed."

"Could you p-p-please switch off those spotties?" I stammered, and immediately began to blub.

Rocky strode across. He held me in his arms, and told me I'd be all right. "*Ça va aller, ma puce.*" Smelling of antiseptic, he kissed me on the forehead. "Come, I will take you home."

With legs like lead, I climbed into his ute.

"I went to the coffee shop, planning to give you a lift home, but the door was locked. I decided to look for you."

"What happened at the vet's?"

"Chocolat's in the back, his leg in plaster, sleeping like a, well, a dog. I had to go all the way to Cairns to get him fixed up."

"I'm so sorry." I gulped back tears. "The accident was my fault."

Rocky turned the key in the ignition, took my hand and said, "*Non.* It was Chocolat's fault. He should learn to hang on better!"

A relieved giggle burst from my throat.

"You know, I found my dog abandoned on the side of the road and feel responsible for his wellbeing. He deserves a decent life, warmth, affection."

"He won't lose a limb, or anything?"

"I am happy to say Chocolat will be frisking about before his plaster is even off." He glanced at me. "I saw you heading for the sugarcane!"

"I was desperate."

"But not too sensible. Taipan snakes live there, rats, cane toads and other things which are deadly."

I shuddered. "I didn't know what else to do."

"Why didn't you stay on the bus?"

"A drunk was slobbering all over me."

"You must always stay on the bus!"

"I s'pose."

He swung the wheel of the ute. We drove along side streets, heading for Glisten Beach, and I heard him murmur, "I would never forgive myself if anything happened to you."

Finding it hard to breathe, I changed the subject. "Do you know if Pascal Manet's in Far North Queensland? Students were talking in Jamesville Tavern about a new French lecturer at Reef University."

"I received a call from Marcel. He plans to come here, but said nothing about Pascal."

"I must've been mistaken."

Still finding it hard to breathe, I noticed we'd entered Arlington Esplanade. We drove past the Amédée Apartments and pulled up outside the All Day Breakfast Café, now closed. I could see the blackboard chalked with the day's specials propped inside the glass door.

"Let's sit on the beach," he said.

"What if Chocolat wakes?"

"We won't go far."

My heart was lurching so badly I was afraid he'd hear it.

We collapsed onto the sand.

Rocky leaned back on his elbows. "It's been a long day," he sighed. He sat up, tucked his hands beneath his legs. "Tell me. Are you able to see the beach, or the water, from your apartment at night?"

Thinking this a strange question, I said, "When the Amédée sign is lit up I can see most things through the coconut palms. But not when it goes off."

"Goes off?"

"The sign's been doing that lately, cutting out. Everything goes dark until it comes back on."

"I see." Rocky hesitated. "You know I'm falling for you. Falling, is that the right word? The same as we say in French?" He gave a half-smile.

"Mmmm." I traced the GIGOLO word on his chest.

Pulling his hands free, he began to play with my Tawdry Tan tips. Pushing the shorn hair away from my face, he kissed me gently on the crease of my mouth and on my lips. He eased my boob tube up.

"A provocative top," he murmured.

Caressing me, his hand then moved down in the direction of my shorts.

"*Que tu es belle*," he whispered.

A whimper came from the tray of the ute, getting louder—until it became a mournful cry, like a baby's.

"*Oh merde.*" Rocky gave a soft laugh. "Chocolat is awake."

I pulled away from his grasp.

Groping around, I adjusted my clothing and scrambled up. He linked his pinkie with mine, and we made our way across the sand to his vehicle. The dog, front leg in plaster up to his shoulder, lifted his head. When he saw us, the heartbreaking cry changed to a high-pitched yelp.

"I'll grab my things." Feeling hollow, I retrieved my tote from the ute.

"I will walk you to the Amédée entrance. I need to be sure you're not attacked again!"

In the road outside Reception, Rocky held me, pushing his body against mine and making moaning noises. He kissed me again, and I knew he wanted the same thing I did. I tangled my fingers in his mop of curls, bright under the light of the sign. And it felt different from my relationship with Stefan, more intense. More grown-up.

Inside my bag, my mobile began to vibrate. We burst out laughing.

The curtains in the Management Apartment moved as I pressed the button. "Hey, I'm busy, Hetty! I'll ring you back in ten!"

The dog gave out a full-blown howl.

Rocky drew away. "*À bientôt!*"

"I'll come up to Kooracoondoo in the morning. I'll bring a bone for Chocolat!"

He climbed behind the wheel, and turned the ignition. The engine gave a throaty chug.

Feeling settled and sorted, alive from his touch, I hurried down the path beside Reception. The lights went on in the Management Apartment as I pushed past one of Claude's new planter baskets, low and at least a metre in diameter. A maidenhair fern poked above the rim. The baskets looked as expensive as they were elegant.

Wiggling the key in the lock of my door, I thought about the curtain moving, the lights going on. I hoped Sandrine wasn't about to tell me off because she'd seen me kissing Rocky.

Chapter 26

Sandrine didn't tap on my door as expected. I stowed my fruit and vegies in the fridge before ringing Hetty.

"I thought you'd be back in Ravella by now!" Her voice boomed over the airwaves.

"Like, I changed my mind." Subsiding onto the sofa, I pulled Rocky's muscle tee from the tote at my feet. "I'm staying in Glisten Beach for a while."

"I see." She took a breath. "My Imperial French History exam went well. It was ace, actually."

"Ace?" What normal person would think an exam was 'ace'? I asked myself.

I heard the lighter flick, the suck of air. "Stefan's looking forward to seeing you. I told him you were coming back."

"Stefan?" I buried my nose in Rocky's muscle tee.

"I was celebrating the end of my exams and bumped into your ex in the bar of the Grand in Kingston. He was drowning his sorrows."

"Sorrows?"

"Win's back on the perfume. Your ex … or, maybe not so ex … gave Win a gift from the hard-earned profits of his Nature Shop: Allure eau de toilette. Next day, the lot was gone. Win said she'd spilt it!"

"Maybe she did spill her Allure." I inhaled the kava farmer's heady earthy smell.

"Nuh, I don't think so!" She blew out. "What are you sniffing?"

"Nothing," I lied. "I just have a sort of, um, sniffle."

"Stefan needs you."

I came up for air. "Wha … he *needs* me? In his dreams, your dreams, everyone in Ravella's dreams! I've got a *new* guy now."

Hetty gasped. "That was quick! Who?"

"A freedom fighter! Way older than Stefan, way more macho-man, way more mature and I can feel sparks! And he's got this sun-kissed skin and over-the-top lips, and a fully sick sixpack—abs, pecs, lats, delts and seriously awesome biceps! He's eye candy, Hetty!"

"Are you nuts, Genna? Or are you on the kava again?"

"No, no kava. Rocky made me do a bungy jump, and he paid, and it cost a bomb, and it was the most amazing ride! And then we were heading back down the mountain, and I opened his ute door to chuck, and Chocolat, his dog, was thrown out on the road and broke his leg. Oh, and lots of other stuff happened."

"Rocky and Chockie?" she burst out. "Heehaw, heehaw! That jump sure scrambled your brain."

Refusing to let Hetty spoil my day, I pressed the button of my mobile and trailed to the bathroom to wash Rocky's muscle tee. As I ran my finger over the ASSASSIN word, I changed my mind.

In the bedroom, I placed his clothing on my pillow. Pulling off my shorts and boob tube, I dragged his gear over my head and climbed between the sheets. Curled up and yawning, I lay there thinking of Win. I remembered her eyes like road maps, ice-blonde hair tousled and speech slurred when she struggled to look after her mother. I tried to feel sorry for my ex-best friend, but my thoughts turned to Rocky. The odour coming from his muscle tee was far more enticing than any expensive French perfume.

Surrounded by his smell, the most incredible BO, I drifted off to the whoosh of the overhead ceiling fan. I dreamt of roadblocks, and dreadlocks, fists raised in triumph as a wild-haired, grinning Rocky was installed as president of the newly-independent New Caledonia.

Dead to the world, I had no idea if the Amédée Apartments sign played up that night. I only woke once. Floundering up from my dreams, I heard a shout.

"Stoppp! *Voleur!* Stoppp!"

With a whine, and a clank, a vehicle moved off, accelerating. Clutching Rocky's clothing to me, I pushed aside my bedroom curtain. A heap of cane swayed in a truck's tray as it careered down the drive from the Beachfront Apartments, flew past the Garden Apartments and disappeared along the road at the rear of the complex.

Starkers, willie whirling as he pounded the concrete, Claude gave chase. *Had somebody swiped his new planter baskets?* I didn't dare find out. Claude in the nuddy was a scary sight. And, in the mood I was in, I wouldn't have known *where* to look.

Chapter 27

I woke to find the window edged in daylight. Doors closed throughout the Amédée Apartments. I could hear the sound of joggers and thongs shuffling along the balconies as tourists made their way, yawning, down to the grass verge outside Reception.

Soon Claude shouted, "See you lat-errrr!"

The Waveripper reef bus surged past along Arlington Esplanade, giving out a hissing noise, before fading off into the distance.

Snug in Rocky's muscle tee, I rolled over and dozed. Having promised to visit Chocolat, I eventually climbed out of bed. I placed the clothing under my pillow and headed for the bathroom.

Under the shower, the comb ran easily through my extensions. I shook my hair dry, applied lipstick and pulled on my fatigues and tank top. I stuffed a spare white mini (to change into for work), plus mobile, keys and wallet in my duffle bag, and set off.

I almost tripped over a Maigret paperback, unwrapped, lying on my doorstep: *Maigret aux Assises.* Maigret in Court? What was that about? I needed to give that to Claude.

On my way to Reception I sidestepped dirt and a shattered maidenhair fern. Someone had definitely pinched Claude's baskets.

Mrs Hays-Bert was behind the counter.

"Where's Claude? I have this book for him." I waved the Maigret.

“Claude’s gone to Cairns with Sandrine.” She made a tut-tut sound. “The poor darling’s planter baskets were stolen during the night. Did you hear?”

“Well, I heard the noise, looked out and saw Claude chasing a truck down the drive.” I placed the book in my duffle bag. “He was in the nuddy!”

Clarissa Hays-Bert turned an interesting shade of pink. “Yes, I did look out, also, and saw, ah”—she cleared her throat—“and I believe they will be going through mug shots”—she cleared her throat again—“after Sandrine’s seen the doctor.”

“Doctor?” I fiddled with an extension. ”Anything to do with her bruises?”

“Bruises?” She stared. “I don’t know anything about bruises, but Sandrine had a terrible miscarriage last year.”

“Yes, Claude told me. Did he see the man who, um, stole the planter baskets?”

“He said the thief had a swarthy face and wore one of those sleeveless T-shirts, plus he had a beanie pulled down over his ears.”

That description fitted Rocky. And, I remembered the beanie in the tray of his ute. *Had my new boyfriend nicked the planter baskets?* Surely not. Then again, what did I really know about Roch Colline? Pascal had told me the gendarmes kept a file on Rocky’s political activities, together with the petty crimes he had committed as an adolescent.

Thinking of Pascal made me wonder if the French examiner was in Glisten Beach.

Mrs Hays-Bert’s voice interrupted my musing. She said, “I repeat, ‘Is there anything else I can help you with?’ You seemed so far away.”

“Um, yes,” I replied, thinking quickly, “I also wish to know if a person is currently staying at the Amédée Apartments. His name is Pascal Manet.”

“That certainly sounds French. I don’t recall, but I’ll check.” Mrs Hays-Bert scrolled down the list on the computer screen. “Manet, Manet … hmm.” Pause. “No one of that name registered here. Is it important?”

“Not really.”

“Anything else?”

“Um, I need a bone for a friend, I mean, for his dog.”

“Well, I don’t have one. Why don’t you try the All Day Breakfast Café? They use ham; they might give you a bone, dear.”

"Okay, I'll try them."

A couple with luggage staggered into Reception. Dodging bulging suitcases, I headed along Arlington Esplanade to the All Day Breakfast Café. Chalked on the blackboard outside the café a sign read:

Specials—Juices: Fruit Tingles, $4.50; Pineapple Bomb, $4.00

I could get the bone, and have a juice for my breakfast at the same time, I decided.

A man wearing an Oasis T-shirt devoured ham and eggs at an inside table. "Ripper eggs, Meggsie!" he called to the chick behind the counter wiping down surfaces.

Meggsie looked up. "Ham fresh off the bone this morning, but." The freckles on her nose danced. "A bonzer way to start the day I say." She saw me. "Can I help you there, luv?"

"A Pineapple Bomb, please. And do you have a spare bone you could sell me?"

"Whaddya want a bone for?"

"For a dog, I promised I'd bring him a bone."

"A talking dog?" she laughed. "Sure, I have a ham bone. Just a sec, I'll do your drink."

Using a cleaver, she split a pineapple in two and shoved it in a juicer. Golden liquid spewed into a tall waxed cup.

"A whole pineapple for four dollars?" I pointed to the jumbo container.

"Sure thing, and is it to take away?"

I nodded.

Meggsie jammed on a lid, and inserted a straw. "I'll go get your bone."

The man eating ham and eggs now slurped on milky tea. "I should have a blue with the wife more often!" he said.

Grinning, Meggsie went into the kitchen. She reappeared with a large newspaper-wrapped parcel. "Here y'are!"

"That's huge!" I stuffed the parcel in my duffle bag. "How much do I owe you for the bone?"

"Zilch, would've just gone in the garbage. Sure you wouldn't like some ham yourself, or bangers and mash? You could do with fattening."

"I'm raw vegan."

"Well, I never! No wonder you look so skinny, eh!"

Sipping on my drink, I swung the duffle bag over my shoulder.

"Have a good one," she said.

Suppressing pineapple burps, I headed for the highway.

The Cassowary Rise bus juddered out of the rainforest.

A salty meat smell pushed through my duffle bag as I clambered from the bus. I scanned the tangle of trucks and utes outside the Kooracoondoo Markets. None resembled Rocky's ute. Lugging my bag, I set off.

Passing racks of T-shirts, sarongs, and eating places decked with hanging ferns, I finally reached 8 Sugarcane Lane. Seeing no vehicle outside, I halted beside the dead snake. What to do? Had my new boyfriend forgotten I was coming?

Picking my way along the path, I pulled open the flywire screen and knocked on the front door. Jiggling the handle, I went from foot to foot. No one came.

I twisted the knob to find the door unlocked.

"Is anyone there?" I shouted into the musty dimness. "Douce? Rocky?"

Silence.

"*Il y a quelqu'un?*" I tried in French.

Should I go in? I wondered.

Chapter 28

A fridge hummed in the kitchen. I decided to leave the bone and return to Glisten Beach. I plunked my duffle on the faux marble bench, and tugged at the zip.

A vehicle crunched over the gravel outside. Had Rocky returned? I rushed to the window. The driver of a well-padded BMW pulled on the handbrake and sat there.

The anodised, sun-shaped clock on the wall clicked over. *Time to get out of here*, I told myself. I eased the duffle zip back up. As I made off down the passage, the front gate squeaked open. I darted into Douce's bedroom, and beside a life-sized grinning crocodile, hid behind the door,

"Thank you for coming," said a woman, who sounded like Rocky's mum.

"*Ça va*," murmured the man. A Frenchman?

They went into the formal front room, where the photos of Douce were displayed.

I tiptoed across the passage. As I squinted through the crack in the door, my heart began to paddle. Jeanne Colline—or Hill, or whatever she called herself—looked up at Pascal Manet. He wore chinos and a business shirt; his face was like a stone.

And I immediately remembered asking the French examiner if I could call him 'Dad' when things got too much in New Caledonia. How could I have forgotten? Now I understood the meaning of Dominick's words: 'Your dad dropped by to see you.'

I tried to concentrate on what they were saying.

"I never would have recognised you. You are a man now." Jeanne reached to touch Pascal's face.

He jerked his head away. "Roch rang Marcel, and my brother passed on your message. You 'ave a problem, and you need my help?"

Jeanne ran her fingers through her cropped hair. "First, tell me about yourself. I see you're doing well … that car."

Pascal gave a slight shrug. "I am a teacher, which is really not so important. I am here because Alliance Française ask me to give lectures for the French Department at Reef University. You are impressed by my hire car?"

"A wife?"

He shook his head.

"You never married?"

He adjusted the rolled-up sleeves of his shirt.

"The stabbing? Is that the reason? Did it affect you, ah, in *that* way?"

"My stomach is very well," he said.

"Do you have a girlfriend, or should I say girlfriends?" Jeanne gave what passed for a girlish smile. Was Rocky's mum flirting with Pascal?

"I do not wish to discuss it."

"Oh, Pascal, you used to confide in me, tell me your problems."

"As you say, I 'ave grown up."

"I missed you, you know."

He appeared tense, almost angry.

"It was agony after I fled from Grande Terre, and K-Mel, and those terrible Events." She pushed at her hair with trembling fingers. "The fire, your brush with death, I longed for you."

My heart began to bang around. Indigestion from the pineapple drink worked its way up my chest.

"*Longed* for me?" His words were awash with incredulity. "I was an adolescent when you departed!"

"I loved you, Pascal."

My gaze burned through the crack of the door hinge.

"*Loved* me? You abuse me from my teenage years. You cheat me of my childhood. You deny me my rite of passage. I became a man while a child. I have a missed step in my life. I wanted to slash my wrists. Is that *amour*? I think not." Unhappiness poured from his body. "I have a noise in my head."

Everything spun. I was finding it hard to breathe, as if I had been punched. Had Jeanne Colline really abused the French examiner? Was that why he never seemed genuinely happy? I was swept to the point of panic. Pineapple burps seared my chest.

I decided to return to Douce's bedroom, grab my duffle bag and creep out the front door. I had heard too much, heard things I'd rather not have known. I should scoot before they saw me.

And yet … I remained frozen to the spot.

Pascal picked up a photo of Douce, examined it and met her gaze. "Why did you really leave *Nouvelle-Calédonie*, Jeanne?"

She stared at him, her grey eyes—like Rocky's, but different from Douce's—huge.

"You were gone when I am home from hospital in Sydney after my operations," he said, running his thumb over the frame, "and wearing a bag for many weeks, and lonely. Why did you go? Was it your fear of the escalating car bombings? Was it Douce? Or was it because of me?" He replaced the photo carefully.

"K-Mel found out about us." She shoved her hands deep into her jeans' pockets.

"Ah, I see." He let out a sigh. "And that will explain why your husband hates me so much. When Yannick Boudaou places his bayonet in 'is rifle to jab me in my gut 'e tells me it is *my* fault those people were slaughtered in the north of Grande Terre." He leaned forward, his face close to hers, his expression menacing. "But it has no sense. I am only a boy. Did K-Mel instruct Yannick to kill me?"

Not responding, Jeanne stared him out.

Pascal backed off. "And did 'e set fire to the family hut because of what we did?"

She slowly nodded.

"*Merde!*" His voice was soft with astonishment. "At last I understand why K-Mel not 'elp me when I am lying in the middle of the road wounded. And why he laughs as flames rise into the sky. For years, I wonder about 'is behaviour."

Silence. Pascal and Jeanne stood there eyeballing each other.

More low talking. I strained to hear, but the words came in fits and starts. I was unable to make out their meaning.

Next thing I knew, they were heading towards the passage where I stood.

I shot back into Douce's room.

"You can persuade your daughter to use the kava leaves?" he murmured.

Kava leaves? He'd said 'leaves'. Not the roots, to be ground up and drunk? Had Douce burnt herself?

"I can persuade her, turn it into a little *jeu*, a game."

"You are sure?"

"I am almost certain."

"I see."

Jeanne dropped her voice. I heard "bungy jumping" and "memory wire". Then: "much older than Douce" before the words became clearer: "As I said, my daughter is different. She could never cope with that."

"You realise it is illegal to bring plant products into this country?"

"But you'll do it for me?"

"I will do it for Douce. I am sure she is a lovely child."

"She is a child in a woman's body." Their voices faded as they went outside. I heard them talking.

"You call yourself Hill now?"

"… business purposes."

Through the bedroom window, I saw the French examiner give Jeanne a formal French *bise* on each cheek. He climbed into his sleek hire car.

As he drove off, my body began to shake like an out-of-control jack-hammer. And I remembered Pascal saying, 'I would 'ave done anything for Jeanne.' Well, he had—as a kid. And now he was about to risk being thrown in prison by bringing illegal plants into Australia. Did he love her? But how could he love her? Jeanne Colline looked tired and worn, and decades older than him. From the things they'd said in the front room, she'd carried out unspeakable acts on Pascal.

I felt as if my skin were splitting.

I was surprised to hear rhythmical thwacks coming from the garden in front of the house. Was Jeanne pulling out weeds, chucking them on the front path? Didn't she have a stall to look after?

Dripping with sweat, my clothing drenched, I saw a ceiling fan above Douce's bed. I turned the knob to low. The blades clanked and ground, making a terrible racket. I switched the fan off. Hemmed in, suffocated by the furry soft toys around me, I felt an itch develop at the back of my nose.

They say you can suppress a sneeze by pushing your tongue against the roof of your mouth. Well, my tongue was working overtime. I desperately needed to get out of there, but I was trapped.

Should I climb through the window? I wondered.

Chapter 29

Edging aside the bead board with my foot, I urged the sash up. A crack snaked across the corner of the glass, and I could see fresh jemmy marks at the side of the sill. Chicko beads lay scattered on her dressing table. Had Douce climbed out of her own room lately? *Or had someone else climbed in?*

Perspiration poured down my face. Hanging onto the old brass catches, I moved the frame bit by bit. I was terrified Jeanne would hear me; terrified Rocky would arrive in his ute and see me shinning from his sister's bedroom window.

After what seemed like an eternity, the space was wide enough for me to get through. Pushing my duffle bag into a clump of bougainvillea below, I poked my head out. The coast was clear. I squeezed my body sideways, gripped the sill and dropped to the ground beside the bougainvillea. Scratching my hands on a cluster of bracts, I retrieved my bag and tossed it over the fence. Wincing at the clunky sound, I levered my body up and sprang over.

Panting and free, I rocked off past the Colline house. I could see no sign of Jeanne. Had she gone back to her stall at the markets? I berated myself for panicking. If I had remained calm, I could have used the front door and not become scratched and sweaty.

Grinding to a halt beside a melaleuca, I reached into the duffle for my mobile phone to see if Rocky had sent a text. My message box was empty.

I began to press buttons. My gaze was diverted by a tree python wriggling up the trunk. Were they truly not poisonous? Or had Douce lied? As a precaution, I moved away. Grasping my bag, I SMSed:

i am w8ing where r u?

The blue Sending Message line hurtled my words to Rocky. I waited in vain for his response. Had he dropped me like a bag of cold chips already? I made up my mind to return to Glisten Beach, and have a relaxing swim before I went to work.

As I set off down Sugarcane Lane, a tall chick in jeans headed towards me, licking on a Kit Kat wrapper.

"Hi, Douce!" I called. "Do you know where Rocky is? I told him I'd visit but I can't find him."

"Who?" Douce looked confused.

"Rocky Colline?"

"Who's he?" Douce wore a brief blouse exposing her midriff.

On the point of blurting out "your brother" I caught myself and said, "Roch. You know, spelt R-O-C-H." Then I remembered Douce was unable to spell. "It's pronounced like 'rock'. Sort of like a stone you find, down there." I pointed in the direction of the Barrabull River.

"Roch? I don't know any Roch."

I thought hard. "The supplier? Do-you-know-where-the-*supplier*-is?"

"Oh." She brightened. "The supplier!"

"Yeah, where's the supplier?"

"He's gone to the fire station."

"Fire station?" I pointed to the building on the other side of the road.

Douce looked worried. "Nah, I think he was going to the cop shop."

My heart plummeted. *Had Sandrine and Claude dobbed in Rocky?* "The fuzz? You mean he's gone to the police station?"

Douce continued to lick her Kit Kat wrapper. Spangles twinkled in her navel, and I could see a muffin top forming over the waistband of her jeans. Was Douce getting fat from too much chocolate?

From across the street a shout: "'Ey, Douche Bag, I'm warnin' you. Stay away from me old man! Or you're history!" The guy wore a singlet, shorts and scuffed Blundstones; his baseball cap was on an angle. "And if yer not careful, Siobhan'll cut ya up into tiny pieces."

"And feed me to the crocs in the Barrabull?" Douce flicked her chestnut curls over her shoulder. "Get stuffed, Quanah! I never went near your old man. You suck!" The bracelets rising up her arm gleamed against the rainforest backdrop.

She licked her wrapper again. Quanah kept walking.

"You're sure the supplier's gone to the cop shop?" I said.

"Yeah, something to do with his dog, I dunno, whatever."

"For Chocolat's licence?"

"What licence?"

I could see I was getting nowhere with Douce. I unzipped my duffle.

"Could you give this to Rocky?" I pulled out the newspaper parcel.

She grabbed the package. "It's heavy!" The Kit Kat wrapper slipped from her grasp and cartwheeled along the footpath. "Wotcha got in there?"

"A bone for Chocolat."

"Smells funny."

"It's ham."

"I like ham. Mama always buys a ham at Christmas, or half a ham, depending on how many safari skirts and stuff she's sold, um, and my beads, too, of course."

"Don't eat that, 'cos the bone belongs to Chocolat."

"Like as if!" She rubbed her ankle. Seeing an etched leaf there I wondered if Douce had done the tattoo herself.

"Well …" I said.

She noticed my hand. "You're bleeding! How'd you do that?"

"Um, on a prickly bushy thing, bougainvillea, I think."

"Yeah, there's one beneath my bedroom window. I've cut myself lots of times."

Hoping she hadn't twigged that I'd scratched myself on the very same thorns, I felt myself go pink.

Her taffeta eyes stared.

Not confident that she'd remember to pass on any message, I said, "Tell Rocky to ring me when he gets back from the cop shop!"

"What cop shop?"

"You said …"

"Whatever …"

"Okay. See ya." Hoisting my lightened load, I continued along Sugarcane Lane, planning to catch the bus back to Glisten Beach.

☆

The bus was late. Hot and sticky and hanging out for something wet and cool, I decided to go inside the markets and buy myself a drink. I could also see if Claude's nicked planter baskets were for sale. I set off through the maze of paths leading to the open space beneath the melaleucas.

The muddy puddles had dried up, but the traders still worked with sweat running down their faces. I adjusted my duffle, and bought an icy cold granita from Curly's. I ambled along, slurping and crunching on my 'pure fruit-based iced drink'.

Stopping to admire some kinky macramé at 'René's Retro Pot Hangers', I said to the stallholder, "These are lovely. But where can I find planter baskets, like, big'uns?" I held my arms out wide.

"Try 'Poppy and Pete's Planter Baskets'." Giving me a toothy smile, René pointed in the direction of 'Joanie's Clothing Corner'.

"Thanks, I'll go look!" Pushing past a tourist in gleaming Reeboks, I dragged on my drink.

At 'Joanie's Clothing Corner', I saw Jeanne take money from the 'Aussie Cold Comfort Neckties' vendor. I gave a quiet, cautious slurp.

"You sure everything's okay, Jeanne?" I heard the trader say.

"Everything's fine." She turned to secure a shirt drooping from the hessian backdrop.

"The look on your dial lately says things is goin' bad for you."

"Leave it will you, Horrie!" she snapped.

"Keep your shirt on, Jeanne!"

Sucking on my straw, I moved away. Arriving at 'Poppy and Pete's Planter Baskets' I saw baskets identical to the ones Claude had purchased.

"Are these new?" Tilting a basket towards me with my free hand, I viewed the dirt in the bottom.

Poppy and Pete exchanged glances.

"Just came in this morning!" Poppy's mouth went small.

"But there's dirt in there!" I crunched on a piece of ice.

"There's dirt everywhere!" She waved her arms. "This whole market's full of dirt."

"And shit as well!" Pete's laughter was forced.

Were these baskets Claude's pinched planters? Should the name of the stall be 'Poppy and Pete's *Pinched* Planter Baskets'? I asked myself.

But I had no proof, and no real reason to believe the baskets had initially been stolen by Roch Colline. If I'd discovered Rocky had stolen them, would it have made a difference to how I felt about him? I wondered. After all, I had swiped money from Pascal's suit pocket when desperate for kava.

Pondering on whether theft was ever justifiable, I threaded my way back to 'Douce's Trinkets'. Douce was still not back behind her stall. I lingered at 'Iris Veivers: Pearls for Girls', running a sticky finger over an intricate freshwater neckpiece in delicate rose.

"That's awesome. Tell me, Iris"—slurp—"did you thread the necklace yourself?"

"I did. And it was *that* difficult, took me almost the whole night in front of the telly!" Her cheeks glowed with pleasure. "Price is reasonable, considering."

"I'm a bit skint." Using my spoon-shaped straw I scooped granita through the hole in the domed lid. "When I get my pay packet," I said, sucking on the grains, "I'll think about it."

"Do you work around here, um …?"

"Name's Genna. Nah, I just serve coffee at Dominick Nicks's in Jamesville Mall."

"I don't often get down the mountain." Iris looked glum.

"Are you *still* minding Douce's stall?"

"That girl fair drives me bananas with her wandering. And 'er bangle buyers are always going 'when'll she be back'." She assessed my beads. "So they can discuss memory wire, how long the spring effect lasts an' that."

"I saw Douce in Sugarcane Lane." I scraped the bottom of the plastic mug. "She was licking on a Kit Kat wrapper."

Iris rolled her eyes. "That girl is majorly chocoholic, and I swear she's putting on weight because of it." Pause. "Weren't you asking about a person called Douce recently, only a Douce with a different family handle?"

"Yeah, it turned out to be the same as your Douce. I got the surname wrong." I ran a fruity tongue over my lips.

"Well, steer 'er back in this direction if you see her again. I've been flat out like a lizard drinking!"

The scream of a bungy jumper rang over the Kooracoondoo Markets.

Choking on the last of the ice flakes, I spluttered, "Do you ever get used to the noise? *I* didn't scream like that!"

"Wow! You had a jump?" Iris looked impressed.

"Yeah, and it was so mygodish! The ground rush was out there!"

"Friend of mine likes doing Tandems, raves about Cliffhangers, and Fruit Bats, and Pendulums, and Psycho Back Dives. Oh, and Cling-Ons. Titanics, too, whatever they are! And Swan Dives!"

"I did a Swan Dive, a Backward Swan Dive!"

"Did you, eh? There's no way I'll jump, Douce neither, and sometimes I think she has the hots for Bungy Malachi the way she talks. You're so game!"

"Nah, I had the *best* time! And the bungy man has the sexiest way of saying 'jumping in paradise' to persuade you to lean back and let go."

"Does 'e?"

I sized up the stallholder. "Haven't you *ever* been tempted to bungy jump, Iris?"

"I've heard things."

"Heard things?" I crushed the plastic container, and tossed it in a bin. "Tell me *exactly* what you've heard."

"Oh, I can't. It's just, you know, accidents and, like, I dunno … *things*!"

"Please tell me!"

She shook her head.

"Why can't you tell me?"

Iris leaned forward, and whispered, "Night-time, Malachi might do something grotesque!" She unscrewed a bottle of spring water and swigged.

"Like what?"

"Like *molest* me!"

Chapter 30

Back from the jungle village of Kooracoondoo—and still no word from Rocky—I trudged along Arlington Esplanade.

Alongside sandwich boards advertising flats for sale and discounted reef tours, Sandrine swayed on killer heels as she farewelled guests outside the Amédée Apartments. "Come back soon for that extra touch of paradise!" Her dress drooped in the humidity.

A beaming holiday-maker wedged his wife into the waiting taxi.

Sandrine's face froze when she saw me.

"I need to talk to you," she hissed.

With the fixed smile back on her face, she waved the taxi off.

"As I said, I want a word with you!" She walked me through Reception, past Claude clicking on computer keys, and into the Management Apartment.

"What's the problem?" I was hanging out for a swim before work.

Her gaze scanned my camo gear. She made no comment, but said, "He's not good enough for you, Geneviève!"

"My name is Genna. And who is not good enough for me?"

"Very well, *Genna*! The rough young man I saw you kissing last night."

"Rough young man?" I suppressed a pineapple burp. "You don't even *know* him!"

"Oh, yes I do! He came here looking for somewhere to sleep, several months ago. I turned him away. Dirty, with bandaged hands and smelling of smoke he walked in and had the gall …"

"Rocky is from New Caledonia! And he really cares for his country, and someone torched his car in the Latin Quarter, and he had to flee." I continued to vent. "And he had no time to wash because there was a cyclone! Aren't you meant to give aid to your fellow countrymen?"

"This man is not a Caldoche!"

"And neither is Claude!" I glared at his *Baby-foot* soccer table.

"Claude, I will have you know, is the nephew of a great chief. *That* man is a mongrel!" Sandrine's eyes had a glaze about them, as though she had taken a hallucinatory substance.

I remained silent.

"He's after your money!"

"Rocky is after my *money*?" By now, I was almost shrieking. "There is no money!"

"He doesn't know that!"

A pineapple burp erupted in her face.

"Do you have to be so crude? Is that how she brought you up?"

"At least *she* didn't abandon me, like *you did*! You left me high and dry, physically and emotionally. And it sucks!"

As always, on the subject of Sandrine and the Procuration, the tears welled up. I gulped them back.

Clad in a cheesecloth shirt, Claude loomed in the doorway. "Will you ladies please stop scrrrreaming? You can be 'eard on Arlington Esplanade, and you 'ave caused me to lose a customer for a veeerrrry expensive cruise."

"Oh, shut up, Claude!"

"Genna is rrright!" He pointed an accusing finger.

"What do you mean?"

"You leave a helpless leeetle baby and expect 'er to forget. And I hear what you say before, and it is *not* your business who Genna kiss."

"I think, um, I'd better go," I murmured.

Claude headed for the side entrance of the Management Apartment. "Come wis me!" Over his shoulder, he said: "Sandrine, you will look after Rrrreception!"

Hoisting my camo bag, I scuttled along behind him to his shed.

"I have your sings for making a sign." He handed me a piece of plywood.

"I'll do the sign this evening, when I get back from work." I juggled the brush and the tiny tin of paint labelled Kelp he'd perched on top of the wood. "I'm desperate for a swim right now. That okay?"

Claude inclined his head. He crossed his arms, and leant against his workbench. The whine of a vacuum cleaner rang out from the top floor of the Garden Apartments.

"I can hear Mercurio cleaning." I glanced through the windows overlooking the pool area.

"One of our guests 'as left and 'e is preparing the apartment for a new arrival. Very few holiday apartments are for let in back." Claude unfolded his arms, folded them again, crossed his legs and settled against the bench. "Most residents in Garden Apartments are permanent."

"Like Mrs Hays-Bert?"

"*Oui*. Madame 'Ays-Bert normally resides in number six, but owners are up from Melbourne." His eyes met mine. "I know zis man you kiss."

A flush flooded my face.

"'E is *indépendantiste* and will do anysing, and I mean *anysing*, for his country. Be careful you not get wounded!"

"You've never belonged to the separatist movement?"

"I do have my sympathies with *indépendantiste* movement, but my heart belongs to Sandrine. Your young man's heart belongs only to his country. Do not be surprised at anysing 'e does. Be veeerrry careful."

I was tempted to ask if Rocky was the person who had stolen his planter baskets, but changed my mind. With Claude's predictions ringing in my ears I made to leave, but remembered the book.

"Um, I have the Maigret thingy." I delved into my duffle.

"When did you receive this?"

"It was on my doorstep this morning."

"You should give Maigret books to me *tout de suite*."

"I had things to do and forgot. Sorry, the book smells of ham." I took a step, and turned again. "Is Sandrine all right? I thought she looked a bit funny just now, sort of spaced out."

"You must ask 'er."

Bothered by Sandrine's mood swings and her bruises, and wondering why Claude needed the Maigret books, I hurried to change for my much needed swim.

A hot wind blew on Glisten Beach. I walked for a while, until I came to the stream with the sign saying WARNING/ACHTUNG. The sign contained an image of a crocodile, jaws apart within a red triangle beside a swimmer with a scarlet slash across his shoulders. *Estuarine crocodiles live in water and on banks in this area*, it announced.

I backed away. Behind the mangroves, the water was murky. Not wishing to be snatched, I headed towards the Coral Sea with only stingers and stonefish to worry about.

Throwing my towel down, I spread out and slipped my arms through the straps of my bikini. Hoping to top up my tan, I sunbathed topless. Relaxed at last, I wondered where Rocky was. Had Chocolat taken a turn for the worse? Or was his failure to appear connected with the stolen planter baskets?

My thoughts wandered to the French examiner, and the sickening conversation I'd overheard. Had Jeanne really molested Pascal when he was a teenager? Did Rocky know his mum was a paedophile? And why had Jeanne asked Pascal to find kava leaves for Douce?

Troubled by these things, and becoming tenser, I rolled onto my back.

A smell of chichi perfume.

"Is it legal to sunbake topless on Glisten Beach?" queried a woman.

"Don't know, darling, but she looks like a wog, and they do that! Anyway, it doesn't matter, they're like mosquito bites," said her friend.

"You're right. She could fall flat on *her* face!"

Rolling onto my front, I muttered into the sand: "I'm not a wog, and my boyfriend says my boobs are perfect!"

Slipping my top back on, I shoved myself up to see the smoothly tanned tourists strolling towards Urupu Point. I jogged to the water, and plunged in.

The sea was warm and soothing. Feeling comfortable, I floated. My eyes began to close. Next thing I knew, I was coughing up water, and thinking of crocodiles. Didn't they move from creek to creek via the sea? Pushing my way out of the limp surf, I collapsed on my towel.

I woke from a brief sleep to find I had strap marks on my shoulders—a pale tan against a darker tan. Worse, I had five minutes in which to get dressed. If I missed the shuttle to Jamesville Mall, I'd be late for work.

Snatching up my towel, I scampered through the coconut palms and across Arlington Esplanade. Passing a yawning Sandrine in Reception, I yelled, "Tell Wesley to wait for me!"

Sandrine rubbed her eyelids. "Very well." She yawned again.

Five minutes later, I found myself on the bus with the same sleaze-bag who had tried to lick my leg.

Chapter 31

Toting my duffle bag (in case Dominick had leftover vegies), I edged past the sleaze.

I sat at the rear of the bus, picking grains of sand off my hands and arms, and praying he wouldn't come on to me. Sober as a magistrate, the sleaze gazed ahead, not even looking in my direction.

At Jamesville Mall, I plunged into the cool of the shopping centre. I examined my Swatch. I had ten minutes to spare. Anton of Drop Zone Army-Navy gave me the thumbs-up sign as I passed. I returned his greeting with a wave, and halted at Lavender Bale's. The T-shirt shop was empty of tourists. Should I order a T-shirt for Rocky? I wondered. Or was it too early in our relationship?

Pale-skinned, with not a sunspot in sight, Lavender Bale wore her hair in a mousy bob. She raised a plucked eyebrow. "Can I help you?"

"What do you have for a guy," I said, "a macho person who goes for black and dirty green, butch-type colours?"

"I have black with a green tree frog on the front, mud-brown with a cheerful crocodile running across the chest. You could have his name in a darker brown, or black, above that." She paused. "His name could be in any colour really, above the frog. I do the name in a rubber substance, washable. My T-shirts are very popular!"

I chose the grinning crocodile. “Rocky’s more of a croc dude and I’d like his name in black, please. The green tree frog is cute, but … nah! … it’s not his style.”

“Rocky, is that his name?”

“Actually it’s pronounced ‘rock’ but spelt R-O-C-H.”

“Then Roch it is.” She handed over paper and a ballpoint pen.

“How long will the T-shirt take?”

“Come back in, oh, should be an hour unless I have a rush of tourists. Do you have shopping to do?”

“I work at Dominick Nicks’s coffee shop.” I pulled out my purse.

“Then pay me when it’s done,” she said.

☆

Dominick gave me my apron. I wiped down tables, served coffee and placed pastries on plates. As I refilled the sugar stick bowls, the telephone rang.

Dominick picked up. “Sure, I’ll get Genna to fill the order.” After hanging up, he said, “Could you take a long black to Seranella’s Locks?”

In the salon the hairdresser waved, and continued removing a client’s rollers.

I placed the coffee on the reception desk.

“Happy with your hair, eh?” asked Sofia.

“It’s a bit salty, ’cos I went for a swim.” I flicked my head from side to side. “But everyone thinks my new look is beyond cool!”

“Excellent! Did you have a bungy jump when you went to Kooracoondoo Markets?”

“Yeah, a friend shouted me, and it was the best!”

“Goodonya! You’re brave! Seranella’s jumped, and she said it was awesome, but I dunno.” She frowned.

“You’ve heard bad things about Malachi?”

“Well.” She played with the chain around her neck. “Only rumours, but. People say he killed someone, an accident.”

“A bungy jumping accident?”

“In a country town down south. In Victoria, I think.”

"You don't know, like, the specifics?"

"Just that someone died, a girl, teenager. And, ah, I think she might've been pregnant."

"Was the bungy man charged?"

Sofia shrugged.

"Well, I'm still here! And I had an absolute ball!"

"Good for you, eh!" She grasped the paper cup. "I better give this coffee to the client."

"Yeah, and I have a T-shirt to pick up before I go back to work."

"Lavender Bale?"

I nodded.

"Make sure she gets the name right! I've heard complaints!"

Worried Dominick might dock my pay, I dashed along the mall. People watched as Lavender erected umbrellas over hairdryers. Hot air blasted onto her creations. The shop was like a sauna.

"I've finished yours," she said.

"Excellent!"

"Do you like it?" She showed me the T-shirt.

"Oh no, you got the spelling wrong," I said. "I wrote R-O-C-H on that piece of paper you gave me."

Lavender glared. "You told me ROCK!"

"No, I said it was *pronounced* 'rock'. My boyfriend's name is French."

"Ferdinand Foch, the great French marshal and commander-in-chief of the Allied forces pronounced *his* name FOSSSSHHHHH!"

"I don't care about Marshal Foch!"

"It must be your handwriting! However, this once, I'll do another, although I *am* out of crocodiles on mud-brown. I only have green tree frogs left on black, cassowaries on pink, crocodiles on purple."

"I'll have a green tree frog on black."

"I can't have your T-shirt finished before tomorrow." Lavender's smile was scarier than a crocodile's. "Will that do?"

"I'll pick it up on my way to work."

The shopkeeper turned to a man in grey shorts. "I think yours are almost done." She peered beneath her plastic umbrella.

Disappointed, I hurried back to the coffee shop.

"You took your time." Dominick's spectacles were misted up. "I've been flat out making flat whites." He twisted his pinkie ring. "Have you been gossiping with Seranella, eh?"

An overweight student with tufty hair and carrying a clipboard ordered a decaf skinny cappuccino and four finger buns. I set to work.

During the next lull, I attempted to ring Rocky on my mobile phone. As usual, the signal was too weak. I left a message on his voicemail. Soon, his SMS shot back:

c u 2morrow am on glisten beach

My heart surged. I snapped his beads against my wrist. Time flew as I served customers, and wondered what to wear the following morning.

Less than an hour to go before knock off, Dominick hissed in my ear as I was loading the dishwasher. "Your dad's arrived, with a friend. Would you like to serve them?"

"What dad?" A coffee cup collided with a plate.

"He just came through the outside door. Good looking bird with him, too."

Uh-oh, Pascal Manet had turned up.

"*You* serve them!" I kept my head below the counter. "I'm busy with the dishes!"

"Don't you want to speak to him? Have you had a falling out with your father?"

"I told you, my dad is dead! This man is not my father!"

"Is he a pervert then? Is that why you don't want to talk to him? Are you avoiding him because he's done something to you?"

"No, he is not a pervert! And, even though he gave me a *rotten* mark in my final French oral exam, I am *not* avoiding him!"

"You're scared of him, then, because he's a French examiner?"

"I'm *not* scared of him … well, not much … and I'm kinda busy at the moment." I continued to stack the crockery.

"Well, if he's not a pervert, and you're not scared of him, why don't you want to serve him?"

Recalling the conversation I'd overheard between Pascal and Rocky's mum that morning, I said, "I just, it's not easy. Like, I dunno."

Dominick peered at me through his specs.

"Oh, all right. I'll *do* it."

Pascal's briefcase was propped on the floor beside him. He chatted across the table with a woman in a leopard print top. Her bronzed skin was impeccable, and she wore bright red lip gloss. They sat at a window overlooking the terrace.

A Velcro feeling took over the soles of my feet as I went to take their orders. I seemed to have rods in my legs.

"Hi," I said, "um, Monsieur Manet, um, I mean Pascal." A trickle of sweat itched at my sticky back.

"Genna!" The French teacher pushed himself up from the table. He grabbed me by the shoulders and gave me a *bise* on each cheek. "*Comment ça va?*" He smelled of Kenzo Air aftershave.

"*Ça va bien,*" I said. Wishing I'd showered before work, I hastily switched to English. "I'm, like, really, really well."

"This is a wonderful tan you 'ave!" His mouth creased with pleasure as he leaned back to look at me. "And you 'ave, let me see, changed your hairs?"

I could hardly say Dominick had forced me to cut off my dreads due to Pascal's toothpaste, honey, eggs and Stately Homes of England beeswax being a health hazard around food.

Instead, I said, "I was so over dreadlocks!"

Pascal ran his eyes across my Tawdry Tan tips, the skinny extensions on my shoulders. "I prefer this one."

"My dreads reminded you of the Events?"

"A little." He turned to his companion. "Genna, I would like to present Madame Christine Delon, head of the French Department at Reef University."

Rising from her chair, Madame Delon gave me a shiny smile and a perfumed handshake. "*Enchantée,*" she said.

"*Enchantée!*" I felt my toes curl in embarrassment. "Can I get you both a coffee?"

"Christine?" Pascal turned in her direction.

"*Café au lait* for me." Madame Delon's English was almost without accent.

"And I will take an espresso." He resumed his seat.

"*Pâtisseries*?"

Each said no.

As I marched off to make their coffees, I heard him say: "Flaubert." He paused. "*Oui, oui, oui.*" He paused again. "*À la fac.*" He added: "*Vous l'avez lu, Christine?*"

Pascal had called her '*vous*'; I realised Madame Delon was not his current girlfriend.

I was busy creating a caramelised crema on Pascal's espresso, when Dominick hissed in my ear. "You sure this dad person is not a pervert? He was *very* friendly towards you, and I heard him say 'oh, la', followed by the F-word."

"*La fac*," I said, "is pronounced like the F-word, but means university in French. And Pascal is *not* a pervert! Even when he had me under house arrest, he treated me like a gentleman." And I remembered Pascal's reaction when I'd thrown up on the back of his jeans. "Well, he treated me with respect most of the time."

"Did you say *house arrest*?" Dominick's specs seemed to totally fog up.

"Pascal is an all right guy. He was acting under my grandfather's instructions." I drew in a breath. "It's complicated."

"You sure have an unusual family!"

"Tell me about it!"

Dominick wiped down tables while I finished making the coffees. Pascal's espresso was impressively black and, assuming Madame Delon's request for a *café au lait* meant she wanted a latte, I poured in the steamed milk before adding foam.

Order filled, I headed for their table.

"Hey, psst." Dominick hissed at me again.

"What's wrong?" I turned.

"You forgot to sprinkle on the *powdered chocolate*!"

"Hers is not a cappuccino, it's a latte," I mouthed.

"If it's a latte, why isn't it in a tumbler?"

From the corner of my eye, I saw Pascal and Madame Delon engaged in close conversation.

"Oh, heck. I forgot. She asked for a *café au lait* and I thought …" I whipped around to fix it.

"That's okay, then," said Dominick. "She'll expect her coffee in a cup."

"Will she? Cool!" I wheeled around again.

With a crash, cups and saucers slipped from my fingers and hit the ground, spraying my legs with coffee. Chips and slivers of china scattered in a circle around me, and settled. Pascal and Madame Delon stopped talking. Dominick looked fizzed off.

Coffee seeped into my sandals, and I stood there, rigid.

Chapter 32

I behaved as I had during my French oral exam. I bolted. I skidded out the door, and along the almost empty Jamesville Mall where the shops were now closed. Arriving at the Ladies loo I barrelled through the swing entrance and thrust myself, breathless, against the hand basin.

Again, I had made a fool of myself in front of Pascal. Running the cold tap, I splashed water over my face, hands and neck before inspecting the damage to my clothes and body. A brown stain almost obliterated the NICK INTO DOMINICK'S slogan on my apron. Spots dotted my legs from the burning coffee. My sandals were sticky with spilt sludge.

Drenching a corner of the pinny, I applied cool water until the sting went away and the burns became less angry. Folding the fabric, I went into a cubicle, locked the door, closed the lid and sat down. Burying my face in the soggy material, I snivelled and felt sorry for myself. A wimpy sense of worthlessness wrapped itself around me like a cloak.

"You loser!" I wailed.

A rap on the toilet door. "You all right in there, luv?" Beery breath blasted through the crack.

"I'm okay," I sniffed.

"You're not thinking of doing something stupid, are you?"

"Just leave me alone!"

"Ya sure, luv?"

"Oh, get lost!"

"No need to be so rude, but!" She shuffled off, making an angry swoosh sound as she left.

Fifteen minutes later, confident that Pascal and his friend would be gone from the coffee shop—but not confident I hadn't lost my job—I mooched back past the shuttered boutiques and tourism outlets to face the music with Dominick.

Uh-oh, the sparkplug of my humiliation was still there. On his own, at the same table, Pascal scratched on a sheet of paper with his fountain pen. A short black was at his elbow.

I could hardly run away again.

"Are you all right?" Dominick looked concerned. "You ran off so quick. Did you injure yourself?"

"I'm fine."

"Sorry, my fault, I mucked you about."

"This needs a wash." I handed him the soggy apron.

Dominick indicated Pascal with his chin. "The bird with him had to leave. Your dad, or Year 12 examiner, or whatever that bloke is to you, said he'd drive you home when you've finished up here."

"Oooh, nooo! I'd prefer to catch the Jamesville Tavern shuttle."

"Are you sure?"

Thinking of the sleaze on the bus, probably in the process of getting ripped right this minute, I reconsidered. "Well, okay."

Dominick looked at his watch. "The customers have dried up, and there's a Dracula flick I'd like to see at the drive-in with Seranella." The dishwasher churned. "If you like, you can go. I'll lock up."

"See you tomorrow, then?" I went behind the counter to grab my things.

"Like some vegies?" He opened the fridge door.

"I haven't finished the last lot." I cringed at the thought of Pascal seeing me stuff leftovers into my duffle bag.

☆

We made our way across the car park. "Take this, please, I need to smoke." Pascal gave me his briefcase. "It has been a difficult day."

He pulled a packet of Gauloises Blondes from the top pocket of his shirt, and slid out a cigarette. Lighting it, he blew wisps into the muggy air.

"You shouldn't suck on those cancer sticks," I said.

"Pfft." He shrugged. "*You* smoke chop-chop, or should I say hhhhash?"

"I told you, I do *not* do dope! Why don't you believe me?"

"Is it not suspicious that I discover pot in your bedroom at Jacques Forestier's house?" He clicked the remote.

I gave a sigh of exasperation. "It wasn't my swamp! It was someone else's!"

"We will never know." He opened the car door.

I gave him his briefcase. "Wow! This is nice!" I squirmed myself into the Beemer, inhaling the leather smell. "Way better than the *Deux Chevaux*." I looked at him. "Do you still have the Deuche, or did you get rid of it when you got your boring Merc back?"

"I keep the Deuche. I do not know why, for sentimental reason perhaps." He twisted the key into the ignition. "Remove that if it annoys you." A hire car rubbish bag dangled from the glove box.

"*That's* not what's annoying me! It's your coffin nail!" I pressed open the automatic window and gasped in a lungful of air. "Are you in FNQ to give lectures on Flaubert?"

"I am." He drew hard on his cigarette.

"Personally, I prefer not to think about Flaubert! It reminds me of my oral exam." I placed my duffle bag strategically to cover the coffee stain on my skirt.

"But you continue to study French?"

Sugarcane whipped past in the dark.

"I deferred my course at South Central Community College to be with Sandrine. Claude rang, said she was unwell." I chose not to tell him about the bruises. "But she seems fine."

We lapsed into silence. The lights on the dashboard glowed subtly, but the cold air blasting through the car failed to dispel his smoke.

Pascal broke the silence. "Do I detect an odour of ham coming from your army bag?"

"I bought a ham bone for Rocky's"—too late, his name was out—"um, dog." I prayed Pascal wouldn't guess I'd overheard his conversation with Jeanne Colline.

"You 'ave seen Roch since you arrived?"

"Is that a problem?"

"I 'ave told you before, Roch is not good enough for you!"

"Rocky's a great guy, and I'm sick of people saying he's not good enough for me! You, Sandrine …"

"Sandrine?"

"She saw me with him."

"What do you mean, '*with 'im*'?"

"Just kissing!"

"You 'ave no future with Roch," he said, abruptly.

Pascal was starting to take over my life again. Had my grandfather asked him to keep an eye on me, report back? Was that why Pascal had made it his business to contact me?

"I do not understand you, Genna. Roch, a poor kava farmer, takes you to nakamals, you drink kava containing cockroaches together, and you become besotted."

"Besotted? Boy, I don't think so. As for cockroaches, I never had cockroaches in *my* kava!"

"There are always cockroaches in kava!"

My stomach began to churn.

Not for the first time, I said, "Don't you get *sick* of always being right?"

Pascal tossed his butt out the window.

"You'll set the sugarcane on fire!"

He told me to let go. "*Laisse tomber,* Genna! I do not need you to be angry with me. My day 'as been difficult enough!"

"Did Jacques Forestier tell you to check up on me?" I tensed. "Or did you come to the coffee shop just for me, to see me for myself?"

We did a right off the highway. "Sandrine tells me you are working in Jamesville." He gave a tiny shrug. "I wish to see you. It is very simple."

"You spoke to Sandrine?"

"She gave me a key to inspect an apartment on the top floor of Beachfront section, a magnificent view."

"But Mrs Hays-Bert said you're not staying at the apartments." *No, no, no.* Me and my *big mouth*; now he'd know I'd been checking up on *him*.

"I am living at Mimosa Sands Resort in Coral Cove and it is expensive, so I would like to buy. I find Sandrine's apartments reasonable in price."

"Did you buy one?"

"I 'ave made an offer through a real estate agent." Pause. "So, tell me, did the dress you purchase in Anse Vata make your little friend fall in love with you all over again?"

"Nope, it's over, and I've moved on."

"Your Stefan is a fool." He eased the Beemer into the kerb outside Reception.

Embarrassed, I murmured, "He has a right not to be keen on me anymore."

Pascal reached to touch the beads on my wrist. "This is very beautiful. Who makes your wonderful bracelet?"

Tempted to say I didn't know, I realised he'd find out. "A girl called Douce."

"It is very lovely."

He looked strained, and I saw the beginnings of a five o'clock shadow. Up close, he was swarthier than I remembered. Handsome, in a way.

"Did Roch give you this?" He exhaled heavily.

"He was wearing it. I admired it and he gave it to me. The bracelet fits 'cause it's on memory wire."

"Memory wire?"

I twirled the bangle off, twisted it back on again. The beads clung and curled around my wrist.

"Is there a place you can join me in a glass of …" He took a breath. "I believe you prefer fruit juice?"

Would Pascal ask awkward questions about Douce if I had a drink with him? I wondered, before saying: "Um, the only café in Glisten Beach is the All Day Breakfast Café, and that'll be closed 'cos the guests are spinebashing for tomorrow's tour." I wagged a finger. "You, know, I *am* eighteen, and allowed in a bar!"

"We could find a bar in Coral Cove, have some wine together?"

I wouldn't have minded an old-fashioned Blue Lagoon to calm me—or even a Fluffy Duck—but replied, "Nah, too glitzy in Coral Cove. I stink of coffee, and I've got to paint a notice for Claude."

"I will be leaving tomorrow."

"Oh?" My heart started to rattle in my chest. I itched with curiosity. Was Pascal about to let me in on the secret of the kava leaves?

"For a short while," he added.

"And when will you be back from Nouméa?"

"How do you know I go to *Nouvelle-Calédonie*?" His blue eyes narrowed as he met my gaze. "I never said anything about Nouméa."

Chapter 33

Had Pascal guessed that I'd overheard his conversation with Rocky's mother? Or had he bought my excuse that I'd made a random stab, I wondered, slamming my apartment door shut.

Stacks of other places he might visit came to mind: Paris to see his mother; Melbourne to check on Alliance Française; Tahiti to catch up with his—current, or was it ex?—girlfriend, president of a pearl-buying company. There were heaps of towns and cities he might have chosen to jet off to.

In a frazzle, I turned the ceiling fan to high. The blades of the fan whipped over my head, flipping my extensions off my shoulders. Dropping my smelly duffle on the floor, I stripped and headed for the bathroom to take a much needed shower.

I scrubbed the ham and coffee odour from my hair and skin. After sweeping the sand and salt away, I stood there until the water ran cold and I shivered. I shoved my soiled clothes in the washer, dragged an old T-shirt over my head and stepped into a pair of plaid boxers I'd stolen from Stefan.

Although hanging out for bed and beauty sleep before I saw Rocky the next day (I no longer cared if he'd nicked those planter baskets), I knew I should finish the Amédée Library sign before I even thought of shut-eye. Turning the fan down a notch, I grabbed a knife from the kitchen and prised the lid off the tin. Stirring the paint with a spoon handle, I dipped in my brush and began to inscribe the words on the plywood. The paint was gooey, the brush turning stiff as I stroked. By the time I'd written 'Self-Service', my eyes were fluttering—the fumes?—and both index fingers were smeared with acrylic.

After writing 'Library' I jammed the lid back on, swished the brush in a glass of water and left it to soak.

Yawning, I ambled to my bedroom, set the ceiling fan on low and collapsed onto the unmade sheets. With the earthy whiff of Rocky's muscle tee filtering through my pillow, my vision blurred over. Eyelid movies shifted and swayed and formed strange shapes before I drifted off.

☆

During the night, the wind started to howl. I awoke to a crash—the sound of splintering timber, or was it a door? The crash was accompanied by a grunt. The sound was close by, as if from the room marked Storage.

I lurched up. The luminous hands of my Swatch read nine minutes past three. I staggered from my bed, and hauled back the curtains in the sitting room. The Amédée Apartments sign was off. The external lights along the Beachfront Apartments' balconies were also extinguished. I ran into my bedroom, and pulled back the curtains there. Through the tropical foliage, I saw that the Garden Apartments' walkways were unlit. The entire complex was swathed in darkness.

The palms gave out a noise like falling rain as the fronds rubbed and scraped against each other.

Back in the sitting room, I saw the coconut trees across the road being flung by the storm. Through curving branches, I discerned a vessel heading out to sea. *Who would venture on the ocean on a night like this?* I asked myself.

Wide awake now, I drew the curtains to, switched on the lights and opened the can of paint. Keeping my ears pricked for unusual noises, I cleaned the bristles on a paper towel and continued to do my library sign. With the wind screaming, I was able to hear little above the din.

Having completed Claude's task, I propped the plywood against the kitchen bench to dry. Head aching with tiredness, I placed the brush back in the water and made for my bed. Hugging my pillow to me, the pungent smell of Rocky's muscle tee overrode the paint fumes. I nodded off instantly.

Chapter 34

I slept through the Waveripper reef bus morning pick-up. Children yelling and splashing in the pool outside dragged me out of the dream.

My Swatch read almost nine—time to get moving. I was certain Rocky wouldn't venture past Reception to knock on my door. He might already be on Glisten Beach, impatiently waiting.

What to wear? Pulling the previous day's bikini from the tangled pile, I felt the fabric, tempted to don it again. Uh-uh, still damp. Did Rocky like bright colours? And then I recalled him admiring my yellow-spotted knickers. Would I dare to appear in my undies again, as a monokini?

Nibbling on a nail, I spied the strap of a bikini in citrus, with a bee embroidered on the backside. Stefan had ogled me when I first swanned around in that crocheted number. Decision made, I slipped on the bikini. Slinging a towel over my shoulder, I set off barefoot.

No Maigret lay on the doorstep. I dodged fallen fronds and steaming puddles on the path leading to the foreshore. Passing Reception, I waved to Sandrine.

"You're looking tired, Genna," she called. "You have shadows under your eyes."

"The storm kept me awake."

"Oh." Pause. "Have you applied your sunscreen?"

"I don't need sunscreen."

"Oh yes you do, SPF thirty-plus protection, at the least!"

As I skirted the sandwich board advertising, I heard her say, "Don't go near any of the streams! A man was taken last night near the creek behind a resort in Coral Cove!"

Pascal was staying at the Mimosa Sands Resort in Coral Cove. "Anyone I know?" My heart began to paddle.

"A Tasmanian, from a place called Penguin."

I relaxed.

She added: "This morning's calm weather and a rising tide mean some early stingers … or maybe late, I'm never sure … have been sighted, so *swim inside the net*. You will find the stinger net further along the beach, opposite the All Day Breakfast Café, and marked by a red and yellow flag. The box jellyfish is dangerous! Take care!"

"I'll be careful!"

I padded across the beach.

A lifesaver, wearing goggles and snorkel, swam inside the net. His see-through red and gold bodysuit gleamed in the sunshine as he rose to his feet and waded from the water. Were deadly box jellyfish in there? The water looked fine to me.

Spreading my towel on the sand, I slipped the tie on my bikini top undone and started to sunbathe. The weather was perfect, and I lay there thinking of Rocky. I was hanging out to see him, dying to find out how Chocolat was coping with his leg in plaster. Had the dog enjoyed the bone?

I could see no sign of Rocky's ute.

I rolled onto my back. Further along the beach another lifesaver dived beneath the water, checking the net. Tiny waves lapped softly, and I congratulated myself on my decision to visit Far North Queensland. Sandrine was friendly, the beach was awesome, and I had a new guy and a new job. Plus a fabbo new hairdo.

The only cloud on my horizon was Pascal. His problems bothered me. Apart from that, my life was perfect.

I lay on my front again, keeping an eye on the cars cruising along the narrow esplanade. *Where was Rocky?* I began to get impatient.

An hour passed. Still no ute, and the sun was beating down. I decided to have a quick dip while I waited. Ensuring the strings on my bikini were securely tied, I sauntered along the beach to the stinger net to join the other swimmers.

"G'day!" Sweat pearled above the lifesaver's lips. "Watch out for that box jellyfish, eh!" He adjusted his red and gold cap.

"Aren't you hot in that bodystocking thing?" I pointed to his wetsuit, made of pantyhose material.

"Better'n being stung, but." He gave me an even smile.

"So I'll be all right if I swim in that big square?"

"Yeah, me and Al … I'm Cliff, and Al's gone across to the All Day Breakfast Café for a bite to eat … dived in a minute ago, had a bit of a swim around. She's A-okay, all clear!" He gave me the thumbs-up.

"What's *that* for, Cliff?" A whopping bottle sat atop a wooden crate.

"Acetic acid, in case you get tentacles wrapped around your legs and other parts of your body. We flood the stung area for half a minute to render the stings harmless. And there," he said, pointing at a bell-shaped jellyfish floating in a nearby jar, "you have the enemy, Chironex fleckeri."

I gaped at the bundles of tentacles on each corner of the box-shaped hollow bell. However, I was unafraid. For years, Stefan and I had trapped blue-ringed octopuses in rock pools. And blue ringers were deadly—one bite and you were paralysed for twenty-four hours.

"Should be sweet, though?"

"I'm as certain as I can be, checked, can't do nuthin' more." Cliff tightened the cap strings beneath his chin. "You from down south, eh?"

"I'm staying at the Amédée Apartments." I shielded my eyes with my hands. "It could become, like, permanent if I decide to stay, and I just might do that! It's a great place to chill out!"

"Goodonya! Ya know you're lookin' beat, as if you could do with a rest, but."

"Right." I didn't *feel* tired, so why was everyone telling me I *looked* tired?

"The Deep North's a fair dinkum paradise, until the wet comes." Turning, he yelled, "Eh buster, use the net, mate!" as a tubby man ran into the water outside the patrolled area. "And divin' in is the worst thing you can do!"

The tubby man kept going. Cliff trotted off, shouting.

Wading into the stinger-resistant enclosure, I sank into the water and began to do laps. Breaststroke at first, followed by freestyle. The sea was magic that day, like crystal. I could see nothing goobie like cone fish, or stonefish, or creepy creatures with tentacles. The water swelled and surged as I swam backwards and forwards inside the jellyfish net. I ceased swimming, rolled on my back and floated.

This was seventh heaven.

"Yowee!" I lifted my arm to punch my fist in the air, but I didn't have the energy. Wallowing, I dogpaddled for a bit.

Stopping again for a breather, I trod water and peered through the palm trees. On the footpath outside the All Day Breakfast Café, tanned flesh and burnt flesh, taut bods and flabby figures lounged on deck-chairs in boardies and bikinis. Skin sheeny with coconut oil, holiday-makers in wraparounds and aviator shades consumed waffles and hot chips, eggs and raisin toast, washing the food down with coffee, Fruit Tingles and Pineapple Bombs. Straightening, I moved to shallower water. Was Rocky also there, eating?

I squinted, but was unable to see him.

The airport bus from Cairns rounded the corner into Arlington Esplanade. The vehicle slowed at the Amédée Apartments, and then continued on to the All Day Breakfast Café where a knot of tourists—some wearing zinc cream—tumbled down the steps.

Secure in the knowledge that Rocky would find me I remained waist-deep in the water, my hand shading my eyes, my bracelet sparkling. I flicked an extension stuck to my cheek back over my shoulder, anchored my feet in the sand and waited.

Without warning, a pain shot through my body.

Chapter 35

I gasped and clutched, did my best to push my way out of the water, but the pain was so bad I was unable to budge. My nervous system had pinned me to the spot. A 'thing' clung to my thigh, and all I could feel was agony.

"Help!" I screamed. "Something's got me by the leegggsss …" My voice faded to a whisper, and it was difficult to breathe. My chest heaved, and the searing went on and on, as I writhed and feebly tried to rip the thing off. "Cliff! Cliff!"

Only a raspy wheeze came out. My heart lurched as though it was about to jump from my chest. Boom, ba-boom, boom, ba-boom, boom, *boom*, BOOM.

Overhead, the sky turned vanilla and mauve and slate grey, interspersed with pinprick stars of brightness. A zillion spring-loaded hypodermic needles jabbed at my limbs. Tingling and pounding, my skin was bursting open, and I felt myself slip down and down. The water, icy now, rose over my head. Everything turned to lapping black … and then to silence.

Peace at last. I lay on the beach in Ravella, the hot sand on my back. The tang of household vinegar wafted up as fingers picked their way across my body, gentle and deft. A tickly feel of metal ran across my skin, and I detected the familiar smell of zinc cream as Stefan poured suntan oil over me—or was it vinegar? *What are you doing, Stefan?* He hung onto my nose and began to kiss me, swallowing me up as he always did before lifting his mouth to—blow out? *Had a blue ringer bitten me?* Taking a deep breath, he turned to blow into my lungs once more. *You always told me to be careful, didn't you, Stef?*

Our chests joined as one. Stefan was breathing for me, and that was how it should be, how it always had been. We belonged together. And my ribcage felt light again. No more effort as he continued to work away. I could taste his zinc cream, and the protection was soothing, cool—way better than a granita from Curly's. *Curly?* I knew no one in Ravella called Curly. And they didn't even sell granitas—only slurpies and smoothies and other slush drinks like melted sorbets. *I wouldn't mind a Lemon Berry Smoothie right this minute!* I told myself.

Stefan ceased blowing air in my lungs.

Keep going, Stef, you have to keep this up for the rest of the day, and into the night. Don't you remember—it takes twenty-four hours for the blue ringer venom to wear off? And if you don't keep going, I'll die! Please keep going? I don't want to die. Please, pretty please. I'll do anything ...

My arms thrashed of their own accord. My muscles ached with a pain I'd never experienced before, yet I kept on thrashing. A hand stroked my cheek.

A voice—like Stefan's: "Chill out, mate. You can relax now. We inactivated the remaining nematocysts."

A voice—like Cliff's: "I'll leave you to it then, eh? She'll be okay. Just keep 'er still for thirty minutes. She may need a narcotic analgesia."

The voice—like Stefan's: "She'll be right. Genna's a gutsy chick. We go way back."

My head swirled, rocked, and filled with blood. Pain came over me in waves. People around me talked in hushed tones. I seemed to be hallucinating.

The voice—like Cliff's: "Whaddya do for a crust then, eh?"

"Got my own Nature Shop, flog marine spiders trapped in sea bubbles, blue-ringed octopuses. I mount 'em in Perspex for the tourists. Oh, and I sell Palaeozoic rocks in sealed cellophane packets. Plus the usual stuff, like crested spoons."

"Knew what ya were doin' with them tentacles, but. You handled them tweezers like a pro! Kept her head well down …"

"I thought she might've had Irukandji Syndrome … Carukia barnesi … at first, seeing as she was swimming in the net. I've read a lot about those and I wondered."

"Nah, definitely Chironex fleckeri, a small one, doubt the tentacles would've been three metres long, more like twenty centimetres. The swell washed it over the side and into the net. Watch 'er, those welts are pretty red and inflamed. None near the face, though, which is lucky, eh? She's a good looking girlie, a real hottie."

A woman's voice cried: "Cliff, another one's been stung. A kid, this time!"

"Strewth, this is like a war zone! Gotta go. Catch ya later then, eh?"

Sand sprayed from his feet as Cliff jogged off.

Silence. My face was being stroked; a finger ran along my cheekbone. I inhaled the zinc cream odour.

Then: "I've wanted to do that since I was ten years old, babe, give you mouth to mouth." The voice continued to sound like my ex, although Stefan never called me 'babe', and he was down south on the Mornington Peninsula—a four hour flight from Glisten Beach.

"It is you, isn't it?" I whispered, not daring to look.

"Shush, don't talk!" Stefan placed his finger gently on my lips. "I'll lie here beside you, keep you company."

I breathed out the words: "What are you doing … oh heck, I feel awful … in Glisten Beach?"

"Don't talk, babe."

"Don't call me 'babe'!" I forced my eyes open to see sweat trickling from his coppery hair and down his temples. He was clad in his usual white shorts and T-shirt, the zinc cream had worn off his cheeks and I could see his freckles.

"I meant to say *mate*, mate. You're my mate, and you'll always be my mate, and be very special to me." A pause. His next words came out in a rush: "I made a mistake. I'm here to ask you to have me back. I still love ya, mate!"

"Don't! Please stop, Stef. I'm hurting so much I can't even think about us and, anyway, you went off with my best friend. I'll never forgive you. Oh, oh, oh, I feel terrible."

"I'm really sorry, babe, I mean, mate." Placing his arm around me, he kissed me softly on the mouth—a comforting kiss. He lifted my bikini strap to kiss me on the shoulder.

"What are you, ahhhh, *doing*?"

"These crocheted bathers always did fall down when you went in the water."

"Ooooh," I groaned. "My bikini didn't come off when they, you, whoever, pulled me out? Please say it didn't!"

Stefan's smile was lazy, his teeth yellow against the white of the zinc cream. He said nothing, just kissed me on the shoulder again, a longer kiss.

"Don't do that, Stef!"

He stopped kissing me. He shouted, "Shoo! Go away!" His body jerked against mine as he flapped his hand. "Stupid three-legged dog! Go on, *shoo*! Get *outttaaaaa* here!"

Paws scrabbling, the dog ran off.

Stefan placed his arm around me again.

My heart, already pounding from the torture, seemed to cease functioning. "Did you say a *three-legged* dog? One of his legs was *missing*? You sure it wasn't set in plaster?"

"Nuh, it was definitely three-legged, an ugly-looking monster!" Stefan lightly tugged my extensions. "You're always changing your hairstyle, mate. Wotcha done, this time?"

"Um, um."

He fingered my Tawdry Tan tips. "Looks complicated! How d'you look after it in this climate?"

"Wash'n'go," I mumbled. "Wash, comb and leave it."

"Excellent!" he said.

My breath jounced and became uneven. "I don't care about my stupid hair! The dog, what colour was the dog?"

"Brown all over."

"That's Chocolat!" I struggled to raise my head, but was unable to move. "Rocky's here!"

A shrill whistle came from the vicinity of Arlington Esplanade, followed by "*Allez viens!*" Scratching of paws as the dog landed awkwardly on the tray.

"Rocky! Don't, *please* don't go!" My voice seemed to blow away on the rising breeze. My legs were swollen and excruciating; I was stuck there.

"Keep still, mate!"

"Stop him, Stefan!" Sweat streamed off me.

"Stop who? The Koori bloke in the grungy muscle tee, ugly as his dog, who just got in a ute with spotties?"

"He's not a Koori. He's a Caledonian freedom fighter!"

"What's he to you?"

Tears pricked beneath my lids. I bit my lip to prevent myself from blubbing. I didn't feel anything, only tasted the blood.

The utility rumbled, throbbed and roared. The engine sounded as wonky as my heart when the ute chugged off down the road. Chocolat whimpered in the back as Rocky turned the corner. The growl of the motor faded.

Stefan called out: "Gimme that acetic acid, Cliff!"

And he flooded my legs with more vinegar.

Chapter 36

Piercing pangs shot through my body. Sweat seemed to gush from every pore. A strange chafing sound rose from my chest with each heartbeat.

With Stefan supporting me, I waited while Sandrine clicked her tongue, and fussed about, and straightened my mucky sheets.

"I detect a bad smell!" She reached beneath my pillow and hauled out Rocky's muscle tee. "What's this?" ASSASSIN seemed to flash like a green neon sign.

I felt Stefan stiffen.

In a river of agony, I attempted to shrug as if I had no idea how the item happened to be there.

"This needs a wash," she said, carrying the clothing from my bedroom between her thumb and forefinger.

Beside me, Stefan compressed his mouth into a slit. "You been boozin' and bonkin' while you've been up north?"

"Who, me? I've done nothing!"

Back in my bedroom, Sandrine finished fixing my sheets.

"Oh, oh, oh, I can't *stand* this!" I willed my breath to become slow and deep, to manage the excruciating feeling.

"Then who owns the muscle tee?" he hissed again.

Lips pursed into an O, I exhaled in short breaths. "I-found-it-on-the-beach."

"Yeah, right! It belongs to the bloke with the three-legged dog, doesn't it? I can tell by the look on yer face, the guilt!" Lifting the memory wire, Stefan flicked my bracelet. "I suppose he gave you this?"

Suffering chiselled through my body. "That's so not fair! Don't quiz me, Stef! He gave me the beads, and shouted me a bungy jump, that's all."

I waggled a feeble finger in Sandrine's direction, shook my head and attempted to glare at my ex. But the glare lost its impact when my eyes welled up from the spasms.

"'E sounds flaky to me."

"I'm hurting!" I gasped. "When will this *stop*?"

Stefan calmed down. "Sorry, babe, I mean, mate. I'm not thinking straight, too upset. I'm feelin' lower than a footprint." Pause. "It's gonna take twenty-four hours at least for what you're experiencing to go away. And then you should take it quiet for the next week or two."

"I don't think I can stand it anymore!"

"You should've worn a stinger suit, mate."

"Oh-oh-oh … but I swam in the *netttt.*"

"You may lie down now." Sandrine turned the ceiling fan to high.

Stefan helped me to climb onto my bed just before I blacked out.

☆

The day dragged on. Cramping, grasping my stomach—someone had changed me into a clean T-shirt and knickers—I pushed myself up on my elbows to see long, whip-like lines, ladder patterns at the top of my swollen legs. And the pain showed no sign of abating.

Sandrine shook her head and tsk-tsked. While Stefan watched over me, she went into the kitchen and brewed me camomile tea.

"I hate hippie tea!" Screwing up my face, I dribbled the tea back into the cup.

"A traditional European herb, camomile cures many things." Her hair was in an untidy knot. "Drink, it is good for you."

"No, no." My mind clutched around. "What I need is a granita. Yes, I need something *really* cool!"

"I think Meggsie does granitas," said Sandrine. "Would you please … Stef, or should I call you *Stefan*? ... go down to the All Day Breakfast Café? It's on Arlington Esplanade, not far from our apartments."

"I know the place. I was there when Genna got stung." Jiggling coins, Stefan slammed the front door behind him as he raced off.

While he was gone, Sandrine changed my sheets beneath me. Brushing away sand from my skin, she said, "You have shadows around your eyes." Peering, she added, "Is that makeup?"

I remembered Claude's library sign. "Probably paint."

"I can remove it with essential oil."

After what seemed like three hours, Stefan was back. "Meggsie pulverised a stack of icy poles." He handed me the cold drink. "This should help chill you down."

I crunched on the lemon-flavoured granita.

Puce-faced and panting, Stefan plonked himself on a chair in the corner of the room. Expelling a jet of air through his teeth, he said in a distracted fashion, "You should stop the blisters from forming, Mrs, Madame … um, Sandrine. We don't want Genna to have permanent scarring! And she needs ice packs for the pain."

He pushed himself off the chair, went to the fridge and rattled around. On his return, his handkerchief bulged with ice cubes.

Placing the pack alternately on my stomach and legs, he said, "You got any frozen peas, mate? I forgot to look."

"You *know* I'm … great, the ice is helping! … raw vegan. Sheesh, the pack's no longer helping. I, ah, don't eat cooked food and I'm sure, like, 'snap, um, frozen' means …" I was feeling delirious.

"Win always has a bag of frozen peas in her fridge!"

Wrenched back into full consciousness by his words, I screamed, "Oh, shut up, *shut up*, SHUT UP! I don't want you even *mentioning* the name of that bit—*person*—in my presence!"

"Sssshhh," said Sandrine.

She began to apply vinegar and olive oil to my legs. Soon, I smelled like a salad. She straightened my sheets again, fiddled and fussed about and called me '*ma petite*'. And I wondered if it was the first time she had ever really touched me.

"Genna needs a crepe bandage on her legs," said Stefan, "although it's probably a bit late for that."

Lightning bolts of pain still shot through my limbs and stomach and chest. My extensions felt as though bugs were playing chasey in my hair shafts.

Sandrine continued to try to make me comfortable.

"I cannot *bear* this! Can't you give me something?"

She handed me a glass of water and two codeine tablets. "Swallow!" .

The painkillers made no difference.

She saturated a face cloth in a basin of cool water and lavender essential oil, wrung the fabric out and placed it over my face. "Breathe deeply," she murmured.

I breathed deeply, but the pain went on and on. I continued to wail and flop about and weep—until I got that squiggly feeling in my stomach.

"I'm going to vomit!" I lurched up.

Sandrine pushed me back. "It's the stress of the pain. Lie still."

"I can't help it! I'm gonna chuck!" I grabbed my chest.

"Could you fetch a towel from the bathroom?" She jerked her head at Stefan.

He slouched off.

"Quick! Quick! Quick!"

In a jiff, Stefan was back.

I heaved lemon-flavoured spew into the towel, heaved until nothing was left to bring up.

"Can't you give me something stronger?" I pleaded.

Sandrine kept feeding me pills. As the daylight turned to evening, I was throwing up just as much. By now, into a bowl.

Stefan hung on to my hair.

Claude came in briefly.

Mwaaah. Splack! Mwaaah. Splack! He gave me a juicy smooch on each cheek, and took my hand in his massive paw. "Can you not *do* somesing, Sandrine?"

"I'm doing all I can," she said.

"I cannot stay, my leeetle cabbage." He squeezed my fingers. "A backpacker 'as parked 'is campervan in front of our *won*-derful apartments."

The aroma of ti-tree oil lingered in the air as he barrelled off. Outside, on Arlington Esplanade, I could hear him yelling.

"I think she needs a narcotic painkiller, a shot of pethidine," said Stefan, as if I were not capable of speaking for myself.

"I don't want to go to hospital," I cried.

Tears ran down my face and puddled, merging with my body sweat. The sheets were clammy from the cool of the overhead ceiling fan and I began to shiver. My teeth clattered about, and it felt as though every hair shaft on my body had gone into shock. I wondered if I could go on.

"Currently we have a medical practitioner in Apartment No. 18. I will see if he has something for the pain." Sandrine scurried to the phone.

Stefan held my hand. "You have awesome skin, tanned and smooth. It's one of the things I've always admired about you." He stroked my arm, and it felt good.

Sandrine dialled Reception to be transferred to the guest's flat.

Her voice was high and anxious. "Doctor Mack, I'm *so* glad I caught you." After that, I could only make out the words 'stinger' and 'box jellyfish' and 'immense pain' before she hung up.

"He's coming," she called out. "I'll put these plates in the dishwasher while we wait."

"I'm sick of this sweating," I said to Stefan. "It makes the sheets go yucky and cold."

"You're not gunna die or anything! You'll be okay as soon as the doc gets the narcotic analgesia into you. The envenomation wasn't as huge as it might've been. You need to get tangled up real good with the Indo-Pacific Box Jellyfish, contacting at least ten feet of tentacles, to die. Did I tell you"—he was back on the subject of Win Winstone—"Win's socking down the perfume again? She needs ya, mate."

"Some best friend she turned out to beeee." My breathing was becoming thready. "For years, she swanned in and out of my place yet never asked me inside her house until she had no choice." A wave of exhaustion came over me

"Give her a break. Her old lady was sick with Korsakoff's Syndrome!"

"She could've let me in on it. I would've helped. Oh, I can't stand this pain …" My voice died to a whisper.

"It was the shame, mate. And I'm worried she's going the same way as Alice. She's even given up Pilates classes, and I think she sometimes lets your ma down in that recycle shop, makes multi mistakes and doesn't turn up."

"Well, I'm sorry."

A knock on the front door.

"Doctor Mack has arrived," called Sandrine.

"Look, I'm knackered, mate. I was up at four this morning to drive to Tullamarine and then catch the early morning flight to Cairns. And you'll be out to it for a while after he sticks the needle in." He let go of my hand. "I'll see you when you come round."

"Where are you staying?"

"Backpackers' hostel in Cairns." His smile was whiter now that the zinc cream had worn off. "I hope there's no mossies, or fleas, or bedbugs in the bunk, plays hell with my, um, condition."

A man with plastered-down hair, in a short-sleeved shirt like an airline pilot's, stood beside Sandrine with his stethoscope.

"G'day, doc!" Stefan edged towards the doorway.

I summoned the energy to call out: "Thanks for saving my life!"

"Was worth the trip," he said, "just to blow air in your lungs, even if you won't have me back."

"I've moved on."

"Yeah, you were *real* attached to that muscle tee of his." Pause. "I'll drop by later, tomorrow, before I leave to catch the plane home. You oughta be awake by then."

"I'd like that."

"Catch ya later, mate!" He closed the front door behind him, and I felt a sort of emptiness.

Doctor Mack listened to my chest. "Bit of cardiac arrhythmia." He swabbed my arm with alcohol. "I hear you've had a nasty confrontation with a jellyfish? This should give you some relief, give your body a chance to recuperate." His chest hair and moustache were as black as his bag.

I barely felt the needle. There were no eyelid movies that night. I passed straight into a pain-free darkness, like the most amazing deep velvet.

Chapter 37

What was in that injection? I wondered when I woke. Stefan still seemed to be seated on the chair in the corner, except he was wearing oversized black-rimmed nerd glasses and his hair, now darker, was done in … *Indian plaits*?

I peered through slitted lids. His legs were solid and pale, and he wore chunky brown sandals. He was clad in cinnamon walk shorts, and his nose was buried in a collection of poetry by Baudelaire.

My mind swirled. I closed my eyes and lay there feeling at peace. I had no pain. I just felt tired, and my muscles were achy. *But why did I feel like an Egyptian mummy?* Groping beneath the sheets, I discovered my thighs were bound with crepe bandages.

"How are you feeling?" Stefan even *sounded* like Hetty Geiger. "You've been out to it for a long while."

My eyelids flew open. "Hetty? Why are *you* here?" My tongue felt thick.

She grinned, gave a little wave. "Hi, Gen, you've surfaced! Stef rang, told me about the drama. My exams were over, so I decided to fly up!"

"He said he'd be here when I woke."

"He was tired of waiting for you to come around, so he caught the plane back to Ravella."

"How long have I been asleep?"

"Two days."

"Wow!" And then I remembered Rocky driving away while I lay there. "Did anyone ring while I was out to it?"

"Not really, only your"—pause—"Namilly Perrier, to see how you were after she heard about the accident."

"My mum?"

"Well, whatever you call her now." Hetty tugged at her plait. "Your other mum keeps popping in and fussing. She seems nice, despite those tarty pink clothes she wears."

"Sandrine?"

"Yeah, Gen. To be frank, I find this relationship thing confusing. Who is the person you actually call 'Mum' these days?"

"Namilly's my *mum*! She's the one who brought me up. Sandrine will always be Sandrine to me. She signed that Procuration document, and I won't forget it!"

"I think she cares, though. She's been super worried. She got in such a tizzy she collided with a cupboard in the kitchen!"

"Don't break my heart! It's time she worried about me!" I lifted my hand from beneath the sheet. "Could you get my mobile? I need to ring Rocky."

"So, you've still got the hots for the insurgent?" Hetty placed her poetry on the floor and fossicked in my bag.

"Rocky is cool, but he was supposed to meet me on Glisten Beach, um, *two* days ago, but drove away just after Stefan finished giving me, um, mouth-to-mouth resuscitation."

Hetty handed me the phone. "Perhaps Rocky didn't realise you'd been stung by a box jellyfish, and thought you were kissing Stefan? Does he know you're still carrying the phone your ex paid for?"

I gave a feeble fidget. "The mobile still works. Why should I buy a new one? I'm not flush with moolah!"

Hetty glared through her megaton geek glasses. "You *sure* Stefan didn't kiss you?"

"Ooh noooo, um, like, well, a comforting kiss and a little one on my shoulder." I cleared my throat. "I told him to stop!"

"*He*, your new guy, didn't know that, and Stefan does, from a distance, look like Kurt Cobain!"

"Surely the guy wouldn't be so dumb. Why would I kiss Stefan? I told Rocky my relationship with Stefan was over. I think the real problem *is* that I almost killed Chocolat."

"Was that when you opened Rocky's ute door to chuck, and the dog flew out of the tray?"

"Yeah, well, he might fill me in." I brought up Rocky's number and hit the green key. The phone rang and rang, before switching to voicemail.

"Hi, Rocky," I said after the beep, "it's Genna. I missed you on the beach. Just wondering what happened. Ring me!" I pressed the Off button.

"Look, I'm getting out of bed." I pushed myself up on my elbows. "'Cos I need to go."

"To the loo?"

I flashed my eyes with impatience. "I have to catch the bus to Kooracoondoo, see Rocky, find out what's bothering him. I also have to pick up a T-shirt I ordered, cute, with a green tree frog and his name."

"*You*, Genna Perrier, are not going anywhere! You're resting!"

"Who do you think you are, my *third* mother?"

"Strangely enough, even though *you* think I'm a dag, and I still remember you shouting, 'Geek alert!' when I first got my specs and calling me 'geek of the week' when I did something stupid like let the tennis ball float in on set point against Eastern Lakes High." Pause. "Or did Fat Betty do that?" She inhaled. "Y'know, I do care about you. Why do you think I'm here? Do you think I travelled all this way just to see your macadocious Caldoche face?" She heaved herself out of her chair.

"Where are you going? To speak to Sandrine, report in? And does my grandfather know? Will Jacques Forestier send in his guard dogs as well? Get Marcel Manet to come here? Alert Pascal?"

"Aren't you being a tad paranoid?" Hetty loomed over me. "Look, Gen, do you want permanent *welts* on your legs? Scarring?"

"Whaddya mean 'welts'? No, I don't want scarring! I'd never be able to wear bikinis again!"

Hetty chewed her lip and went, "Hmmmn." And then, "I dunno. A bit of a scar at the top of your legs could be kinda interesting!"

"You are gross! I am so getting outta here!" I tried to swing my legs off the bed, but they refused to move. "Wow, I feel shocking. I'm aching all over!"

"Sandrine told me to make you a camomile drink. Although, personally, I think *tisanes* are disgusting."

"I hate hippie tea!"

"Well, we agree on one thing." Hetty stomped off. "Guess who I saw at Cairns airport when I arrived yesterday," she called from the kitchen, "catching the flight to Brissie?"

"No idea. Who?"

"Remember the cool chalkie in the shiny grey suit who conducted our Year 12 Frog Orals? I'd forgotten how hot he was! Why would *monsieur* be going to Brisbane?"

"Hot? Hot!" I squealed. "Pascal is a pompous dude. How can you think he's *hot*?"

"Boy, he so is!"

And I recalled Pascal saying he would have to be away from his lecturing job at Reef University for a short while. "He was probably on his way to catch the connecting flight to Nouméa," I shouted. "What's so attractive about Pascal Manet?"

Balancing steaming mugs of camomile and a brown paper bag, Hetty re-entered the bedroom. "Like, he's got the best baby blues and a lean, mean physique. Makes me go all, oh, you know!"

"Don't be a dork! You like anyone in pants who's got a halfway decent body! Anyway, there's serious stuff you don't know about Pascal."

"What stuff?"

"Oh, things I'd rather not talk about." I eyed the paper bag. "Wotcha got in there?"

Hetty placed the mugs on the bedside table and handed me the parcel. "It's from Stefan, a 'remorse gift' I think."

I waved a finger at her. "It's as well Stefan an' I broke up. He's shaping up to be like his old man, knocking off those cashier chicks."

"Stefan doesn't have any cashier chicks."

"He will! You just wait 'til he goes IDB."

"Into Daddy's Business? You think he'll run the servo?"

"Absolutely! What's in the bag? I must check out this so-called 'remorse gift', a gift for having dumped me I suppose." Ripping the paper off, I saw the word SUGAR inscribed on an anodised lid. "What *is* it? Sheesh, it's a," I screamed at the top of my lungs, "BOX JELLYFISH!"

I dropped the stinger. Hetty lunged. She grabbed the jar, jiggled and juggled and finally hugged the container to her chest.

"How *could* he?" I huffed.

"Well, *I* think the pressie is rather special. Stefan says it's the very same jellyfish that actually stung you, moving at a speed of four knots. The lifesaver, Cliff, caught it and Sandrine supplied the jar, and it's now in formalin so you can keep the Sea Wasp, or Marine Stinger, as a souvenir!" Her face had turned bright pink.

"That is *so* disgusting!" My gaze recoiled from the toxic bunches of tentacles on each corner of the blue-tinted body. "Take it away! Chuck the yucky thing down the toilet so it can be gobbled up by an equally revolting cane toad! Stefan Becker is one totally *sick* dude!"

"I don't get it. You've been stuffing blue ringers in snap-lock bags for as long as I can remember. A box jellyfish in a jar is, like, not much different."

"It's *very* different! That particular box jellyfish tried to kill me!"

"Okay. I'll get rid of it." Hetty made for the door. "Are there really cane toads in the toilet up here?"

"I've never seen one, but it's about all I haven't seen."

"Have you seen *mud wrestling*?" Behind the coke-bottle lenses, her eyes were huge.

"Well no, I haven't actually *seen* mud wrestling, or foam parties, or wet T-shirt competitions. But I have done a bungy jump. And I know where I can see those things. I've also been near taipans in the sugarcane, *and* I heard a man was eaten by a croc in Coral Cove." Pause. "How did you find out about mud wrestling?"

"Those brochures on your coffee table."

I waved my hand. "Get rid of that creature before I start to spew again!"

Hetty marched into the bathroom. I heard her struggling with the screw top.

"Aaargh!" She let out a shriek. "This is sooooo *repulsive*!"

I had a flash of inspiration. The stinger could be cool as a trophy, like having your appendix in a jar for everyone to gander at.

"Hey, Hetty!" I yelled. "Hold it! Don't tip the contents down the loo! Leave the goobie on the kitchen bench! I might keep it, 'cos people could be interested for, um, scientific, Chironex fleckeri, reasons."

"You, Genna Perrier, are as sick as Stefan!"

"As if."

A knock.

"I'll get it!" Still clutching the jellyfish, she opened my front door. "Oh, hi, *monsieur*! *Elle va bien ce matin.*" Like a true brainiac, Hetty began to rabbit on in French.

Having finished discussing my health, Claude strode into my bedroom in lawn bowls gear and carrying his bowling bag. He adjusted his starched hat.

"You are awake now, Genna. Do you know what day ees it, my leeetle cabbage?" He enveloped my hand with his warm, long fingers.

"Sure, it's Saturday!"

"Ve-*rrry* good!" Teeth whiter than his outfit, he said, "How you know?"

"Dominick said to tell you he'd see you at lawn bowls on Saturday if he could get away, so it must be Saturday. Although, I guess he'll be short-staffed now I'm laid up."

Claude smiled again. "Can I get you anysing, *mon petit chou*?"

"Thanks, but Hetty's looking after me."

"Sandrine give me your lovely sign and I place it on ze library door … *merci beaucoup!* ... and I find your words to be most professional." Claude squeezed my paw. "You are very much betterrrr now?"

"Much better now the pain's gone. For a while there I thought Genna Perrier *Memorial* Library would've been more appropriate!"

"But you 'ave survived."

"Yeah, and did you see the monster that stung me?" I said, chuffed to have my very own Indo-Pacific Box Jellyfish.

Claude peered from a distance. "Pfft, berk! She is ugly!" He cleared his throat. "I must go bowl my ball. *À tout à l'heure.* See you lat-*errrr*!"

Striding from my room, he pulled the front door to behind him.

Hetty's gaze latched on to mine. "How come your birth mother hooked up with *him*?"

"You mean his teeth?" I giggled. "He says his pearly whites are vinyl-coated, but I think he means *ceramic-veneered*, or something."

"Nooo, it's just …" She lowered herself heavily on the chair.

"Are you being a snob, Hetty Geiger?"

"Nooo, but he's, like so …" She crossed and uncrossed her legs.

"So *big*? I know. Claude used to be a mine worker in New Cal, but he's kind and he loves Sandrine, which is all that matters. And he's about as different from my birth father as you could possibly imagine. I think that's probably the attraction, on *her* part anyway, and they're devoted and they've been trying to have kids and Claude told me he's worried Sandrine might want children for the wrong reasons, just to really get up her father's nose, 'cos Jacques Forestier is a very, very racist person."

"However did they meet?"

"At *Papi's* house." The 'grandfather' word seemed to pop out naturally. "I mean Jacques Forestier's place in Nouméa when she was still grieving over my birth father's death. That's what Marcel Manet told me."

"Wasn't Marcel the guy who tracked you down on the information super-highway, in those chat rooms where you gave out your home address like the biggest fruitcake? Like, really." Behind the thick lenses, I saw her eyes roll. "And then he rocked up in Ravella?"

"Yeah, I did a dumb thing. But Marcel's a good mate of Roch Colline, and I would never have met my new guy otherwise."

My mobile burped. On the screen was an envelope icon. *A text from Rocky?*

Hetty levered herself up. "Well, I'm going outside for a cig. You okay for a while?"

"Sure."

I opened the SMS.

Chapter 38

An invitation to join a flash mob in Cairns, protesting against the culling of crocodiles, filled the screen.

"Oh, *merde*!" Had Rocky not received my message? Or was he ignoring me?

Disappointed, I wondered if I should send him an SMS. Or would he think I was coming on too strong? I gnawed on a nail as I considered what to say: *where r u?*—nope, too demanding; *i w8ed on beach but u neva Rived*—definitely too whiny; *how r u?*—a tad boring; *i miss u*—pathetic!

I decided to enquire about Chocolat's health—awkward, as Stefan claimed the dog's injured leg was missing. After more nibbling of fingers, I tapped out:

i hope chockie is bak 2 normal

I sent the text. Aching all over, yet pleasantly sleepy, my eyes began to close. Soon I was dreaming of dogs with three legs, dogs with plaster on all four legs and dogs with no legs at all—which suddenly sprouted tentacles. Smooth-coated and slimy the tentacles slid towards me, slipping and squirming, until I was bound by doggy medusa.

"Hetty!" I screamed. "Help me! I'm being strangled by dog tentacles."

"Help you? Sandrine is involved in something dodgy. What is going on?"

My eyes flew open.

Hetty stood in the doorway, looking puzzled. "Have you ever been in that room tucked away against the side entrance of the Management Apartment, marked Storage?" Behind her geek glasses, her eyes were like het-up goldfish.

"Well, I pushed open the Storage door once. There were bags of linen, and something shiny, like the barrel of an air rifle. And maybe an old bike, plus wooden boxes."

"Aha! Yes! Crates with *rope handles*!"

"Are 'rope handles' a big deal?" I yawned. "Rocky had his Scrabble board set up on one of those things."

"Guns! People carry *guns* in crates with rope handles. AK47s, and such."

Unable to recall if the box in Rocky's bedroom was fitted with rope handles, or leather handles, or anything at all, I knuckled my eyes. "You're imagining it."

"I'm not! I've got brothers!" Hetty yanked one of her plaits in an agitated fashion. "They shoot rabbits, and talk about these things."

"I need to pee."

"There's no need to be rude!" She glared.

"So, whaddya want me to do about the boxes? Confront Claude? Anyway, I do need to use the loo. Can you help me out of bed, please?" I watched her back away. "I don't want you to wipe my behind, or anything!"

"That's a relief!" Grabbing my hands, she pulled me into an upright position.

"Now swing my legs over the edge of the mattress."

Waves of dizziness swept through me when I stood.

"Now help me walk."

My lucky legs resembled Michelin man. I edged along, with Hetty supporting me by the elbow.

"I think I'll take a shower," I called when I'd finished.

"No!" Hetty bellowed from the other side of the door. "You'll wet the bandages. *Do not have a shower* until Sandrine says so!"

"But I haven't showered for three days, and I stink. I'll take the dressings off before I wash."

"DO NOT REMOVE THE BANDAGES." Her voice was hoarse. "Promise me you won't?"

"I'll think about it."

By now, I was curious.

Placing the toilet lid down, I manoeuvred myself into a sitting position, lifted the metal clip securing the dressing and peeled back a corner of the smelly crepe. I kept unwinding until—"Oh no," I whispered. Brown whip-like scars crisscrossed my upper left thigh. "I won't be able to wear bathers ever again!" In a free-for-all of fingers, I unwound the dressing off my right thigh. Same.

As if in a bad dream, I calmly wound the crepe back into place. Reattaching the clip, I hunched over and clasped myself around the waist.

"What's going down in there?" Hetty called out.

"Oh, I'm just"—and I gulped the tears back—"like, enjoying being upright and"—I swallowed a wad of mucous—"um, thinking. I'll be, be, be all right. You shove off. Why don't you go take another walk, suss out those, um, wooden boxes?"

Silence from the other side.

"Or do some book bashing while I, like, sit and sort of …" A gob of phlegm clogged my throat.

Tears trickled down my cheeks. *No wonder Stefan hadn't waited for me to wake*, I told myself. He knew the box jellyfish sting would leave bad scarring. He went straight back to Win. So what if she was socking down perfume, pretending she'd spilled it? Her body was perfect from the outside.

"You sure you're okay?"

"Yeah." Gulp. "Yeah, yeah, I'll come out, like, when I'm ready."

"Cool. I'll help you back into bed when you call me." Her footsteps faded.

A storm of silent tears shook my body. I slumped on the toilet quietly weeping, choking back the sound until I thought my eyes would pop out.

In no time, my lids were like slits, as puffy as my swollen ankles. Plastered to the loo seat, I rocked and rocked until the tears dried up. Night fell outside, and I could see the Garden Apartment lights glowing through the bathroom window. Someone flip-flopped along the walkway outside my apartment, stopped, coughed, and hawked spittle into the Jungle Walk ferns before moving on.

The concrete clang of footsteps on the stairs competed with the whine of the lift. Had the Waveripper reef bus just dropped off the tourists?

Finally I pushed myself up and, gripping the plastic towel rail, propelled myself to the hand basin. In the mirror, I saw tear track stains. I hastily washed the marks off, splashed my face and re-examined my image. The paint smears beneath my eyes had almost gone, but my cheeks were hollow, and my extensions were like rats' tails.

You are now a certified loser, I said to myself. *No guy will ever look at you again.* You're going to end up like Namilly, NO MAN IN SIGHT, with a bad heart and spending your life looking after other people's kids. Caring for strays, like Win and Alice.

Tears began to gather again. I splashed my face once more, and straightened my shoulders. Using the vanity as a prop, I dragged my way to the washing machine, past the overhead dryer to the stainless steel laundry tub. Turning the faux-wood handle of the bathroom door, I swayed. Urging myself on, I made it to my bed and flopped down.

"You okay, Gen?" Hetty called from the living room. "Sorry, I got involved in Paul Verlaine. You remember that poem we had to learn in Year 10 for the Alliance Française exam, *Chanson d'automne*? The last line is so true, that in the end we're carried this way and that by the wind, like a dead leaf."

I felt exactly like a dead leaf, but said, "And you received a *Mention Honorable*?"

"Sure did."

I was about to pull my pillow over my head and weep some more, when I heard her say, "And now I'm in the middle of a Maigret book."

I dropped the pillow. "A M-M-Maigret book?"

"Early this morning, while you were still out to it, a guy with the coolest dreadlocks right down to his shoulders, and with a fierce dark face, knocked on the door and gave me *Maigret et la Grande Perche.* His accent was drawly, as if he came from some Pacific island. You know, one of those former colonies like Vanuatu, or even New Caledonia. So I spoke to him in French, and he said it was for your library. *Presses de la Cité* edition."

Maigret et la Grande Perche had been the title Sandrine first mentioned. "You haven't given the book to Claude yet?"

"Why should I give the book to Claude?" Hetty sounded petulant. "I haven't finished the story. It's strange, though, on the imprint page someone has circled '*2 et 3*' in biro, towards the end of the first sentence which goes '*La loi du onze mars …*'"

"Okay, okay, just give it to Claude," I shouted.

"Don't get your knickers in a twist, Gen. Chill out." Pause. "What sort of nosh would you like for dinner?"

"Get me a Pineapple Bomb from Meggsie at the All Day Breakfast Café. I'll pay you back. Oh, and a granita of any flavour to follow. As icy cold as you can get it."

"Boy, you must be thirsty!" She poked her head around the architrave.

"My mouth is dry as chips."

"You look a bit peaky."

I quickly changed the subject. "There's only one bedroom. Where are you sleeping?"

"The living room sofa pulls out, and the bed's made up."

"Oh, right. I forgot." The breeze from the overhead fan ruffled the sheet over my swollen legs. "Dominick's leftovers must be off by now so, if you want fresh vegies, there's the Fraiche Mini-mart up near the highway. They've got everything, even fishing tackle and beachwear." Wearily, I took a breath. "Claude might drive you, if he's not too busy."

"And everything is fresh?"

"That's what I thought at first. No, the owner is called Eddie Fraiche, and he has a beer gut and burps a lot."

"Sounds gross."

"He means well." A heavy sigh. "Now don't forget to give that book to Claude! He's usually in Reception at this hour, but could be in his shed."

"Sure." Hetty waved the paperback. "I'll be as quick as I can with your liquid meal."

She pulled the front door to. As I blew my nose, I wondered if Claude would be antsy at receiving his Maigret so late. And who was the man with the dreadlocks? Yannick Boudaou, the leader of the independence movement in New Caledonia? If so, why was he in Glisten Beach?

My thoughts began to drift.

Chapter 39

I woke with a start to find my bedside lamp on. A granita—now melted—and a Pineapple Bomb—juice separated into fibre, floating on liquid—sat on my bedside table. I prised the domed lid off the granita, which smelled of mango. Opting for the Pineapple Bomb, I took a long, thirst-quenching sip.

As I swallowed, I detected an alien odour.

"How dare you smoke dope in my apartment, Hetty!" I muttered.

Shoving my hands beneath my knees, I lifted my lucky-legs-turned-stumpy-legs over the side of the bed, wobbled upright and edged into the living room. The lights were out. Hetty's plaits were unleashed; her hair flowed across the pillow like rippled seaweed. She lay on her back, snoring.

The curtain rod, stuffed with items of clothing, caught my gaze. A stray booby trap strap drooped down, encircling the image of a printed fish. Specs and mobile phone and books jostled on the coffee table.

"I can smell grass!" I gave a hefty sniff. "And why are your bloomers and those undies hanging over the window?"

"Wha...wha...wha..." Panting and swallowing hard, Hetty pushed herself up. "It's that thing, makes it impossible to sleep." She pointed to the Amédée Apartments sign glowing through the curtains. "I only just nodded off a moment ago!"

"I *said* ... someone's been smoking a joint."

"What's the time?" She peered myopically at her man-style watch.

I consulted my Swatch. "Two minutes to two."

"Everyone's been asleep for hours, no night-life whatsoever in this place. Is it always as quiet as this?" Lifting her waist-length hair, she dropped it down behind her shoulders.

"Sure is. No parties or booze-ups in these holiday apartments. Everyone's in bed early so they can get up at sparrow's fart to do tours … reef, rainforest, outback, crocodiles, hot air ballooning, you name it."

Hetty reached for her specs.

Shuffling to the shell-shaped light, I flicked the switch and sniffed again. "That sweet smell seems to have disappeared. Where's your ashtray?"

"Over there, on the floor. You can check, but you'll find it empty, not even a chop-chop cig butt." She indicated a delicate branch lying beside the sofa bed. "Your birth mum smokes wicko, though. There's the proof!"

"What proof?"

Adjusting the puffed sleeves of her shortie pyjamas, she picked up the plant and, leaning her elbows on her knees, twirled the stem in her fingers. "Have you ever been in the Jungle Walk?"

I shook my head.

"Well, I found this."

"So you found a bit of a plant in the Jungle Walk. Big deal."

"Yeah, but look closely. It's GRASS! Your birth olds, or whatever you call them, are growing weed in the Jungle Walk!"

I shambled to a nearby chair and clung on. "How d'you know the plant belongs to Sandrine? It could be Mercurio's. He's always hanging about in the garden. And how do you know the stuff's marijuana?"

"Derr, Genna. Don't be a dorkbrain! Believe me, and I've got brothers. I know!"

"I thought you only smoked chop-chop."

"I do only smoke chop-chop, but I know dope when I see it."

"Mmmmn. I seem to remember you swallowing a roach end before your oral exam. You were sucking on swamp then!"

"That's different, I was stressed." Pause. "Anyway, who are you to talk? You owned a porno grammar book."

"*Merde! The French Your Teachers Never Taught You* wasn't porno, just slang."

"Stop changing the subject. I think your birth mum's growing weed. I saw her come out of the Jungle Walk and she pretended not to see me, the reason I went in. I never used this." She waved the frilly, pointy leaf. "I just found it."

"Sandrine wouldn't grow an illegal product! Think of the damage to her livelihood if Amédée Apartments was raided by the police!"

"There's funny stuff going on in this place!"

"Wrong! She'd be deported, sent back to French territory and … oh, heck, I still feel pooped, all I wanna do is flake out. Now I know you, *personally*, are not into the yarndi, at least, not in my apartment, I'm off for more sack time."

I waddled to the wall light, and hit the switch. Simultaneously, the outside sign faded, plunging the room into darkness.

The sofa bed springs squeaked. "What's up? The lights have gone out!"

"Some power problem. It happens every so often." I remembered the Maigret book. "Did you give Claude the paperback?"

"Uh-huh, Claude was in Reception and I did as you requested. Although I don't understand why, as *you're* the so-called librarian, I couldn't have finished reading it."

"He told me to give him any Maigret immediately."

"That's odd."

Was there a connection between the lights going out and the delivery of the paperbacks? I wondered. "Hey, could you check if the balcony lights on the walkways, both Beachfront and Garden, have gone out as well?"

Hetty almost knocked me flying as she blundered past. I continued to cling to the chair as she flicked the switch in the bathroom.

"Light's on in here."

"I *know* the power works in the bathroom! Cut the switch, and have a look out back, at the pedestrian areas."

"You mean, turn the inside light off?"

"Yep."

A click.

"Now tell me what you see through the bathroom window."

"The glass is frosted. I can't make out a thing, only vague shapes."

I sighed. “Slide the frosted panel back, and squiz through the flywire!”

A scraping sound. “Right, I’m at the window, looking out. I can feel the hot night air in my face, hear palm fronds rustle, smell wet tropic mould and gecko poo and, whoops, you’ve got a frog on your outside wall, or maybe a cane toad.”

“What else can you see?”

“What am I *supposed* to see?”

“Those lights along the balconies, the external ones, are they out as well?”

“Nup, they’re still shining! It must be the Amédée Apartments dooverlackey out front that is dodgy.”

Disappointed, I said, “Yeah, maybe the sign’s playing up. Well, I’m off to bed.”

As I plodded into my room, she called, “Wait a sec! The lights have gone out! The whole complex is in darkness!” Silence from the bathroom.

“Yeah, and?”

A hoarse whisper: “I can hear grunting, the padding of footsteps, someone in bare feet, a slinking sound as if something’s being carried. Is that supposed to *mean* anything?”

“Dunno.” My mind scrambled for an answer. “Has Claude replaced the planter baskets?”

“Huh?”

“He had planter baskets at either end of the balconies.”

“Um, I never noticed. No one said anything to me about baskets.”

“Someone stole his planters, so it could be thieves taking more stuff!”

“Well, I don’t have anything to pinch.” She slammed the window shut. “So I better make the most of this darkness, get some zizz while I can.”

Unable to sleep, I massaged my legs below the bandages, afraid to touch the welts, fretting about whether I’d ever wear a bikini again.

Soon, I heard Hetty groan. “Rats, the sign’s back on!”

On my clock radio, the numbers clicked over to 3:00am.

Chapter 40

Next morning, Hetty burst into my room. "The crates are gone from Storage!"

"Perhaps someone stole them?"

"You, Gen, have a thief complex. I still think Sandrine and her partner are gun-running. Is Claude active in the New Caledonia independence movement?"

"He says he sympathises, but basically only cares about doing what Sandrine wants. And, as I don't *hang out* in the Management Apartment, the info I have about Sandrine and Claude is pretty limited."

"Well, those guns are definitely gone."

"But how do you know *guns* were in the boxes?"

Before Hetty could blather about her brothers, I rolled over and pretended to sleep.

The days dragged past. Hetty mopped floors and damp-dusted my apartment. She took messages from people who rang to see how I was: Stefan and Namilly daily; my Ravella friends (apart from Win) at least once.

Roch Colline continued to ignore my texts and telephone calls. "Do you have a photo of him?" Hetty looked thoughtful. "Is he *really* cool?"

"Rocky doesn't like to have his photo taken."

"I'm beginning to wonder if this guy exists!"

I twisted the bangle Rocky had given me.

Hetty marched back and forth between my apartment and the All Day Breakfast Café, purchasing mango granitas, Pineapple Bombs (and sometimes Fruit Tingles) from Meggsie. She concocted carambola salads, diced up pineapple and scooped out avocados. She did whatever I asked her. She filled me in on recent Amédée Apartments' arrivals.

"There's a bunch of suburban Buddhas drinking their beers beside the barbecue."

"Huh?"

"You know, barrel-chested granddads in blue singlets and thongs and shorts."

"Glad I'm lying here in bed, then."

My brainiac friend turned out to be a true pal. She scrounged A4 paper from Sandrine, glue from Claude and knife-like nail scissors from Mrs Hays-Bert. She sat on the floor of my flat repairing spines, smoothing curled pages and wiggling grains of sand from the popular fiction rejects donated by tourists to my miniscule library.

We discussed Sandrine.

"Did you see the bruises on her arms?" I asked. "Reckon Claude hits her?"

"No way, Gen. Claude thinks the sun shines out of Sandrine's derriere. She bumps into things, and that causes the bruises."

"You still reckon she's a pothead?"

"Absolutely! Can't you smell it?"

"I did kinda have my suspicions." I chewed my lip. "You think that's why she bumps into things?"

"Could be." Hetty dabbed glue on a spine-sized slice of A4. "Mind you, it could've been worse, like discovering your birth mum was a prostitute, or a people smuggler, or a murderer." She sighed. "Damn. I've glued the paper down and now it needs cutting. Can you give me those?"

I handed her the scissors.

"Like she could have a brain tumour," she continued, "and it's the reason she collides with stuff."

"You think she's *really* sick?"

"Well, her eyes are sometimes bloodshot. Maybe she's got a problem with her vision, and needs to see a doctor?"

"I think she's done that."

Again, I began to worry about Sandrine's health.

Finally Sandrine removed the bandages, and I was able to take a shower. I was all cried out about the welts, resigned to being scarred forever.

Gradually, my legs went back to their normal size.

Hetty and I took long walks on Glisten Beach. We trudged all the way to Urupu Point, past the mangroves and inlets where crocodiles lurked. We went to Coral Cove in the opposite direction, where we checked out the glitzy tourist resorts and watched girls in bikinis ride past on Vespa scooters. We flicked marked-down sarongs on racks in beachwear shops, searching for bargains. And I showed Hetty the Mimosa Sands Resort, the sprawling white building where Pascal Manet was staying.

We peeked into the foyer. Large screenlike pieces of cloth moved the air about in a backwards and forwards motion.

"What are those?" I whispered.

"Punkahs. In India the fans used to be operated by people, punkah wallahs. I've read about it."

"Looks groovy, kinda classy."

"Mmn." Her eyes grew dreamy. "*I* wouldn't mind being paid to keep the French examiner cool."

"You are so crass, Hetty Geiger!"

"He's the man!"

"Don't talk about Dad like that!"

"You call Monsieur Manet … Dad?" Her eyes grew round.

"Yeah. In New Cal when I was in deep, I needed *somebody* to call Dad."

"He doesn't look old enough to be your dad."

"Well, no … but." I decided it was best to change the subject. "Let's go around the back and see where the Tasmanian was taken by a crocodile."

We hoped to spot nostrils poking from the muddy water, but saw nothing. Bored, we crossed the road to the Coral Cove beer garden.

I had never confided with Hetty about the marks on my thighs, but I knew she knew when she said, "You could always wear a skirted tankini, like I do."

"A skirted tankini? How revolting!"

She looked hurt, and remained silent for at least eleven minutes before saying, "You could always turn your scars into tattoos!"

We fell about laughing.

I was reminded of Douce with her bottle of ink and safety pin. "A garland of leaves at the top of my legs could look cool," I said.

Sandrine gave me moisturiser, and told me to keep out of the sun.

When no one was around, I swam along the black lines of the pool. I did laps early in the morning, after the Waveripper reef bus had left. I completed more laps later in the evening, when everyone was tucked up in bed.

No more Maigret books were left on my doorstep, none given to Hetty to be passed on to Claude. And the Amédée Apartments sign never faded again while Hetty slept on the sofa bed.

"OMG, that thing's still shining," she complained every night.

Battered tomes, now mended, found their way back to the cupboard housing Claude's and my library. Their spines were solid and free of sand.

Hetty decided it was time to go back south.

Before she left, she christened the Chironex fleckeri. "I pronounce you Rex, Prince of the Kingdom of Marine Life Monsters!" She tapped the lid with a carving knife.

After she'd packed her bloomers and booby traps, walk shorts and T-shirts, tankinis and poetry by Baudelaire, I gave her a bamboo biro and a piece of staghorn coral as a parting pressie.

Adjusting her nerd glasses on her newly peeling nose, she said, "I can't wait to discuss the impact of physical trauma on the subconscious, with relation to the limbic system, in Psych 1001:03, particularly from a Chironex fleckeri perspective." She patted the stinger jar. "See ya, Rex!"

Wearing a frangipani behind her ear, Sandrine called goodbye from Reception. "*Au revoir*," she said. "*Et merci!*"

Claude settled my friend on the shuttle bus.

"Yo, Hetty! Check you later!" I waved until my arm ached, and Wesley turned the corner.

A tsunami of homesickness threatened to engulf me. Once more, I made up my mind to quit my job, farewell Sandrine and return to Ravella.

But first, I needed to confront Rocky.

Chapter 41

Next day, I was tired and achy but determined to go to the jungle village of Kooracoondoo.

After showering, I carefully arranged my hair—now a smidgeon longer. Spiking my Tawdry Tan tips with gel, I draped my extensions over my shoulders. It was too hot for jeans or camo pants, and I feared people might notice the whip marks on my legs. Would the dusky-pink pareo I'd purchased in Anse Vata be too dressy? I asked myself.

Wrapping the gossamer fabric around me, I brought the ties forward and crossed them in a halter around my neck. Clutching the beaded edging, I retrieved the matching kitten-heel sandals and slipped them on.

Switching the ceiling fan to low, I grabbed my tote. Another Maigret lay on my doorstep. The book was titled: *Un Noël de Maigret.*

I flicked through the pages to see if any numbers or words had been marked, as in *Maigret et la Grande Perche.* I discovered two tiny dots between two digits. On Page 148, if you peered, you could—maybe—make out 1:48. Was that a clue? *Was the Amédée Apartments sign due to be turned off at1:48am?*

Smoothing down the pages, I made for Claude's shed and handed him the paperback.

"You are most beautiful today." He placed the Maigret face down on the workbench. "You are celebrating your recovery from a ve-*rrrry* nasty jellyfeeeesh attack?" Half-moons of sweat showed beneath his armpits.

"Well, after I pick up a T-shirt I ordered from Lavender Bale's, I'm going up the mountain."

"For bungy jump?" His eyes widened.

"Ooh, not today, too pooped. But I'm, kinda, getting there."

"Dominick wishes the time when you will be healthy enough to do his work."

"I'll let him know."

"*Bon courage!*" Claude continued to plane a warped apartment door.

A scream as I climbed off the Cassowary Rise bus. Malachi's bungy jumper was having a great time.

Clutching my tote—bulky with Rocky's hand-painted T-shirt—I dodged past tourists and set off for his house. My calves kept cramping from the unaccustomed walking as I made my way past half-price shark jaws, and carousels of hairclips spinning in the wind. Crowds jostled at fast food outlets. A couple sat on faux bamboo chairs at a faux bamboo table, eating Devonshire tea off a shell-enhanced tray.

Hanging on to the beaded edges to prevent my pareo from blowing open, I hurried along the footpath. As I neared 8 Sugarcane Lane, I saw Jeanne attempting to unload a box from the bull-barred utility.

I hid behind a melaleuca.

The wire door squeaked open. Rocky, hair wild, strode towards his mother.

"*Donne-la-moi!*" His biceps bulged as he hefted the crate.

"I'll miss you helping me, son," she said in English, following him inside. "Do you really have to go?"

Overcome with dizziness, I clung to the melaleuca. *Was Rocky leaving Australia?* Or just Kooracoondoo?

A tree python slithered along a branch above my head. I didn't move or cry out, just stood there like a dill. Should I catch the bus back to Glisten Beach? I wondered. Or confront him?

Silence.

Crack. A twig broke off a gum tree.

Voices in the gloomy passage.

"At least you don't have to worry about the dog," I heard him say. "That's one less burden."

"Don't desert Douce, please! Your sister needs you, Roch."

"*Non, c'est pas vrai!* Douce needs her *maman*, not a brother she never knew existed, still doesn't know exists. I feel sad about it, but *c'est la vie*."

"I'll tell her who you are, then?"

"And risk her following me to *Nouvelle-Calédonie*? Douce doesn't speak French, and it's a difficult life growing kava."

"It's the movement, isn't it? You think Yannick Boudaou and his foolish *indépendantistes* can rule the country without French subsidies, European money?"

"We have nickel to provide us with all the money we need! The new Kanak state will be a rich one."

"Bah. Overseas investors will desert in droves. They'll go elsewhere, invest in a stable, nickel-rich country like Canada, or Australia. Stay here, Roch! It's a huge island, a continent. There's a future if you care to look."

"I'm sorry, I cannot."

"Please, please don't go!"

"I promise I'll be back, ah, sometime."

"If you're not killed." Jeanne sounded bitter.

A scuffling sound.

"Let me pass, *s'il te plaît*!"

"It's the girl, isn't it? Sandrine's daughter is the reason you're leaving. I can see the hurt." A pause. "Douce told me."

"Douce knows little, and understands even less. *Laisse-moi partir!*"

Carrying a worn canvas bag, Rocky appeared in the doorway. He picked his mother's fingers off his arm.

I stood by the front gate, feeling like a floozy in my pareo.

Rocky's eyes had a glaze about them. "What are you doing here, Genna? I thought you'd changed your mind about me, like your constantly altering hairstyles."

"That's so not true!"

Silence.

"Um, I bought you a gift. You said you'd meet me on Glisten Beach?"

"I came, but you were busy with a gentleman friend … your current *copain*?" He edged his way through the gate.

"A *gentleman friend*?" I lifted an extension from my sweaty shoulders. "Boy, that's a good one. Stefan is my mate!"

"My poor little flea, people who fall out of love do not kiss on a public beach!" His sculpted lips narrowed.

"Are you really so dumb?"

"Dumb?" His mouth became a fist. "*Oui*, I was dumb, a stupid *con* who fell for you. But, of course, you are a Caldoche, too good for me, a Caldoche *garce*." He scraped the toe of his T-Boot in the dust.

"*Garce*? How dare you! I'm not like that! And you're no angel! You pinched Claude's planter baskets!"

He stepped towards me. "I WHAT?" He lifted his hand, as though to strike, before saying, "I do not hate you. I cannot hate you."

"You nicked …" I faltered.

He lowered his hand. "You will not provoke me."

Our eyes locked, and I knew—"You've drunk kava, haven't you?"

Rocky shrugged. He repeated the words like some mantra: "I do not hate you. I cannot hate you." He added: "I simply feel sorry for you."

I recalled him telling me that it was impossible to hate after drinking kava. "Where did you get the kava, not here in Queensland?"

"A Koori … Joey, Jacky or some such name … lives in a cottage by the Barrabull River. He made me a drink, of the powder, not fresh roots." Rocky gave a short laugh "He strained the liquid through a household rag, a Chux he called it, rather than the traditional palm fibre cloth. He offered me kava flavoured to taste like chocolate mint fudge. I told him I preferred it natural." He gave me a soft smile. "So, you see, my mood is unaffected."

"Rubbish! You'll be scratching next!" My face flushed with anger. "And where's Chocolat? Did you give him the ham bone?"

"Unfortunately, on the day you came I was at the vet having the dog's leg amputated."

"Amputated!" I gasped. "You could've answered my texts, told me?"

"I was distracted."

"What happens to the dog now? You swore you'd never leave Chocolat."

"He is dead."

"Chocolat is *dead*?"

"Put down this morning."

"Oh." The ground began to tilt. "I would've looked after him."

Rocky shook his head. "No one wants a three-legged dog."

"But *I* would've cared for him!"

Tourists hurried past speaking Italian, saying, "Bungy, *pericoloso*", before disappearing down the steps to the railway station.

"Stefan wasn't kissing me. He was giving me," I said, desperate to explain, "the kiss of life, after I was stung by a box jellyfish. I stopped breathing …"

"… and he *happened* to be there?"

I opened my mouth to protest.

A train pulled into the station. Japanese tourists scurried along the road.

"I do not believe you. I know the difference between the kiss of life and lust, but I forgive you." He turned to leave. "*Pardon*, I have a train to catch." His hoodie flapped as he threw his bag over his shoulder, and strode away.

"I've got the scars to prove it," I yelled, parting the folds of my pareo.

Jeanne inhaled sharply. "My son was right to call you a *garce*!" she hissed. "You're a bitch with no conscience, a slut, no different from your mother! I know what they used to say about Sandrine Forestier before she married that man with the bourgeois name. And when she became a widow, I used to hear them whisper."

"It's not m-my-my fault Rocky's leaving." I choked back the tears.

"Jacques Forestier will be pleased you're no longer sleeping with my son."

"Sleeping? Wow! I've never had relations with your son! And Jacques doesn't even *know* I know Rocky."

Jeanne ran her fingers through her hair. "That man knows everything! He pays good money for information!"

A rattle of rusty wheels. Douce flew up the road on her battered bike, crystals flying from her neck, wrists and earlobes. Her muffin top bulged.

"Where's the supplier off to, Mama? I saw him go down to the station." She jammed her foot on the pedal. "Jeez, these Chicko beads weigh somethin' terrible!"

"The supplier has to leave."

"He's gone for ever and ever, hasn't he?"

She threw down her bike. Legs at odd angles, Douce fled across the road and down the steps to the station. Carriages flowed past planter baskets stuffed with fish ferns and, for the first time, she pronounced his name correctly.

"Rocchhhh! *Rocchhh*! ROCCCHHHHKKkkkk!" Her voice made a long squawk.

The straps of my sandals pierced into my skin; my legs felt like lead.

Douce came hurtling back. She picked up her bicycle, swung her leg over the bar and, peddling hard, vanished down beside the railway line.

"Where's Douce off to?" I wondered aloud.

"If my daughter peddles fast, and it's downhill along the boardwalk over the rainforest, she might reach Barrabull Falls Station to see Roch when the driver pulls up for the tourists to take a final holiday snap. The Barrabull Falls bifurcate." Extracting a hanky from the pocket of her jeans, Jeanne clamped it on her nose. "I doubt she'll make it." She stuffed the hanky back in her pocket. "Not the way she is."

Energy spurted into my stumpy-legs-turned-back-to-lucky-legs. I flew across the road, careered past the railway line and onto the board-walk. The tops of tropical trees flashed beneath my feet. Bits of bottle-brush peeped through the gaps in the planks as I ran.

I belted past feathery casuarinas down the suspended slope. Beads and drops of crystal left behind by Douce rolled on the timber and settled in the cracks like bright petals of broken bougainvillea. A rainbow cloud of parrots rose into the sky. I dodged past people strolling along taking in the view, overtook a power-walker in Lycra, and was just able to make out Douce flying along in the distance. The wheels of her bicycle clanked and squeaked as she sped towards the Barrabull Falls railway station.

The locomotive curled around the bend like a monstrous centipede. A long wheeze, a squeal, and the engine hissed to a standstill. Camera-waving tourists tumbled out, heading for the mesh fence. People took photos of one another in a snapping frenzy, before giving a brief geek at the stream tumbling from the escarpment.

Out of breath, I slowed. Douce hurled her bike to the ground and galloped along the platform, peering in every carriage and bailing up passengers.

I lost sight of her as I resumed my descent.

As I rounded the corner, I saw her again. Wrapped in her brother's arms, Douce's chestnut hair blended with his burnished locks.

I knew I should go no further. I remained high above the station until the tourists climbed aboard, and the horn made a mournful sound. The guard swung on, and the train slid away slowly.

Douce flung her arms about like a crazy person. “ROCCCHHH.”

Standing on the tender, Rocky waved to his sister.

Her voice wafted upwards. “KKKKkkkkkkk …” The sound echoed off the mountaintops. “KKkkkkkkkkkkkkkkkkk …”

Chapter 42

Removing my ratty sandals, ruined on the boardwalk, I sank to the cool of my apartment floor. Drawing my knees to my chin, I considered my options. With Rocky gone, should I return to Ravella? Or should I remain in Glisten Beach for a while, maybe go up the mountain from time to time, and keep an eye on Douce?

Reception was closed for the evening, and with no Hetty to talk to, I was hanging out for a natter. I connected my computer to the phone and went online. Few people were in the chat room. I logged off, rang Dominick and told him I'd be back at work the following afternoon.

"Thank heavens for that!" he said. "I've been running around like the proverbial headless chook. So you're better, eh?"

"Yep."

"Goodonya! There are people who don't live to tell the tale after what you've been through."

I hung up, gave the stinger jar a not-so-friendly tap. "'Night, Rex! See ya in the morning!" Tentacles dangled from the cuboid shape, swayed and swung in the soupy formalin.

After showering, I patted my body dry and examined my welts, resisting the urge to scratch. Did this itchiness mean my scars would perhaps disappear? Pulling the T-shirt I'd purchased for Rocky from my tote bag, I folded it neatly and placed it atop the ASSASSIN muscle tee. I climbed into bed in knickers and a singlet.

Beneath the click of the ceiling fan, I thought of the things Rocky had said. Was I really so lacking in commitment? So selfish he should feel sorry for me? Was that the real reason for his going back home? Or was the ongoing independence movement calling him back? Would the people who'd caused him to flee in the first place—the kava dudes who'd removed his father's fingernail—kill him as soon as he stepped off the plane at Tontouta?

As I lay there the grainy feeling took over, the feeling of breaking up, and tumbling and swirling into a black hole …

My eyes sprang open. On my bedside clock, the numbers clicked over to 1:45. I remembered the tiny dots on Page 148 of the Maigret book that I'd passed on to Claude.

I hauled on a pair of cut-offs and scampered into the living room. Drawing back the curtains, I saw a pale shape in the distance, like an ocean-going yacht? I was able to make out a smaller vessel being lowered over the side and into the water.

The Amédée Apartments sign began to flicker and fade. Soon I could no longer see the palms on the other side of Arlington Esplanade. Then I wondered: *dare I go outside among the mangroves?* Discover first-hand what—if anything—was going on?

Clicking open the door leading onto the patio, I slid back the glass and tiptoed through the fern garden. I crossed the road and crept past the coconut palms, until I came to a pandanus whose roots were clumpy enough to hide behind.

To the rear of me, the Beachfront Apartments and Garden Apartments were now bathed in darkness. A cloud blotted out the moon, and I hugged my knees to my chest.

A plop and a grunt. I could hear something being pulled through the water—the swish of oars. A whistle. Whispers in French.

"*Nous sommes là! Par ici! Vite! Vite! Vite!*"

Shifting, flicking sand, a pounding as footsteps headed for the water.

"*Salut, mon pote!*"

The words were followed by the sound of two people kissing. Mwaaah. Splack! Mwaaah. Splack! Two Frenchmen?

The cloud shifted from the moon. I saw a guy with his head shaved, and wearing dark-coloured yachting gear and boat shoes, help his beanie-clad friend into a rubber ducky. The yacht continued to bob in the distance. Squinting hard, I saw the name on the side: Marguerite. Marcel's yacht was called the Marguerite.

It dawned on me: Marcel Manet was here, in Glisten Beach, picking up Rocky.

Crouching, I watched until the clouds covered the moon again. I heard laughter across the water. The breeze began to blow. The palm trees rustled. Spits of rain dropped on my face and hair. Wet sand spurted on my toes, and I scrambled up.

It was time to get out of here.

As I scurried across the road to the Amédée Apartments, the sign surged back on, flooding the street with its glow. The rain stopped, and the lights along the walkways of the complex lit up. The building resembled a great, white fortress guarding the foreshore.

Beneath the sign, inside the Management Apartment, I saw the curtains twitch.

Chapter 43

Life was almost back to normal. The Waveripper reef bus woke me in time for an early morning dip in the pool.

Still concerned about people seeing my thighs, I dragged on thrash wash jeans after drying off. Donning a white Indigo singlet, I went for a walk along Glisten Beach to get me in the mood for serving coffees to university students and rubbernecking tourists.

I'd gone one hundred metres when I came across looping letters scratched in the sand. Approximately two feet high by eight feet long, the message was swollen from last night's rain. I struggled to decipher its meaning. *Je*, I told myself, sounded French. Or was the J a T? No, the stroke curved at the bottom. Then I made out an A, followed by ME. Next, I saw an 'I' tucked between the letters A and M.

Back and forth I went. Was that a 'T' inserted between JE and AIME? Yes, I decided, definitely a T. Wow, someone had written JE T'AIME in large letters!

Up and down and around the words I went. Had they been inscribed by Rocky, as he waited for Marcel to take him to his yacht? Had he meant for me to find the message, telling me he loved me? Surely not. After all those terrible things we'd said to each other?

I searched in vain for a G, anything to tell me Rocky had dug out the words with a piece of driftwood, just for me. Not able to discover anything resembling a G, I stood there until the waves lapped over, and wiped out the inscription. As the water sucked back, I saw a row of tiny shells embedded in the wet sand, curved in the shape of … a G.

A smile snuck over my face as I crossed the road to have a shower before breakfast.

Sandrine called out from Reception, "We need to talk. I have something to tell you."

"Is it important?"

"Later will do."

Making for my flat, I saw Claude chatting to a guy astride a gleaming Harley-Davidson.

"Great gear," I murmured, taking in the leathers, the biker boots and the shiny black helmet. I ogled the long legs encased in the reinforced jeans, the elegance of the form-fitting jacket. "Wicked cool!" I said under my breath. "Hot!"

"*À tout à l'heure.*" Claude farewelled the motorcyclist and headed for the pool area, where Mercurio leaned on his skimmer.

The bikie—a Frenchman?—lowered his visor. Turning the vehicle, he unexpectedly flipped the visor back up.

"*Bonjour, Genna!*"

"Oh, it's only you," I said to Pascal Manet.

"Thank you very much!" His cheeks creased with amusement.

"I didn't know you owned a Harley." My gaze took in the blizzard of zips on his attire.

"She is new." He ran a gloved hand over the engine.

"I can see that." I moved up close. "You told me you were an apnoea diver before your, um, accident but, like, you seem too sorta stitched up to be a bikie."

"*Au contraire*. I 'ave competed in many motocross events in *Calédonie*."

"Bodacious!" I said. "Excellent. I never realised you could be, um, like, *cool*."

"Claude tells me you 'ave been very sick. Would you care to have a ride with me on my *moto*?"

"Um, I'm not sure. I've never been on a bike." And then, hoping he'd say no, I said, "I don't suppose you have a spare helmet?"

"Of course!" Pascal turned to lift the flap of the pannier, undid a drawstring bag and pulled out an open-face model covered with orange flames.

Furrowing my brow, I took the helmet. "I don't know what to do."

"You will need these," he said, giving me a pair of goggles, "to keep the bugs from your eyes. Hold on very tightly to me and do what I do."

"Okay, well, I s'pose I'll go with you."

Goggles in place, I attached the strap of the helmet, and—grateful I'd worn jeans—reached my leg across and eased my butt down behind him.

"You are ready?"

"Sure. Could you take these?"

Zipping my keys and mobile in his pocket, he dropped his visor down.

"Where are we going?" My arms encircled his waist. "Around the block?"

His reply was muffled.

"Not too far, I hope."

The rev of the engine whipped away my words. A throaty throb started up between my legs. Vroom, doom, *vroom, doom*, VROOM, DOOM. Inhaling the smell of leather, Kenzo aftershave and Gauloises cigarettes, I clung on.

A bug-eyed Mrs Hays-Bert watched us edge into the street.

Off like a rocket—VROOM, VROOM, VROOM—we burned around the first corner, swerving past cars. Slowing down to turn left onto the highway, the bike went rumble, rumble, rumble, shake, shake, shake.

We were off like a rocket again. With my arms clamped around Pascal's waist, I'd never been so terrified, so fazed I didn't even find it odd to be gripping onto him. Rocky's beads dug hard into my wrist, and I barely noticed. All I cared about was not becoming road kill.

As we edged past a low loader, I buried my scaredy-cat face in Pascal's back. The sound pounded up my spine and out my ears. VROOM, VROOM, VROOM, *doom*, doom, DOOOOOOMMMM.

Burning rubber, we roared past walls of sugarcane.

The road widened. Through slitted lids, I saw traffic lights ahead.

The lights were green. We chucked a right onto the winding mountain road leading up to Kooracoondoo. The exhaust growled, and the bike swayed around a bend. Leaning into the curve, I did my best not to pull away as I found myself eyeballing the bitumen. My nose was so close I could smell the tar and see myriad tread marks of trucks and buses and motorbikes, and the discarded burst tyre of a pushbike. *A mangled sock?* Had somebody's foot been cut off in an accident? I suppressed the urge to scream.

Passing curtain fig trees, banana plants, tropical vines and ragged bougainvillea bushes, we wound our way up the mountainside. A large goanna lay on the roadside, sunbaking. After a while, I began to relax, to sit up and enjoy the smell of the bush, inhale the rainforest aroma. I could hear the parrots squawk as they lifted above the treetops. I admired the flame trees, marvelled at the lushness of the undergrowth.

We came to some road works. A guy held up a stop sign.

One foot planted on the road, Pascal twisted in his seat. "*Ça va?*" he shouted.

"Fazzo! I am *so* having a great time!" And I meant it.

His face grooved into a grin.

The workman turned the sign to 'Slow', waved his hand and we were off again.

Twenty minutes later, we pulled up outside the Kooracoondoo Markets.

"I 'ave a package to deliver." Pascal parked his Harley-Davidson, cut the engine and said, "Are you wishing to come with me, or you prefer …"

"Absolutely I'm coming."

Tingling from the ride, I drew my leg over the seat of the motorbike. Recalling the conversation in which Jeanne had asked Pascal to bring her kava leaves, I asked myself: *Were kava leaves in the package?* And why? What was the big secret?

"I can check out the stalls, catch up with Iris Veivers and maybe Rocky's sister, if she's not wandering around the countryside, eating chocolate and hanging with just about anyone, while you do what you have to."

Ruffling my hair loose, I handed him the helmet.

A scream rang out.

Pascal started. "What is that?"

He lifted off his head protection to reveal a red paisley scarf. I stared at the jaunty material. This dude was revealing a side to himself that I had never suspected.

"It's only a bungy jumper," I murmured.

"And is it so scary to do this?"

"Sort of, but not really. Malachi's cool. I had a fabbo time when *I* jumped."

Pulling the scarf off his head, Pascal tossed the drenched fabric in with the helmets. "To protect sweat from coming in my eyes." He placed his gloves with the gear.

"Brill colours," I said.

He buckled and locked the pannier. "*On y va?*"

Nodding, I followed.

Chapter 44

The Kooracoondoo Markets seethed with people. A babble of bartering burst in my face as I followed Pascal past a stall I'd never seen before. At the 'Noodle Nest', a guy was busy serving stir fries, rice and succulent satays. Above, a sign read: *Barney's my name, satay's my game.* Sweat streamed down the vendor's face.

Striding along in his biker boots, past aboriginal art and wooden dinosaurs, Pascal headed straight for 'Joanie's Clothing Corner', not looking back to see if I was following.

At 'Discount Opals', I halted and lingered, hoping to overhear his conversation with Jeanne. A smile flooded her face as the French teacher approached. He gave her two *bises* and, reaching inside his jacket, pulled out the parcel.

I sidled past the opal stall. "Can I help you, love?" The trader smelled of jasmine oil.

"Just looking." I strained to hear what Pascal was saying.

"*C'est pas trop tard?*" he said in a low voice.

"No, it's not too late. Douce is ten weeks gone," Jeanne replied in French. "Shouldn't the leaves still work?"

Pascal's shrug was tense.

"K-Mel's growing kava again? You got the product from my husband?"

Pascal nodded yes.

"I hope you didn't tell him why you needed the leaves?"

He shook his head.

Glaring, the opal seller pushed back her hair. "Sure you wouldn't like to try on a ring, eh?"

"Oh, well, yeah, okay." I pointed towards vibrant blues, greens and reds. As I slid the band on my right ring finger, a lightning strike of yellow blazed like a warning.

"No problem bringing the leaves into Australia?" Jeanne continued in French. "Customs didn't question you?"

Pascal shook his head again, before saying: "The father?"

"Malachi," she answered. "The man who operates the bungy jumping and who has seven children … I lose track, or is it eight? … and some older than Douce. You know, I'm grateful." Jeanne's voice rose, as though she assumed no one would understand her. "All I have to do now is persuade her to put the piper methysticum in the place where babies come out, and it'll be over. She'll be disappointed, but I won't be here forever."

Was it her Australian accent? I understood Jeanne's French perfectly.

Pascal reverted to English. "I 'ave never met your daughter, not as an adult."

Jeanne leaned forward. Stretching up, she whispered in his ear.

"*Non!*" He frowned, lifted his hands, and held out his palms defensively. "*Non!*"

"Didn't you ever guess?"

"*Jamais*," he said. And then in English: "*Nev*-errr! Nev-*err*! It is not possible!"

'Aussie Cold Comfort Neckties' Horrie stopped serving a customer and stared.

"Go to Douce, talk to her. She's as beautiful as her photos. She's over there at her stall." Eyes scanning the market, Jeanne said, "I can't see her, but I know she's around somewhere."

"I will buy something from *your* daughter." Pascal gave her a *bise* on each cheek.

My face was flushed from having eavesdropped. I turned to the opals. The entire stall seemed to be flashing a kaleidoscope of colours, as if I had a migraine. Blue, green, red, yellow, blue, green, yellow, red—my brain drummed.

A voice murmured in my ear. "Can I buy it for you?"

I jumped back. "No! No! *No way*. Opals are bad luck, Pascal! I shouldn't have touched the ring, let alone tried it on! I hope nothing horrible happens. They're so awesome that it's hard to believe they are cursed."

His smile was distracted. "It is very hot in the markets. Do you have thirst, as I do?"

"Yes, I'm *really* thirsty!" I struggled to sound as normal as possible.

"I will find you something to drink."

"I know what." I returned the band to the stallholder, now antsy. "You can buy me a granita! Do you like granitas?"

"Are they very cold? Where do we buy one of these confections?"

"Curly's!" I was flustered and jittery, but not surprised to discover Douce was pregnant. "F-follow me. We'll buy two icy cold granitas from Curly. You want lemon or mango?"

He did not reply. His face was blank of emotion.

I tried to think of something to talk about, something chatty, not too serious but not goofy. I said, "Does your brother still work for Jacques Forestier?"

Pascal looked pensive.

"My grandfather, does Marcel still …?"

"Why do you ask?"

"Oh, no reason."

We threaded our way past 'Poppy and Pete's Planter Baskets'.

"Marcel is now independence activist and no longer works for your *papi*. And, now I am here in *Australie*, I no longer work for 'im either. So with his house still in a state of disrepair from our cyclone, Jacques is confined to Bouchon. You remember Bouchon?"

"Sure I remember his deer farm! After being forced to watch the dogs tear a stag apart, I had nightmares for weeks!"

Creases formed in Pascal's forehead. He abruptly changed the subject. "Is Douce as beautiful as everyone tells me?"

"Beautiful? She has stunning skin, and covers herself in stacks of beads. So I'd say beautiful, but not pretty. She has unusual taffeta eyes."

"Taffeta eyes?"

"Grey, shot with blue. But she talks in a slaggy way, skanky, as if she's the town bike, although I don't think she is. With all those stuffed toys in her room, she seems too innocent." Pause. "Sometimes she's vague and off the planet, and you wonder if she's a shingle short." We came to Curly's and I said, "But I don't think you'd like her. She's ditsy, can't read or write and she used to wag school."

"I am sure I would like 'er."

"Well, you'll be able to find out. 'Douce's Trinkets' is up the incline, right next to 'Iris Veivers: Pearls for Girls'." I pointed at the list of flavours. "Which do you prefer, lemon or mango?"

"Citrus Grandis." Pascal indicated the sign.

"Two granitas, please," I said. "One grapefruit, one mango."

The butterfly in his left ear winked as Curly took the money from Pascal.

Grasping our granitas, we set off. Slurping and crunching, we climbed the slope, making for Douce's stall. Scooping grains of granita through the domed lid, I used the spoon-billed straw and sucked on the coldness.

Douce was not serving her customers. Instead of being refreshed by the gravelly iced drink, my stomach began to churn for no good reason. The adjacent stall, 'Iris Veivers: Pearls for Girls', was also empty.

I broke into a half-jog, expecting to see Iris chatting with a trader in a nearby aisle.

No sign of Iris.

I rushed past jangling wind chimes and wooden puzzles shaped like a map of Australia, eye diagnosis and mozzie coils. Magnetic wrist bands. Antimacassars and lace baby bibs. Hair wraps. Still no sign of Iris.

A foreboding swept through me as I traipsed back to 'Douce's Trinkets'.

Reflective, Pascal nursed his granita. From a basket brimming with bracelets on memory wire, he picked one up, examined it, placed the bracelet back, and picked up another.

I halted.

He ceased browsing. "There is something wrong?"

"I've got a funny feeling. Douce wanders off all the time, and Iris watches her things. She knows Douce is scatty and looks out for her, but I can't see Iris either."

The words were barely out of my mouth when Iris appeared. Tucking her hair behind her ears in a frenzied fashion, she flip-flopped along, knocking her pearl display as she went behind her stall.

"Can I help you?" she said, and then paused. "Oh, hi, it's you, Jennifer! How ya going, eh?"

"My name is Genna!" I pointed at Pascal—now examining a necklace made of glittering Chicko beads, onyx and green garnet. "This is a friend from New Caledonia, come to Queensland to give lectures." I licked the end of my straw. "You look kinda bothered."

"Bothered? I'm packing death!"

"What's wrong?"

"Douce has decided to jump!"

"Nooooo."

Iris leaned forward. "She's been feeling a bit under the weather lately and Malachi told her to go see a bloke called Joey in a shack down along the Barrabull River, said Joey'd give her a drink to make her feel better. Then Douce'd feel calm enough to have a bungy."

"But Douce said she'd never jump, no way! Did she drink kava?"

"Dunno. She told me Joey gave her a chocolate mint fudge milkshake this morning. Although why she had to go all the way to some dump on the Barrabull for a milkshake, I dunno. She's been strange ever since, calm. Douce can be difficult, but she was polite to customers, holding up her beads, gazing and smiling." Iris's voice dropped to a whisper. "And *then*, fifteen minutes ago, she says, 'I gotta go see …'"

"See who?"

"'Malachi, I'm gonna have a bungy.' And she's got this dreamy look on 'er face."

"Rocky was offered a chocolate mint fudge milkshake by the same man!"

"You mean the supplier that Joanie … Jeanne, as some prefer to call her … took in because she felt sorry for him?"

I was about to scream that Rocky was Jeanne's son, and Douce's brother, but gulped back the words. With a sinking feeling, I said, "He told me that, in fact, he drank powdered kava, and it made no difference. But I don't believe him. I bet that's what Douce drank, and I'm petrified at what she might do from having chug-a-lugged *kava*."

"What's kava, eh, a drug?"

"Sort of, but legal and it makes your tongue go numb and you don't, like, worry about a thing anymore. It tastes *disgusting* but gives you this awesome feeling. Joey's disguised the muddy taste with chocolate! Douce'll be so calm and clear-headed she'll be capable of anything!"

Iris's eyes were like dinner plates.

"After what everyone says about the bungy man, I've got these bad vibes!" Despite the heat, the granita was freezing my fingers.

"Well, it's too late now. She's climbing the tower this minute!"

"But she mustn't jump, not in her condition!"

"Condition?" Iris looked rattled. "You don't mean? Nah, Douce is just chocoholic, pudgy around the middle. She says she's done it with Malachi, but I don't believe her. Why would she? A man his age, and a wife, Siobhan, and all those kids, and creepy with it!"

Pascal looked up briefly. Did he think this was just girl talk? He began fiddling with the memory wire again, unwinding a bracelet, letting it curl over his hand. He moved the beads down his wrist, as if thinking.

"Look, I'm off," I said. "I'm gonna try to stop Douce before she's all strapped up, and something shocking happens."

Pushing aside a sunburnt dude in lolly-striped trousers, I dodged didgeridoos, bird feeders and twirling mobiles. Dashing up the path, I headed for the tower.

Chapter 45

The chick with the hennaed hair and pierced nose wasn't in the ticket office. A woman with long, grey-flecked tresses sat there. A row of silver hoops sprouted from each eyebrow. Her lips were deep red, almost black

Was this Siobhan?

Before I could speak, she said, "Bungy jumpin's closed for the rest of t'day. No more jumpin' 'til tomorrer. My husband is a very safety conscious man, and the harness needs its usual checkin'."

"I'm not here to do a bungy. I've come to stop my friend from jumping!"

A group of guys guarded the tower steps near the boardwalk. Quanah, in his Blundstones and baseball cap, stood beside the raven-haired Seamus. The young man in shorts and Reeboks who'd laughed at my unfounded fear was also there, this time unsmiling.

All stared silently.

Peering through the scaffolding, I saw Douce mount. Dressed in a white peasant blouse and frilly trousers, she slowly placed one foot after the other, as though in a dream.

I cupped my hands together, and screeched, "Douce! Come back down!"

Carrying what looked like her bead board, she kept going.

"Come down this minute, Douce!"

She took no notice.

"You have to stop her!" I yelled at Malachi's sons.

"Don't spoil 'er day. Me dad's givin' her the jump for free," said Seamus.

"But it's dangerous in her, um." I paused. "It's just like dangerous."

"She's quite safe," said the guy in Reeboks. "I've done it …"

"Yeah, I know, a trillion times! You already told me." I tried to push past.

Quanah shoved me hard; I almost lost my balance. "You're not goin' anywhere, slag!"

"Lads!" I turned to see Siobhan shake her head. "That's enough rough stuff." Her brows made one long shiny caterpillar, as she eyed me with her gaze. "Do I have to be explainin' again? My husband takes his safety very seriously. We can't be lettin' every Tom, Dick and Jane climb the tower when a jump is in progress. Do you get me drift?"

I gave one last try. "Please stop her," I pleaded.

Siobhan shook her head no.

"*Douce!*" I screamed at the top of my lungs. "I'll buy you a carton of Kit Kats if you come down immediately!"

Douce stopped for a moment, as if confused. She glanced down at the bead board in her hand, and continued on.

"*Arrête cette connerie!*" Behind me, Pascal Manet placed his hand on my shoulder.

I whipped around. "Stop my stupidity? You don't understand."

"*Non*. *You* do not understand. Jeanne will make 'er daughter use kava leaves I bring from *Nouvelle-Calédonie*, so she loses baby anyway." His eyes looked bleak.

"Baby! Baby?" I cried. "I'm worried about *Douce*!"

"Why?"

"You really don't get it!" I shrugged his hand away. "I intend to stop her!"

I darted back inside the markets. The soles of my feet oozed sweat, and I slithered as I negotiated hammocks and goanna oil and garden art. Heritage linen. I crashed past palmistry readings, a parrot in a cage chewing on a muesli wrapper, skirted pecan pies and macadamias, home-made jams and high-fibre figs. Gluten free food. Spinach and fetta cobs. 'Creole Spices' collided with a 'Saucy Salsa' sign. And the glands in my hands also poured out perspiration.

With the aroma of fresh Turkish bread in my nostrils, I emerged into the cafeteria and fast food section. The smell of deep-fried food made me feel like chucking as, gorging on hot dogs, greasy hamburgers and baked spuds, people rose from their benches to head for the railing.

"Think she'll do a Water Touch, or an Elevator?" someone said.

Still clutching my granita, I thrust my way through the throng.

"Nah, I'd bet on the Pendulum, or the Titanic."

"The Titanic, you reckon? Well, she's big enough to make one helluva splash."

I heard someone whisper "Psycho Back Dive" and then giggle.

"Do you mind, I was here first!" An obese woman waved food in my face.

"My friend's about to jump," I said.

"So? Doesn't give you a licence to be rude, but!" Yellow juice ran down her chin as she bit into a pickle. "We all wanna have a look, *don't* we, eh?"

"Pardon! *Merde!*" To the rear, Pascal battled his way through. "I must pass."

"Bloody Frog!" said a bloke with a beer gut. "They're all the friggin' same, just think of the Rainbow Warrior!"

The tattoos on Malachi's arms were tanned and oiled. His face was masked, and he remained high on the deck, waiting for Douce.

"I did the Cliffhanger when I jumped," a girl whispered to her friend, "and I wanted to go again today but they said no, that the bungy was closed."

By now, Pascal stood to the right of me.

Douce arrived. The crowd roared and cheered. Malachi moved forward. Kissing Douce on the cheek, he tried to remove the bead board from her grasp, but she clung on.

He raised her arm and shouted, "Ladies and gentlemen. We have a Spanish lady here, come all the way from Catalonia."

"She is French, not Spanish," Pascal muttered in my ear.

"Yeah, he just says that." I relaxed a little as I recalled my incredible Backward Swan Dive. "Malachi makes stuff up, to get people in the mood."

"Darlin' Douce will entertain us with bungy jumpin'," announced Malachi, "such as ye've never seen in yer life."

Placing the harness around her waist, and between her legs, he pulled the webbing tight. He cuffed her ankles together. Douce, as tall as Malachi, gazed across the treetops with an eerie smile on her face.

"Don't jump, Douce!" I formed a tunnel with my fingers. "Go back! Turn around! Descend that ladder!"

A bray of sound. "Jump! C'mon, jump!"

"Don't jump!" I yelled.

"Jaaarmp!"

Seamus was back in his boat, waiting to haul in Douce. Reeds poked from the billabong. Was the pond drying up?

"Don't jump! Don't jump!" I screamed. "There's not enough water!"

"Jaaaaarmp! Jaaaaarmp, Douche Bag!"

I hissed at the beefy bloke behind me. "How dare you! You are *so* disgusting!"

"Aaagh! Get a life!" he replied. "Just a bit of fun. Girl's a screw loose, anyway."

Malachi seemed oblivious to the noise from below as he connected the cord to her waist, secured it with the massive silver clip and attached the fat elastic hanging from the overhead beam. Remembering the whiff of grog on his breath, I wondered if he'd been drinking.

He whispered in her ear, before crying, "Ladies and gentleman, our Spanish lady will now perform the rare and difficult, and most un-us-u-aaaal, Bead Board Tambourine!"

Douce looked fixedly ahead. She held her arms out wide as if to jump. Instead, Rocky's name came out. "ROCHHKKKKkkkk! ROCHHHKKKKkkkk!"

Low and mournful, the sound flowed over the stand of palm trees, wafted across the shivering tree ferns and ricocheted around the jungle.

"KKkKKKKkkkkkkkkkkkkk …"

Tremors ran down my spine.

The crowd fell silent.

Pascal tensed up. "What is happening?"

"I don't know." I turned to him. "This is weird. Douce never knew her brother's name before, never knew Rocky *was* her brother, always called him 'the supplier' until the day he left. And now, it's as if the word Roch is wired into her subconscious and she can't stop saying it."

"She's jumped," someone gasped.

I whipped my head around.

Dropping in a Forward Swan Dive, Douce resembled a big, frilly bird. My heart stuck in my throat as she plummeted. The rebound kicked in. She bounced up.

I relaxed.

"I worried about nothing!" I swivelled my body to look at Pascal. "Douce's gonna be fine! She'll really enjoy this, totally love the ground rush!"

In my peripheral vision, I saw Douce drop the bead board. Her body twisted and plunged. Down she went to the reeds and the mud, and Seamus in the boat. But instead of the rope pulling her back, she seemed to keep on going.

Pascal clamped his hand across my eyes.

A dull thud.

People screamed. Surf pounded in my ears. The granita slid from my fingers. Liquid ran over my toes as Pascal shoved me away from the railing and into the crowd, now surging forward.

Malachi's cry pierced the air. "Ooooh, nooooo. Me daaaarlin' Douce! Me daaaaarlin' Doooooce!"

"*On y va!*" Pascal removed his hand from my eyes and pushed me past 'Reiki Therapy' and 'Twista Pouches', 'Knots and Wheels', 'Try Some Puzzles' and 'Stop Itches Fast'.

"What's going on? I saw her drop, and you stopped me from looking. What happened?"

Relentlessly, he moved me towards the exit. "The elastic has broken."

"But Douce'll be all right?"

People ran past shouting, yelling into mobile phones: *There's been an accident, accident, accident. Call the ambulance, quick before it is too late. Get a move on, move on, move on …*

"She's gonna be all right? Please tell me she's gonna be okay!"

Pascal's face was the colour of wet papier-mâché. Muscles clicked along the edge of his jaw as he murmured, "Douce land on the side of 'er head. Her neck is snapped."

"Her neck's broken?" The ground beneath me swayed. "What does that mean? Will she be in a wheelchair? And how do you *know* she broke her neck?"

"I 'ave seen such a thing before, when I compete in motocross events. My close friend falls off his bike and is deceased in the same fashion. It happens instantaneously, like *zat*." His fingers were unsteady as he attempted to snap them.

"But, but you could be wrong?"

"*Elle est morte, j'en suis sûr.*"

From his expression, I knew he was telling the truth.

Douce was dead.

Chapter 46

I slouched against the cyclone fence surrounding the Kooracoondoo Markets. I dug my fingers into the hessian tacked across the wire, trembling from the horror of Douce's death. I didn't weep. I just hung on while my world tipped and slewed, rocked and shook.

Pascal gazed down the street, saying nothing. He pulled a packet of Gauloises Blondes from inside his jacket. Using a glitzy gold lighter, he lit up, and blew smoke into the air. He walked around in circles, found a tree stump and lowered his butt. He threw his lighted cigarette on the ground, and leaned his elbows on his knees. Placing his head in his hands, he sat, still as a statue.

People streamed from the market wearing shattered expressions. Tears ran down cheeks; people wiped their noses. Mostly the crowd was silent.

My teeth continued to chatter from the shock and, through blurred vision, I saw Poppy and Pete lugging planter baskets. Looking distraught, they loaded the tray of a utility. Seeing the planters reminded me: *Who would break the news to Rocky?* I thought of Iris, Horrie of 'Aussie Cold Comfort Neckties' and, of course, Jeanne.

"Shouldn't you h-help Jeanne, y'know, go and c-comfort her?" I called in a choky voice.

Pascal didn't budge. He sat there like a stone, elbows on his knees, holding his head in his hands. Other vendors emerged lugging crates and containers which they loaded into flat-bed trucks, battered utes and station wagons.

A fire engine came clanging up Sugarcane Lane. Wielding axes, men jumped out and ran through to the bungy tower where people jostled and gathered, and screamed out questions. Further down the road, a vehicle spun its back wheels in a tight circle, kicking up clouds of dust. The noxious smell of burnt rubber filled the air.

"Where is the ambulance?" I murmured.

A strange hysteria welled up through my chest, and burst from my throat. Tears rolled down my face. The tears soon dried up. I pushed myself off the fence, approached Pascal, and pressed my fingers into the leather of his jacket.

"What about Jeanne?"

"*J'ai mal.*" Not looking up, he held the same position.

His body shook.

"I'm hurting, too." I exhaled. "Aren't you hot in that jacket?"

He said nothing.

I stood there kneading his shoulders.

After a few minutes, he reached for my left hand, pulled it forward and held it hard against his cheek. I felt the wetness, and I knew he was weeping. Which I found odd. I'd never seen a grown man cry before. Pascal was so arrogant that it seemed even more unexpected.

"Why are you so upset? You didn't even know Douce."

And I remembered those whispered conversations I'd overheard, the things he'd told me in the kitchen of his home in Baie des Citrons, the flash of blue in Douce's eyes, the colour of her skin so different from Rocky's.

A light bulb switched on in my head. "You're, you're Douce's dad, aren't you?"

His reply was muffled. "She says that, but it is not true."

"But, but, how old were you when all this happened?"

"Very young, my early teens."

I was shocked by his answer. "How cruddy! I mean, that's awful! When did you find out?"

His head was still down, and I felt him shrug. "Per'aps twenty minutes ago, but she lies!"

A squiggly feeling ran through me. "I'm sorry. Now I know you are, or might have been, a dad, I shouldn't really call you Dad."

A raspy laugh. Eyes red and swollen, he pushed himself up. "*J'ai envie de te prendre dans mes bras.*"

"Me, too."

So we stood there hugging, gently rocking and weeping and comforting each other, until we both smelled the same: a mix of Kenzo aftershave and biker leather, Gauloises cigarettes and stinky tropical sweat.

An ambulance screeched up the street, followed by a police car.

"I still think you should go see Jeanne," I said. "Even if you hate her, she needs you."

"*Non.* She needs K-Mel, Roch." Pulling a hanky from his pocket, Pascal blew his nose.

"Rocky should be told! Who's gonna do that?"

"I will ring Marcel on my *portable.*"

"I still think you should …"

"I need to walk, perhaps along the river."

We headed towards the Barrabull River, passing bongs and rainforest yoghurt, floral skirts, herbal packs and printed T-shirts limp on their hangers.

On Sugarcane Lane, no one ate Devonshire teas. Knots of people stood around, talking in hushed whispers about Douce and the bungy man: *a terrible tragedy, tragedy, horror, horror, I didn't know her but … I hear she was unusual, couldn't read or write, you could say not normal, used to hang out on the river and the railway line, but beautiful, and those beads of hers, marvellous memory wire …*

Subdued tourists filed into buses for the long ride back to the beaches, or Jamesville Tavern for a stiff drink. Maybe they were off to Cairns to catch the plane back home.

Those who remained tried to come to terms with this 'tragedy'. Would the tourists stay away? Or would even more people stream up the mountain to go bungy jumping with Malachi?

"I'm certain the bungy man did it," I murmured.

Pascal, immersed in his thoughts, turned to look at me.

"They say a girl died doing a jump with Malachi before, down south in Victoria. And this other girl was also pregnant."

"But 'e would be incarcerated, locked up if it were the case."

"Rocky said the same thing when I tried to wimp out of doing my jump. But, I dunno, it's kinda dodgy … two girls pregnant, two girls dead, and the common denominator is Malachi."

Pascal ran his fingers through his hair. "Surely there will be an inquest."

We came to the cottage with the snake tacked to the gatepost.

"Aren't you going to leave a note, or knock, or something?"

He gave a slight shake of his head.

"I never took you for a coward."

With a heavy sigh, Pascal pushed aside the front gate. He strode down the path and rapped on the flywire. Pulling the door open, he called out, "*Il y a quelqu'un*?" After a moment, he said, "No one is home." The hinges squeaked shut.

"Oh, well, at least you sort of tried. But I still think …"

"*Laisse tomber*, Genna," he said.

I decided not to test his patience. "Okay, I'll drop it."

A jetty on wonky pylons covered in lichens and mosses stretched over the mangroves on Barrabull River. A water dragon plopped. I marvelled at the darting mullet and stately barramundi, thinking how peaceful it was. A kingfisher swooped and flew off, lugging a flapping mountain fish. A pied currawong took to the sky.

Pascal nudged my elbow. "Crocodile!" He indicated a ripple, and a pair of muddy eyes. "We must move."

"Yeah, makes sense."

Passing an acacia with a green tree snake sliding up the trunk, we came to a shack with a broken front window. A feather was stuck to the front door. A wisp of smoke rose to the rear of the building.

"Do you think that's Joey's place?"

"Joey?" Pascal seemed uninterested.

"He's the Koori who gave Douce kava, according to Iris. Didn't you hear us talking?"

Expecting him to rant about the perils of drinking the root of the piper methysticum plant, I was surprised to see him look at his watch.

We headed back along the squelching ground of the riverbank. A whipbird cracked. Giving out an iridescent flash, a Ulysses butterfly winged past. As we turned into Sugarcane Lane, I saw rusty cars, trucks parked at odd angles and, among them, a ute with bullbar and spotties.

"She's home. You can offer your condolences."

Pascal huffed and puffed as I pushed him up the path and into the house, now chock-full of traders carrying platters of finger food.

Horrie of 'Aussie Cold Comfort Neckties' stood in the passage, facial hair twitching. "Jeanne's having a lie down." He offered me an asparagus roll.

"Thanks, but no."

"She doesn't wanna talk to nobody." He wandered off sniffing.

Tears streaking down her apple cheeks, Iris Veivers approached. Flinging her arms about me, she covered my neck with body fluids. "I told ya, but. Didn't I say Douce never shoulda had a bungy?" Iris smelled of baby powder and BO. Her body shook like a jackhammer.

Wearing Iris like a scarf, I turned to Pascal. "Go and talk to Jeanne!" Freeing an arm, I flapped it in the direction of her bedroom.

"*Et toi?*"

"No, she hates me, says I remind her of Sandrine. She called me a Caldoche bitch."

"Bullsugar!" Iris snivelled into my hair extensions. "I think you're lovely, Jennifer, the grousest person."

"Name's Genna."

"Right." A long gorby snort. "You cared about my friend, weren't never stuck-up, never said nothin' bad about 'er."

"I need a glass of water," I said.

Still wearing Iris, I passed Jeanne's room in a hop-stepping motion, making my way to the kitchen. Astonished at first to see the book-lined shelves bulging with French classics—Balzac, Flaubert, Voltaire, Victor Hugo, Émile Zola and others I'd never heard of—I recalled Rocky saying his parents had met behind the barricades in Paris, May '68.

A vendor staggered into the house carrying cartons from Jeanne's utility. He dumped the boxes in Rocky's room, and I spied a crate with rope handles in there. Had the crate carried guns? I decided now was not the time to be thinking about guns.

In the kitchen a chick with a pierced upper lip heaped party pies on a platter. Beside her, the 'Discount Opals' trader efficiently arranged ribbon sandwiches.

"You a rellie?" asked the chick with the piercing.

“Nope, I’m a friend of the family.”

“Figures.” She paused to pick up a fallen pie off the bench. “Joanie doesn’t seem to have any rellies. And she only ever had the one child.”

I bit my tongue.

Iris detached herself. She grabbed a ribbon sandwich from the tray and sank her teeth into the spongy bread.

I opened a cupboard and extracted a glass. I filled it with water, sipped, and headed back to wait for Pascal in the front room—now overflowing with mourners.

Chapter 47

People milled among the photos, picking them up, staring, putting them down carefully as though Douce had been fragile. Everyone's eyes were red-rimmed. And only one word could be heard: *beautiful.*

Poppy and Pete gave me cautious watery glances. Barney the satay seller talked in a low voice with a guy whose beard was done in grey dreads. A dude with Allergy Free printed on his T-shirt leaned on the mantelpiece, wiped his nose, wept some more and wiped his nose again. A kid in a checked pinafore tossed a Slinky. Dogs with jangling collars dragged leads around the room.

Every now and then mourners went outside for a smoke. After dropping ash on the wild orchids, they returned to slurp tea from china cups offered by the girl with the steel ball on her upper lip.

Pascal was gone for ages. The sun began to go down.

Traders left. Others arrived. Everyone brought food. With a jolt, I remembered Dominick and my job in the coffee shop. I was already late. I told myself he'd be ticked off if I didn't turn up. Trouble was, my mobile phone was still in Pascal's pocket.

Pooped and puffy-eyed, I peeked around Jeanne's bedroom door.

Pascal leaned his back against the bookcase, right leg loosely crossed over his left. He nodded when Jeanne said, "Please see Marcel looks after Roch. He's all I've got."

"Excuse me." Edging my way in, I made for the zips on Pascal's jacket.

"What are you doing?" he said, as I prodded my fingers around the padded sleeves, negotiating the pockets, trying to find my phone.

"I'm looking for my mobile."

The ceiling fan ruffled papers on the bookshelves. My gaze latched onto a small, black and white photo of Jeanne and K-Mel carrying banners in Paris, wedged alongside Jean-Paul Sartre's *La Nausée*.

"So, if it isn't Sandrine's daughter! I hope you're happy." Stretched out on her bed, Jeanne pushed herself up on her elbows.

"I do have a name. And that name is Genna! And that is totally gross, so off, a shocking thing to say! Who'd want to harm Douce? I tried to stop her climbing the tower, prevent her from doing that bungy jump and I'm really upset!" My chin began to tremble.

"Now my son's left, I see you've got your hooks into his best friend's older brother!" Jeanne's eyes were like gooseberries.

"Who, the French teacher?" I continued to poke around for my mobile. "I don't think so! He's way too ancient!"

I could feel Pascal's body shake, as if with suppressed laughter. He reached for a zip, ripped it open, pulled out my mobile and handed it to me. "*Voilà!*" Despite having been briefly 'amused', he looked wrung out.

"Thanks."

I scooted into the passage, brought up the number of the coffee shop and pressed the button.

"Yeah, Dominick Nicks speaking. Can I help you?"

"Hi, it's Genna here. Sorry, there's been an accident and I'm kinda running late."

"You're fired!" Dominick's voice boomed over the airwaves.

"Really?" I squeaked. "That's so not fair."

He seemed to calm down slightly. "Look, I feel sorry for you. You've been through a bit. I tried to ring Claude to find out where you were, but Reception is on voicemail."

"They were both there this morning. I spoke to Claude briefly, and also Sandrine, who said she had something to tell me. They sometimes go to the doctor."

"Skim flat white?" I heard him say to a customer. "Look, Genna. I have to go. I'm really busy. I wish you all the best. And I'm sorry it didn't work out."

"I could come tomorrow. Is that cool?"

The line went dead.

My life was turning into one humungous disaster. I'd just lost my job. The top of my legs were itchy, and my muscles were aching. Was the box jellyfish poison still in my system? And would I remain scarred forever?

Mooching along the passage to Rocky's room, I settled myself on his still-unmade bed. Among the crates and boxes, I twisted the bracelet he gave me, thinking about Douce and wondering where Rocky was. Wishing I could be near him to hug the hurt away when Marcel told him about the accident.

The room was dark. I must've dozed off.

Next thing I knew I was swimming with box jellyfish and poisonous tricot rayé snakes. My dreads hung out like sea sausages as I danced with the stripes, whirled with the tentacles. Swirling, swirling, swirling. Weightless—until I felt my waterlogged cut-offs pulling me down. Pascal yanked and hauled and sang out, "Genna! Vite, quick it's a snake!"

I lurched up, crying, "Too late. It bit me!"

I expected to see the weight of the water dragging down Pascal's shorts so that they sat on his hips, revealing the scar on his abdomen. Instead, he stood there in the gloom in his jeans, biker boots and leathers, shaking me by the shoulder.

"*Vite*, it's late. Time for us to leave!"

Chapter 48

A mist hung over the mountain. The jungle stayed hidden and mysterious as we made our descent.

Few cars were on the road and I could hear wild pigs squeal and snort in the bush. I wasn't so afraid on the way back, didn't cling so hard to Pascal. I leaned into the curves when he leaned into the curves, not even thinking of resisting.

Soon we were v-v-vroom-v-v-rooming along Arlington Esplanade, puttering to a standstill outside the Amédée Apartments. Hopping off the bike, I handed my goggles and helmet to Pascal. He sat there, engine chugging, watching as I crossed the road. I made for the path leading to my apartment. The Reception lights were out already. I looked at my Swatch—not yet nine o'clock. Were Sandrine and Claude having a well-deserved candlelit dinner?

Pascal continued to sit there, Harley idling.

Was it his gaunt appearance?

I turned and went back across the road, strapped the helmet under my chin and climbed aboard again. Not a word was spoken as we took off. We zigzagged down streets leading to Coral Cove. Slowing at the Mimosa Sands Resort entrance, Pascal edged the motorcycle into the parking lot at the side of the building.

Still clutching my headgear, I trailed behind through the side door of the hotel. We threaded our way along peaceful passages, on cushiony wall-to-wall carpet embroidered with coral, shells and starfish.

Pascal pulled a key card from his pocket. After swiping the card through a slot beneath the handle, he pushed open the door to his air-conditioned room.

I hesitated.

What did he expect of me? Was it just someone to unload on, get things off his chest?

"You would like a drink?" He dumped his gear on a white-painted cane chair.

"Yeah, sure."

Placing my open-face helmet with his things, I followed him past a king-size bed draped with mosquito netting—which reminded me of the attic room in his house at Baie des Citrons. In the lounge filled with chairs and tables and a bar fridge, an overhead fan turned smoothly.

"You will 'ave a glass of this?"

Raising an eyebrow, Pascal picked up a bottle of Jack Daniel's—the same brand of whisky his brother drank. And I remembered the burning sensation when I'd gulped down the drink Marcel gave me in Ravella after he'd broken the news about Sandrine being my birth mother.

"Um, is whisky raw vegan? I mean, like, is there any heat involved in the process?"

His weary gaze held mine. "I 'ave no idea," he said.

"All right, then. I'll have one with you anyway."

He splashed the spirit into two tasteful tumblers, fossicked around in the refrigerator and dropped in ice cubes. Handing me my drink, he indicated a cane sofa for me to sit on.

"*Santé.*" He lowered his padded denim butt beside mine, took a thirsty swig and plonked the glass down hard on a cane occasional table.

"*Santé.*" I sipped. The whisky seared my throat, and I forced back the cough.

Unzipping a pocket, Pascal grasped his BlackBerry and began to scroll down, checking his messages.

"It's so *humid*," I said. "Aren't you going to remove your jacket?"

"*Je pue*," he replied.

"Yeah, well I stink, too. So I won't even notice."

Pulling out his cigarettes, he eased off his jacket to reveal a Lacoste polo—once light blue, now dingy with perspiration. He tossed the biker gear on a nearby chair, kneaded his temples for a moment, lit up and sat back. Blowing out a stream of smoke, he sighed and said, "*Merde*" to nobody in particular.

We sat there in silence. I sipped my drink. He got up and poured himself another. Leaning over, he stubbed his cigarette in a fish-shaped ashtray, lit up again and started to pace. Backwards and forwards, he went.

I felt we should discuss Douce, get the issue out in the open. "Douce, the name is so pretty," I said. "It means soft, sweet, gentle and, I think, dearest."

A long pause. And then he said, "*En douce*."

"I beg your pardon?"

"*En douce*." His voice was harsh. "You know what that means?"

"Um, actually, no."

"My dear Genna, is your French so *affreux* that you do not know the meaning of *en douce*?" His voice rose with anger.

"I'm sorry, um, I don't know what the expression means." I began to tear up. I took a hasty sip of my Jack Daniel's drink.

"There was a film, *L'amour en douce*, with Daniel Auteuil and Emmanuelle Béart, made in France at the time of the Events. You 'ave heard of it?"

"Nup, I don't think. No, I don't know the movie."

He stretched forward and whispered, "*En douce* means 'on the sly'!"

"On the q.t., oh, you mean 'secretly'?"

"Exactly! And that is the reason Jeanne calls her child Douce!" Pouring another drink, he swigged the lot in one gulp. "A silly *jeu de mots*, a play on words!" He banged his glass down. "A *game*, it was all a game!"

In an effort to make him talk rather than drink, I said, "How did it happen? I mean, like, between you and Rocky's mum."

A short laugh.

"Well, obviously I understand *how* it happened. I mean *why* did it happen?"

"Man does things he is not even capable of imagining," he murmured. "I know Jeanne has an *affaire* with the fish supplier from Yaté. I know she does these things."

"Yeah, but …"

"It was my mother's fault," he said abruptly.

I stared.

"Axelle would be ashamed of course to hear me blame her for asking me to take over bits of this and that, clothes and food." He paused as he thought. "Jeanne and K-Mel were poor, and had trouble affording shoes for Roch, you know. We were, maybe not rich, but comfortable, easy. I was tall for my age."

Beginning to get the picture, I regretted having asked the question. Emptying my glass, I held it out for more whisky.

"Jeanne wore skimpy pareos, her hairs in little Rasta plaits with beads." He picked up the Jack Daniel's bottle, poured with an unsteady hand. "You see, as one says in English, one thing led to … and it *'appen.*" Pause as he gave me the drink. "But I never complain, never tell Jeanne that what she is doing is wrong, *never say no.* I turn up often, when K-Mel is away at the markets in Baie de la Moselle, and maybe she believes I am older than I am." His speech was becoming slurred; he slumped into a club chair. "*Mon Dieu ... putain, putain, putain!* But I never think we will make a b-baby! She lies, she lies …"

Having not eaten all day, I felt woozy, out-of-body. Vaguely thinking I should leave while I was still able to walk back home, I didn't move. I continued to sit there drinking whisky. An unsettled feeling rose from my stomach.

About to throw up, I said, "Quick! Where's the bathroom?"

He waved a vague finger.

I made the basin before chucking. Just.

Struggling with the gold-plated taps, I stood there shivering, head bursting and cleaning mess off the marble with a fluffy white face washer. Reflecting on how I always seemed to be invading Pascal's personal space and mucking things up, I staggered past his bed on rubber legs.

The mosquito netting was tempting.

I lifted the frothy fabric up, crawled beneath and flaked out.

An electric drill in my head, going on and on and on …

I prised my eyelids open to discover time had stood still. I was lying in bed in a strange house in New Caledonia. A sea of white flowed over my head, a soft moving ceiling. An overhead fan whooshed smoothly. My legs were leaden, my throat parched. But I had no doona over me. Instead, I was lying on top of a tightly-stretched sheet. I had the same gummy lids. And I could see a man shape, lolled sideways in a cane chair with his head thrown back. Snoring.

As I had then, I remembered shaky dreams. Only the dreams weren't caused by a cyclone, and a car bombing. The dreams were a nightmare, a bungy jumping nightmare, and Rocky hadn't been killed. Instead, it was his sister who'd had the accident. And there was no doubt, no chance of *that* accident turning into a happy ending.

Tears brimmed over and ran down my cheeks. I lay there, choking them back, thinking I should leave.

I must've dozed off again.

When I woke, the window was framed with light, and I could hear water running. Someone was having a shower. I sat up. The cane chair was empty—time for me to go.

Wondering whether to knock on the bathroom door and tell Pascal I was leaving, I decided to scarper rather than face him. I let myself out. Heading along cool corridors, I passed through the foyer with the punkahs, smiled at the uniformed person on duty and crossed the road to Coral Cove beach.

Head hammering, I trudged along the sand, making for Glisten Beach and the Amédée Apartments.

The sun was barely up. I was sticky and smelly. Checking to make sure no one was about I dragged my clothing off and, forgetting about the perils of Chironex fleckeri, plunged into the ocean.

Splashing about in the tepid seawater, my head felt clearer, until, with a jolt, I remembered Rex and bolted for the shore. Face to the sun, I closed my eyes and stood there topless, in my knickers, feeling the warmth. Which made me think of Douce. I repressed the urge to cry. An ache filled my throat as I reached for my Indigo singlet—scungy and tacky and no longer white. After putting the top back on, I looked back along the beach. In the distance, I saw a guy, bare-chested and wearing shorts. He gave a brief wave, turned and walked away. I knew it was Pascal, making sure I was all right.

Slinging my jeans across my shoulder, I trudged along the sand. As I passed the still-closed All Day Breakfast Café, the Waveripper reef bus hissed around the corner and pulled up with a jerk outside Reception. Tourists in hats with towels and beach bags staggered up the steps, yawning.

Nervous at the prospect of being sprung arriving home late—or would Sandrine think I'd risen early?—I ducked behind a coconut tree, and pulled my jeans over almost-dry knickers. I waited for Claude to emerge, expecting to hear the words, "See you lat-errrr," followed by his usual hand slap on the side of the vehicle.

Claude did not appear. The Waveripper reef bus took off.

Picking up pace, I arrived at Reception to find the doors closed and the sandwich boards advertising tours stacked on the office floor against the inside glass.

Thinking Sandrine and Claude had taken an extended break—an evening together, at last—I headed for my apartment. Arriving at my front door, I snaked my fingers into my jeans' pocket. No key, no mobile. And then I remembered I'd left my things zipped inside Pascal's jacket. I was hanging out for a shower, for my shades, and desperate for an aspirin.

Running a tongue over my salty lips, I went to the side entrance of the Management Apartment and rapped. No answer. I rapped again, and listened for footsteps.

Nothing.

I knocked louder.

A gecko scuttled over the top of the door.

Still no one came.

Chapter 49

Claude's car was not in its parking space. I rattled the door of his shed—locked. Rushing up and down stairs, I ran along balconies randomly tapping on doors, trying to find Mrs Hays-Bert. And then I recalled Claude saying she normally lived in Apartment No. 6, before the Melbourne owners recently turned up for a holiday. Had they gone back yet?

Hurrying to No. 6, I knocked.

Wearing rollers in her hair, Mrs Hays-Bert pulled the door ajar and peered at me blearily through the safety catch.

"Oh, it's you, dear." She closed the door, lifted the catch and opened up. "Can I help you?" Her cheeks shone with face cream.

"Sandrine and Claude seem to have gone!"

"Oh, they've probably driven in to Cairns to see the doctor. Sandrine has an eye appointment today. Laser surgery, I think she said, *in* the surgery." She giggled, and then smirked.

I checked my Swatch. "Surely they wouldn't be at the doctor's? It's barely six in the morning."

"Perhaps they went in last night, stayed over?" A sigh. "They never said anything to me about the office, though. It's a quick procedure, I'm told. I'm sure they'll be back soon." Another smirk.

"Look, I lost my key," I said, thinking it was easier to lie, "and I wonder if you're able to access Reception so I can use the duplicate. I am so desperate for a shower!"

"One moment, dear." She closed the door. Her footsteps faded across the floor tiles.

Mrs Hays-Bert seemed to be gone forever. I was on the point of leaving, trudging all the way to Coral Cove to find Pascal, when she opened up again in full makeup. Her hair was brushed into a helmet shape.

"Follow me!" she said, frog-print shirt flapping.

Mercurio's bingle-patched, buffalo-horn-painted car clanked into the car park as we made for Reception. The office was tidy, ready for business.

Lifting the duplicate key from the row of hooks beside the cold drinks freezer, I said, "Thanks, Mrs Hays-Bert. I'll leave you to look after things."

"Oh, it's no trouble."

Running my fingers through my gooey hair, I eyeballed her. "You don't think they're away, on holiday or something?"

"Certainly not. Darling Claude always tells me if he needs me. No, they won't have disappeared like that." Her eyes homed in on the floor.

Reflecting it wouldn't be the first time my birth mother had 'disappeared like that', I rocked off to have a long, cleansing shower.

My flat was musty. I turned the ceiling fan to high. Dropping the duplicate key on the kitchen bench, I saw an object under the stinger jar. Rex's tentacles swooped and swayed as I lifted the container. My name was inscribed on an envelope. Seeing the word *Geneviève*, my chest began to lurch. I opened the flap, and pulled out the piece of paper. Beneath yesterday's date, the handwriting was neat:

Sorry we were unable to talk this morning. The results of the tests came back from Italy. Our DNA match. We are biological mother and daughter. I do not plan ever to be a burden to you. Bisous et à la prochaine fois,
Sandrine

Confused by the strange letter, I subsided onto the sofa. What did Sandrine mean by 'I do not plan ever to be a burden to you'? Above her signature she'd written 'love' in French, followed by 'until next time'.

Did this mean she planned to see me later today, next week or maybe one day we might cross paths again—if I was lucky?

My brain felt as though a big piece of lead had fallen on it from a great height. Shedding clothes as I went, I made a beeline for the bathroom. Thinking hard, I stood under the shower soaping myself. I stayed beneath the water until I had goose bumps.

A knock on my door. Wrapping myself in a towel, I opened to find Mercurio waiting.

"Whaddya want me to do first, eh?" He ran the back of his hand across his sunburnt nose, and sniffed.

"What do *I* want *you* to do?"

"Yeah, Mrs Thingummy said Claude and his missus have gone away for a few days and you'd know what needs doin'."

"Gone?" I thought quickly. "Yes, they have taken a break. I dunno, um, start cleaning the gecko poo off the external walls of the buildings."

Mercurio slouched off.

After hastily dressing, I darted to Reception.

"What's happening?" I cried. "Mercurio said Sandrine and Claude …"

"They've gone!" said Mrs Hays-Bert. "I checked. His *Baby-foot* soccer table is no longer there."

"Soccer table?" I stared. "Maybe he got tired of it, sold it."

She crooked her plump forefinger.

I trailed after her into the Management Apartment.

"Doesn't look much different to me, just his footy game gone, oh, and the cagou print is missing."

In their bedroom, Mrs Hays-Bert wrenched back the mirrored sliding doors. Empty hangers clattered.

"They *have* left! How could they?" My breath came in gasps. "Why? 'Cos Sandrine discovered she's definitely my birth mother? Was that the reason?"

A rat-a-tat-tat in the distance.

"I have no idea, dear, but someone's knocking at Reception. I need to open up."

Hard on Mrs Hays-Bert's heels, I headed for the office telephone. "Look, I've lost my mobile. Is it okay if I ring, um, I need to talk to someone?"

"I can't see why not. After all, you say you're Sandrine's daughter. You're in charge now." She unbolted the external glass doors.

An angry guy marched in, wearing Levi's jeans and waving his wallet.

"Sandrine here, eh?" he thundered. "I paid big bucks for a group gourmet cook-up and tour of the Daintree with damper and billy tea included. And I don't have the tickets yet! And the chauffeur-driven maxi-campervan is due to set off in half an hour!"

Leaving Mrs Hays-Bert to sort out the problem, I dialled Namilly's number.

The phone rang and rang before she picked up.

"She's gone," I fumed. "She's walked out on me again!"

At the other end of the line, Namilly gave a wheezy yawn. "Who *is* this?"

"It's me, Ma."

"You know I don't like to be called …"

"Yeah, Ma, but she's left!"

"Who's left?"

"Sandrine. She's deserted me all over again, and the only thing I've got to remember her by is a *stinger in a sugar jar*!" I started to snivel.

A long, long silence. And then: "Don't you think it's time you accepted this woman for what she is? You're eighteen, grown up now." Long wheeze. "I did my best, tried to protect you, but you insisted on finding out the truth, went into those chat rooms, offered personal information and ignored the most basic rules of online safety …" On and on my mum went, ranting and rambling.

After a while, I began to feel calmer. "Hey, hang loose, Ma. Perhaps Sandrine has taken time out? I'll catch you later when I know for certain."

I hung up as another irate tourist marched in—clad in a Mossimo top and brandishing a cheque book.

The air was filled with menace. Peed-off guests kept arriving at Reception, a suspicious number of them having paid for tickets to go on cruises and tours: rodeo rides, reef viewing, dingo parks, outback safaris—and I was amazed how many people were into croc feeding. Most had not received confirmation. For the most part, Mrs Hays-Bert and I were able to placate them.

During a break, I ran and fetched Rex. I placed the stinger jar on the counter to frighten people away. But the complaints kept coming, and one of those complaints set me thinking.

Featherstone and Lahey Finance Company rang. The man asked to speak to Claude.

"Claude's not here right now. He'll be back soon. I belong to the family," I said—*big mistake*. "Can I help you?"

"Claude and Sandrine are behind in their mortgage payments," the dude barked over the airwaves. "Could you get one of them to ring me back post haste? The person who went guarantor is getting edgy."

Before I could digest the implications, Body Corporate Services called. "Just touching base re the AGM next week," the chick chirped down the phone. "If Claude could bring the absentee landlords' Voting Papers with him, I'd be grateful. Don't forget we desperately need to update on the Sinking Fund Budget and Contributions, oh, and the Administrative Fund Budget. Is he still going ahead with the extensions to the Resident Manager's Office and upgrading the pools and surrounds? And what about the connection of Private Line, using existing cable?"

"Um, I'll check," I said. "I mean Claude'll get back to you as soon as he … he'll get back to you!"

A workman in overalls poked his head in the door. "G'day. It'll take at least two days to lift and re-lay the tiles in that fourth floor apartment. Meanwhile, Claude'll need to flog the guests in the surrounding flats reduced tours to keep 'em out and keep 'em happy." Trailing powdery grout, he headed for the lift.

No time for lunch.

I managed to ring the Mimosa Sands Resort at Coral Cove and ask for Pascal.

"Mr Manet checked out this morning," said the concierge.

"You're kidding! He's got my keys and mobile. Or did he leave them with you?"

"I'm very sorry, ma'am."

The phone burped immediately after I put the receiver down. "Dr Mann here! Could I speak to …?"

Had I misheard? Was this Dr Mack from Apartment No.18?

"Oh, doctor, thank you soooo much!" I said. "That injection you gave saved my life!"

"The name is Mann, with an n, in fact two of 'em. Is Mrs Sandrine Bass Salary Day Lions there?"

"She's not available."

"My receptionist tells me she also goes by the name of Forestier."

"I'm her, sort of, daughter, and she's not …"

"She missed her appointment this morning. Has she been using the drops? If she doesn't have laser surgery, well, to put it bluntly, I *refuse* to have a patient of mine go blind. She's already lost a substantial amount of peripheral vision. Could she ring me urgently? She tells me she's been smoking cannabis for the condition. Please tell her marijuana is not, and I stress, *not,* a cure for glaucoma. It's an urban myth!"

I now knew Hetty was right. Sandrine smoked dope, believing it would cure her eye disease. Her loss of vision caused her to bump into things, the reason she wrote those words about not wishing to be a 'burden' to me.

A grinder whined upstairs.

My head whirled.

The grinder stopped. A workman called out: "Management must've spent the Lift Levy money. Bring that new box of tiles up via the stairs, will ya? Frog's changed his mind."

'Frog'? It seemed Pascal now owned the apartment on the top floor.

Chapter 50

I kept hoping Sandrine and Claude would return.

One afternoon, when it was quiet, I mooched into the Jungle Walk to check out the plant Hetty had found. Everything was overgrown and tangled in there. I saw no wicko. Perhaps I didn't know what I was looking for?

A policeman in short sleeves and a wide-brimmed hat showed up, requesting the key to Storage.

"What happened to the bungy man, Malachi?" I asked when he'd finished rummaging.

"Arrested and charged with murder," he said.

"I heard another girl died in a bungy accident elsewhere, pregnant like Douce?"

"Too right. The bastard had the same excuse as last time. He said a kid, lighter, jumped just prior to the young lady. The rope malfunctioned when he tried to shorten it to accommodate the extra weight."

"And you don't believe him?"

"Once is carelessness, second time is murder in my book!" He fixed me with his gaze. "But to the reason I'm here. Have you seen any suspicious boxes around the complex, eh?"

Hoping I didn't look guilty, I shook my head. "Is it important?"

"The French government contacted us, claiming a boat was seen off Glisten Beach, picking up guns."

"Ooh, no, not from Amédée Apartments. There are too many tourists!"

"The best crimes are carried out right under people's noses." His eyes bored into mine. "The guests all take tours during the day, flake at night, I imagine?"

"Yeah, s'pose." I prayed he wasn't checking on dope as well. "You're only, like, worried about guns?"

"Should I be worried about something else?" He gave me a sharp look. "Tell management to let me know if they see anything suspicious. Arms' trafficking is a serious offence."

"I'll tell 'em!"

☆

Mrs Hays-Bert received a call from her sister—her brother-in-law had fallen off a roof—and left to go south. Still no word from Sandrine, or Claude, and I told myself they'd just taken a break.

That was, until an owner arrived from Adelaide. "Who's gonna look after my flat, now that Claude's done a runner?"

"How do you know he's 'done a runner'?"

"Picking up my Hertz car at the airport, I saw his station wagon in a non-parking space, abandoned, a bunch of fines beneath the windscreen wiper."

"How do you know the vehicle was Claude's?"

"That pink flamingo thingy hanging from the rear-vision mirror."

As soon as he'd grumbled away, I snatched up the phone, and rang Jacques Forestier.

"Genna here. Is Sandrine with you?"

"Why do you ask?"

"Her, their, car was found abandoned at the airport."

"I haven't seen Sandrine since you were in *Nouvelle-Calédonie.* We haven't spoken since, and she would be unable to get into Grande Terre even if she wanted to. Marcel has left to join the insurgents, influenced by that *métis* kava farmer friend of his, and fighting has broken out. I am confined to Bouchon." His voice sounded shaky; he seemed less certain of himself. "Even my farm manager has departed, taking his wife and baby with him." His voice changed to a whine. "You remember Didier?"

"I do." Unwanted images of slavering dogs flashed through my mind, but I decided to hang tough. "Look, um, *Papi*, some finance people are leaning on me. They seem to know I'm related to Sandrine. You see, the two of them owe all this money."

"I'm sorry." Jacques was alert now. "I'm not in a position to help, even if I did wish to assist the piece of detritus who ran off with my daughter. She's lost money before, that bathing costume shop in Surfers Paradise. I'll need all I've got to buy myself out of this situation!"

Was Rocky involved? I now understood why Claude and the others had warned me off Roch Colline—who, I had to admit, hadn't been totally honest with me.

"Do the freedom fighters have guns?"

"Of course they have guns, brought in from somewhere north of Cairns! Where are you at the moment?" Before I could answer, he went on, "The President of the Southern Province has been taken hostage in a shoot-out! And they say prisoners have escaped from Camp-Est."

My breath seemed to choke in my throat. "I'm sorry, *Papi*, but I gotta go."

I'd barely hung up when the chirpy chick rang back about the fast approaching Annual General Meeting. "Body Corporate Services is, ah, concerned about rumours." She cleared her throat. "Is it true the managers have upped and left, leaving massive debts?"

"Not at all. Until Claude and Sandrine return, I'm in charge." I could feel a dark cloud looming. "I'm in the loop. I'll be up to speed and have the papers ready for the meeting."

Wondering where I could even find any paperwork, I closed my eyelids and allowed the breeze of the ceiling fan to cool me down as I thought.

A familiar voice intruded on my head trip.

"The elevator is not working, and I 'ave four valises and a video-conference to attend at Reef University." BlackBerry in one hand, my mobile in the other, Pascal stood at the entrance to Reception. He wore a floral shirt so hectic it made my vision spin.

The dark cloud lifted. "Oh boy, am I glad to see you! Can you fill me in on AGMs?"

"Why do you ask?" he said, giving me my mobile.

"I have a meeting."

He lifted an eyebrow. "And why do *you* have an annual general meeting? Where is Sandrine? Where is Claude?"

"I've taken over until they come back, but I don't know where they've gone."

"We need to discuss," he said.

"Then we'll have to, like, talk here. I can't leave the office unattended."

Pascal pulled out a Post-it pad. He scribbled 'Back in 5 minutes', stuck the yellow square to the glass door of Reception and said, "*Viens*!"

We sat under the mango tree at the far end of the pool.

"I cannot conceive what you are saying!" Pascal shook his head slowly when I'd finished filling him in. "I now know my brother did you a disservice in leading you to Sandrine. But you must accept that part of your life is over. She will never change. When will you believe it?"

I gave a shrug. "I kinda expect her to suddenly love me or something. And it doesn't happen." I gripped the inside of my bottom lip with my teeth.

"You must go back to your little town, continue with your French course, and do something useful." A pause. "You are young."

"I am eighteen!"

"Ah!" He held up his hand. "I repeat, you are too young to take over all those debts and responsibilities."

"I can't afford to go back. I lost my job and it's a long way and I'm, like, well, I don't have enough dosh to buy …"

"I will pay for your ticket."

"But, but that's not right, not fair."

He abruptly changed the subject. "Marcel asked me to pass this on." Delving in his top pocket, he pulled out a crushed envelope and gave it to me.

My heart banged about beneath my T-shirt as I ripped the letter open.

Pascal pushed himself up. "I will leave you to read while I carry my valises up the many stairs to my apartment! There is no one?"

"Nope, Mercurio didn't turn up today."

The paper smelled as I expected, earthy and smoky, but with an added hint of gunpowder. A smudge of grease marked the top right-hand corner of the page. My eyes raced across his words:

Ma belle, I am writing this behind the barricades! Marcel has joined me in our quest for an independent Nouvelle-Calédonie. We have blocked the RT1 to prevent traffic entering Tontouta airport, and instructed men to lie on the runway to stop planes from landing. Everything is in place. It will be a long struggle. But we will prevail.

Douce's death tore my heart into tiny pieces. I am bitter, finding it hard to forgive Jeanne for not informing Douce I was her brother. I know the importance of forgiveness. And so I ask you to forgive me. Pascal passed on to Marcel the details of your jellyfish attack and how ill you were. I behaved like a child. I was jealous. I am ashamed. While waiting for my friend to ferry me to his boat on the night I left, I dug some words in the sand on Glisten Beach with a stick. I wrote Je t'aime. Did you find my message? I am only a simple kava farmer, Genna, but my country needs me. So, even though I feel this way about you, I am not in a position to make a commitment. At this point, I'm unable to imagine when I might next be in Australia. Will you join me here, when it is safe? I will contact you.

Je t'embrasse,
Rocky

With a sense of elation mixed with disappointment, I re-read his letter. But was there a future for Rocky and me? I took the piece of paper and folded it, and folded it, and folded it again before pushing it right down into the pocket of my jeans.

My mobile rang.

It was Stefan. "Your old lady's real worried about you, mate. She thinks you're getting in too deep up there. And she's been having palpitations, bad ones. She said not to say anything, but she needs you."

"Tell Namilly I'm coming home. You can also tell her she was right about Sandrine."

"Okay, I will." Pause. "Hetty's been giving me heaps, loading it on since she got back, chewing me out for what I did to you." Long pause. "And she's right." After an even longer, really heavy, meaningful pause: "Can't wait to see ya, mate."

"Ditto. Oh, and Stefan?"

"Yeah, mate."

"Tell Ma she's not allowed to say 'I told you so'."

www.ingramcontent.com/pod-product-compliance
Lightning Source LLC
Chambersburg PA
CBHW061602170626
46811CB00001B/284

* 9 7 8 0 9 8 7 4 5 5 4 4 4 *